HOT SINGLE DAD

CLAIRE KINGSLEY

Edited by Elayne Morgan of Serenity Editing Services

Cover by Cassy Roop of Pink Ink Designs

ISBN-13: 978-1979190930

ISBN-10: 1979190933

www.clairekingsleybooks.com

Created with Vellum

A big shout out to all the great dads out there. Keep doing what you're doing, loving your families, leading by example, and showing the world what it means to be a man.

ALSO BY CLAIRE KINGSLEY

Book Boyfriends

Book Boyfriend

Cocky Roommate

Hot Single Dad

The Always Series

Always Have

Always Will

Always Ever After: A Short Story

The Jetty Beach Romance Series

Must Be Love (Nicole and Ryan)

Must Be Crazy (Melissa and Jackson)

Must Be Fate (Cody and Clover)

Must Be Home (Hunter and Emma)

The Back to Jetty Beach Romance Series

Could Be Forever (Finn and Juliet)

Could Be the One (Lucas and Becca)

Could Be the Reason (Gabe and Sadie)

1

CALEB

An endless stream of people come down the escalator, but so far, none of them are the girl I'm waiting for.

"Where's Linnea going to sleep?" Charlotte asks.

"We have an extra bedroom," I say. "You know that, Bug."

My six-year-old daughter sits in my lap. Her brown hair is down and I notice it's a little tangled in the back. I should have brushed it again before we left the house, but I didn't want to be late.

We have a good view of the escalator from where we're sitting, and this way it's easier to keep Charlotte close. I keep a protective arm wrapped around her waist and I have to stop myself from giving the side eye to the people walking by. A crowded airport is one of those places where my dad-instincts get sharp.

"I know, but what if she sleeps with me in my room?" Charlotte asks.

"Aha, now I see why you're asking. I think Linnea is going to want her own room." I tickle her tummy and she squirms, giggling.

"Stop it, Daddy."

My phone buzzes in my pocket so I pull it out. It's my brother, Alex.

"Hey, man."

"Hey, where are you?" he asks. "I'm at the gym. I thought we were shooting hoops tonight."

"No, I'm at the airport." I scoot Charlotte higher up my lap. "Sorry, I thought I told you I couldn't make it."

"Airport?" he asks. "What's going on?"

I take a deep breath. I haven't told my family about the situation yet. It all happened so fast. Just last week, Charlotte's grandparents were talking to her on their Skype call. Next thing I know, I'm sitting at the airport waiting for a flight from Michigan.

"I'm picking someone up," I say. "Kind of a long story, but it's Melanie's sister, Linnea."

"Oh, wow. Just Linnea, or are Melanie's parents coming too?" Alex asks.

"No, Steve and Margo aren't coming." Which is a relief. My relationship with my former in-laws is strained at best—always was. They thought Melanie and I were too young to get married —afraid it would interfere with her career. We were still in medical school, and we *were* young. But when Melanie set her mind to something, not even her parents could stop her.

After Melanie died—she was killed in a car accident when Charlotte was a baby—her parents' opinion of me didn't get any better. They didn't exactly blame me—and they couldn't, I wasn't even there when she was hit—but I know they still felt like I took Melanie's life and turned it sideways. Maybe if she hadn't married me, she wouldn't have moved to Houston to do her residency, and she wouldn't have been on the road that day.

"Is she coming out to visit Charlotte?" Alex asks.

"Not exactly." Charlotte moves into the seat next to me, and I stand, angling myself so I can still see her but can talk more privately. "She's coming to be Charlotte's nanny."

"Hey, that's great."

"Yeah," I say, and I'm sure he can hear the skepticism in my voice. "It's not really my idea, but I'm stuck with it at this point."

"How is it not your idea?" he asks.

"Steve and Margo insisted," I say. "I guess Charlotte told them about the disaster that was Brittany."

"Right—Brittany forgot to pick Charlotte up from school, didn't she?" he asks.

"Yep," I say. "When I literally had my hands inside someone's abdominal cavity. Thank god for Kendra."

"No kidding," he says.

Since we moved back to Seattle, my sister Kendra has been there to bail me out when I needed someone to watch Charlotte more times than I can count. And, to be fair, that's a lot of why we moved home. Being a single dad isn't easy, and my erratic schedule as an ER surgeon makes it even harder. I wanted to be closer to my family, and there's no doubt in my mind it was the right thing to do. But I really need a regular nanny—someone I can trust to take care of my little girl. So far, I haven't had any luck finding the right person.

"Anyway, they were on their Skype call with Charlotte a few days ago and she said they wanted to talk to me. I usually just stay out of the way, you know? I let Charlotte talk to them as long as she wants, but I don't know, it's awkward. I got on the call and Margo said she had a solution to my nanny problem."

"And the solution is Linnea, I take it," he says.

"Yeah. She graduated college not long ago and has been living with them. They didn't really give me much of a choice. When Margo gets an idea in her head, it's pretty hard to dissuade her."

"Huh," Alex says. "Is she in medicine, like Melanie was?"

"No, she's a musician, I think. Piano, maybe? Anyway, she's on her way here."

"You sound incredibly unenthusiastic for a guy who really needs a good nanny," he says. "Or are you worried Linnea will flake out too?"

I glance down at Charlotte, but she's looking at one of the books she brought in her little pink backpack. Still, I lower my voice. "It's not really that. She might be fine with Charlotte, I don't know. But that's the thing—I *don't* know. When I was married to Melanie, the rest of her family lived in Michigan and we didn't see them very often. I barely remember this girl. The last time I saw her, she was this surly teenager who almost never spoke. She wore these big hooded sweatshirts and sat in the corner, not talking. It was weird."

"That is weird," he says.

"I think she was just shy or something. But honestly, that's the last thing Charlotte needs. She's already so shy, she needs someone to bring her out of her shell. Help her learn how to talk to people and make friends. As it is, I don't think Charlotte has any friends at school. She won't talk to anyone. Her teacher wants to have a conference about it."

"Wow, I didn't realize."

"Yeah, the little girl you guys see is not who she is around other people," I say. "And it's getting worse. She's always been quiet. But she's shutting down at school completely. At least when she was in kindergarten she followed directions. Now she has days where she won't even do that."

I glance at Charlotte again before I continue, but she's still reading.

"Anyway, the point is, Charlotte needs a nanny who can help her open up, not someone who's arguably worse than she is socially," I say. "Plus, what the hell am I going to do with some sullen kid who won't talk? This just feels like it's making things harder, not easier."

"Yeah, that's not great," Alex says. "Sorry, man."

"I'll deal with it," I say. "I figure I'll give it a few weeks and then I can put her back on a plane to Michigan. But I should let you go. Is Weston there already?"

"Yeah, he just showed up."

Weston is our new brother-in-law. He married Kendra a few months ago in a ceremony that surprised the hell out of everyone. We all got a text asking us to meet them downtown, and when we got there, they were dressed up outside the courthouse. If it was anyone else, I would have said they were nuts—they hadn't been together very long. But Weston is crazy about her, and Kendra knows what she's doing.

"Okay, I'll catch you guys next week."

"Sounds good," Alex says. "And good luck."

"Thanks."

I hang up and check the time before I pocket my phone. Linnea landed twenty minutes ago, so she should be here soon. I wish I felt better about this, but I can't see how this is going to work. I guess the good news is, Charlotte says she knows Linnea from her Skype calls with her grandparents. Maybe she'll actually talk to her. Even if Brittany—the last nanny we tried—hadn't forgotten Charlotte at school, she wasn't working out anyway. Charlotte wouldn't speak to her, even after several weeks.

But like I told Alex, I'll deal with Linnea for a few weeks and then I can send her back home. Her parents won't be able to argue if I say we gave it a shot and it didn't work out. It's not my responsibility to make sure their daughter has a job.

I watch the people coming down the escalator and keep my eyes out for Linnea. I don't remember exactly what she looks like, but I think I'll recognize her. Maybe. I know she looks nothing like Melanie. Mel was olive-skinned with brown hair that she kept cut in a short bob. I seem to recall Linnea is blond, but I could have that wrong. I just remember wondering where Linnea came from; she didn't look like the rest of their family.

In a way, I'm glad Linnea doesn't look like her sister. I'm worried it's going to be hard enough to bring home a living reminder of what I lost. The pain of losing Melanie is just a sadness in the background—something in the past. Honestly, I miss her more for our daughter than I do for myself. I hate that my little girl has to grow up without a mother. I do everything I can to be what she needs, but I know in some ways I fall short.

"Daddy, what's this word?" Charlotte asks.

I lean down and look at the page. "That says *bike*. The *e* at the end makes this a long *i* sound."

Charlotte goes back to reading, tracing her finger below the words, and I look up at the escalator again. A pair of red high heels catches my eye. I follow the legs they're attached to as the woman rides down, my eyes taking her in. *Holy shit.*

I shouldn't stare, but my gaze moves up a pair of shapely legs to round hips in a form-fitting gray skirt. White blouse, tucked in, showing off a narrow waist. Then—oh sweet Jesus, she is *stacked*. That blouse is barely holding in a set of incredible boobs. Long blond hair, full red lips. This woman is smoking hot —she's built like a pinup—and I can't take my eyes off her.

She steps off the escalator, shouldering a brown leather handbag, and looks around. I have this insane urge to go talk to her before she leaves and I never see her again.

Her beautiful mouth parts in a wide smile and she waves at someone. Almost involuntarily, I glance over my shoulder, wondering what lucky bastard is picking her up.

Charlotte jumps off the chair and runs. I lurch forward, trying to grab her.

"Charlotte, where are you—"

The woman crouches down in front of Charlotte. "Hi, Bug!"

My daughter throws her arms around the woman's neck and hugs her while I stand a few feet away, gaping at them like an idiot.

Oh my fucking god. Is that Linnea?

The woman hugging my daughter looks nothing like the teenager I remember. How long has it been since I saw her last? Five years? Can someone have changed that much in such a short period of time?

Linnea's eyes lift and she smiles at me. She squeezes Charlotte, then stands and takes her hand.

"Hi." She brushes her hair back from her face and adjusts her handbag. "It's been a while."

Say something, Caleb. Stop staring at her like a creeper. "Yeah, wow. Hi. Sorry, I didn't recognize you."

She smiles again and her blue eyes sparkle. "That's okay. I recognized Charlotte. And you."

My brain is not reconciling my memories of Linnea with the stunning woman standing in front of me. There's no way this is the same person.

But Charlotte is terrified of people she doesn't know, and she just ran into this woman's arms. She wouldn't do that if she didn't know her. I guess I should have been paying more attention to their Skype calls. I would have seen Linnea on the screen and been a little more prepared. As it is, I'm still gaping at her like I forgot how to talk.

"So, I have a couple bags," Linnea says. She points to the baggage carousels. "Maybe we should see if they're ready?"

"Right." It feels like I snapped out of a trance. "Bags. Okay. Bug, can you take your backpack?"

"I think I'm right over there," she says and points to one of the monitors.

We wait a few minutes for Linnea's bags to come around the

carousel. She chats with an unusually animated Charlotte, and I try not to stare at her. She leans forward to look at something Charlotte is holding, and I get a view straight down her shirt. Oh my god, those insane tits are in a white lace bra. I tear my eyes away quickly.

Holy shit, what am I doing? Linnea is twenty-two, just out of college. She's here to take care of my daughter while I work. And let's not forget, she's my dead wife's younger sister.

But my dick is not interested in the facts. I have to adjust myself when the girls aren't looking.

She points out her bags when they come around the carousel. They're both large, but that makes sense. I was thinking this arrangement would be temporary, but what I actually agreed to when I talked to her parents didn't have a specific end date. The fact that she's drop-dead gorgeous shouldn't be making me rethink my *send her back after a few weeks* plan. But holy hell.

We head toward the parking garage, Linnea pulling one of her rolling suitcases while I pull the other. Charlotte walks along beside her, holding her hand. I try to force myself to keep my eyes off her ass, but it's almost impossible. The way it moves in that skirt. She looks back at me over her shoulder and flashes that sweet-as-sugar smile again. I smile back, but swallow hard when she turns around.

I'm in big, big trouble.

2

LINNEA

Is there such a thing as an insta-crush? A moment when you see someone for the first time—or maybe the first time in a while—and you're instantly so attracted to them, your tummy is filled with butterflies and you imagine little hearts and stars sparkling around their head? Because that just happened to me.

Caleb smiles at me when he gets in the driver's seat of his car and it sets those butterflies to fluttering all over again. How did I not remember how gorgeous he is? Maybe I didn't notice before. The last time I saw him, we were all still in shock over my sister's death. And before that, he seemed so much older than me, the way Melanie always did. I hardly paid attention to her husband. Back then, I would have been too scared to talk to him anyway, especially if I thought he was cute.

But now I'm sitting in a car with a man who has deep brown eyes, tousled dark hair, and a stubbly jaw that is one of the sexiest things I've ever seen in person. And I'm moving in with him.

Of course, it's to be his daughter's nanny. But still.

I take a deep breath and adjust the handbag I'm carrying in

my lap. It was a long flight from Michigan, but my tiredness was driven away by the jolt of adrenaline that hit me when I saw Caleb. I didn't see him at first. I noticed Charlotte when I got off the escalator, and she came running toward me. It wasn't until I looked up that I saw him standing there. And I've been a jittery bundle of nerves ever since.

I was furious with my mother when she told me she'd talked to Caleb about sending me to Seattle to be Charlotte's nanny. It's not that I mind the idea of being a nanny to my niece—I'm thrilled about that part, actually. Charlotte is the sweetest little thing, and it's been sad to only see her on Skype calls. I love that I'll be able to spend so much time with her—really get to know her.

But my parents didn't ask me if I was interested. They didn't even tell me until after they'd already brought it up with Caleb *and* bought the plane ticket. My mother walked into my room, told me to pack my things, and said I had a flight to Seattle in two days.

Typical.

I did *not* want to move back in with my parents after graduation, but I didn't have much choice. I worked hard for my music degree, but being a classical pianist isn't exactly the fast track to self-sufficiency. I've been teaching piano lessons since high school, and that's a good supplement. But if I want to make a living playing piano, I'm going to need to land a spot with a large symphony.

Which is the plan. I was living with my parents so I had time to practice for auditions. That shouldn't be a problem now. Charlotte is in school, so I'll still have practice time during the day. And I'm going to need it. Pianist positions are few and far between, and there's always a lot of competition.

The hard part is, as much as I love music—it's my life—performing is difficult for me. I love music for its own sake, and I love to play. But I get so anxious when the pressure is on. I'm terrified before a performance, and I'm left exhausted when it's over.

But, as my parents are fond of reminding me, if I'm going to pursue music, I have to give it my all. Go as far as I can. Be the best I can be. They expect me to take advantage of my natural talent with a lot of hard work.

It's a lesson they emphasized with both their daughters. My parents are doctors—my father is a neurosurgeon and my mother works in cancer research—both at the top of their field. Melanie was on her way to becoming some kind of superstar surgeon. So naturally, they want me to be the best in my chosen profession.

However, they were laying the pressure on thick, and I was getting frustrated. My mother was increasingly impatient with the lack of audition opportunities—as if somehow I could control when a major symphony had an opening.

That was why I agreed to come to Seattle. I was angry that my parents didn't consult me before making arrangements with Caleb. But once I thought about it, I realized it was perfect. A new city. A job waiting for me. A place to live. A chance to start fresh, without my mother breathing down my neck and pestering me about auditions.

Of course, I hadn't counted on developing an insta-crush on Caleb.

I take a deep breath. I'm sure this feeling will pass. I'll get used to looking at him—I peek at him from the corner of my eye and oh my god, he is so dreamy—and I won't feel so jumpy anymore.

"Linnea, do you want to sleep in my room with me?" Charlotte asks from the backseat.

Caleb laughs and looks at her in the rear-view mirror. "Bug, we talked about that. Linnea needs her own bed." He coughs. "I mean, her own room."

"Okay," Charlotte says, sounding disappointed.

I twist around in my seat. "Hey, maybe we can have a slumber party sometime. Like on a night when your dad is at work late. Would you like that?"

She nods. "Can it be a pajama party?"

"You bet," I say.

"What kind of pajamas do you have?" she asks. "Most of mine are pink."

"Hmm, I don't usually wear pajamas, so I guess I'll have to get some before our party."

"Then what do you sleep in?" she asks.

"Just something comfortable. Like a tank top."

"And panties?" Charlotte asks. "What kind of panties do you have? Mine are *My Little Pony* and *Strawberry Shortcake*."

My face warms and I know I'm blushing. I try not to look at Caleb, but I peek anyway. He's looking straight ahead, both hands on the steering wheel. "I'm afraid I don't have any that are as fun as that."

"Yeah," she says. "I don't know if they make them in grown up sizes."

"Probably not." I turn back around, hoping she's done talking about my panties. Maybe I should change the subject. "So, Charlotte, have you ever played piano?"

"No."

"If you want, I can teach you," I say.

"I don't know if I'm big enough," she says.

"Sure you are," I say, glancing back at her again. "I started playing when I was younger than you."

Her forehead tightens, her little eyebrows drawing together. "No. I don't want to."

"Oh, okay. That's fine."

"Why not, Bug?" Caleb asks, his voice gentle.

"Because of concerts," she says.

"Concerts?" Caleb asks.

"Sometimes we do music at school, and the teacher showed us a video," she says. "It was a concert and all the music players had to play music in a big room with a lot of people."

"Oh." Caleb turns to me and lowers his voice. "She thinks if she plays piano she'll have to perform in front of an audience. She's not acting like it right now, but most of the time, she's incredibly shy."

My heart melts in my chest. I was painfully shy as a child; I know exactly how she feels. "Aw, Bug. If you want, you can learn to play piano just for yourself. You don't ever have to play in front of people. Maybe just me or your daddy. But no concerts, unless you want to."

"Oh," she says, her voice brightening. "Okay."

Caleb smiles at me, his eyes crinkling at the corners. I smile back, but it feels like my heart just grew wings and it's trying to fly right out of my chest.

Half an hour later, we pull up to a cute little two-story on a quiet street. Caleb helps me get my bags and the three of us go inside.

"Sorry for the mess," Caleb says. "We moved in a month ago, but I haven't really finished unpacking. We were in an apartment before, so I don't even have furniture for all the rooms."

The floorplan is open, with a cozy living area, kitchen, and dining room. There's a formal living room with a fireplace near the front of the house, and stairs leading up. A few boxes are stacked in corners, and some of Charlotte's toys are strewn about. But it doesn't seem that messy to me.

"Don't worry about it," I say. "I can help organize if you need me to."

"I don't want you to feel like you have to clean up after me," he says. "I just work a lot, so it takes me a while to get everything done at home."

"Well, yeah, you're doing everything by yourself," I say.

"Yeah," he says, and I'm struck by the tiredness in his eyes. "Let's get your stuff to your room so you can get settled."

We haul my things upstairs and he shows me around. Charlotte's room, bathroom, my bedroom. He points to a half-open door and mumbles something about that being his bedroom. I'm dying to peek, but of course I don't.

"I hope you'll be comfortable in here," Caleb says, gesturing to my new bedroom.

It's plain, but perfectly functional. There's a queen-sized bed flanked by two small nightstands, a dresser, and a closet.

He rolls my suitcase in and puts it near the closet. "You'll have to share a bathroom with Charlotte. I hope that's okay."

"Of course," I say. "This is great."

"You sure?" he asks.

"Yes," I say, looking around the room. "This is perfect."

Charlotte tugs on my hand. "Can we have our pajama party tonight, Linnea?"

"Not tonight, sweetie," Caleb says. "It's past your bedtime."

"Please, Daddy," she says. "We won't stay up very late. Just a tiny bit."

He picks her up and kisses her cheek. "Sorry, Bug. It's already late."

"Okay, Daddy," she says. "Can Linnea put me to bed, then?"

Caleb laughs. "Not tonight, Bug. Remember, she lives with us now, and she's going to be taking care of you when I have to work." He glances at me. "And hopefully she'll stay for quite a while. She'll have plenty of chances to put you to bed."

I smile at them. "Exactly. I'll see you in the morning, okay?"

She nods and leans her head against Caleb's shoulder. He rubs her back and with a little smile at me, he takes her to get ready for bed. I shut the door behind him and lean against it, letting out a long sigh.

Well, that was not what I was expecting when I got on a plane today.

I need to get my little insta-crush under control. Caleb is almost ten years older than me. I'm here to be his daughter's nanny. And let's not forget, he was married to my dead sister. The thoughts I'm having about him right now are so inappropriate.

But I'm sure it won't last. I just need to keep my silly hormones from taking over.

3

CALEB

I come downstairs, pulling on a t-shirt, and blink the sleep from my eyes. Charlotte usually wakes me in the morning, but it's after nine, and she never came in. It felt good to sleep late, but I wonder how long she's been up. Soft voices carry from the kitchen. I walk around the corner and stop in my tracks.

Linnea is standing at the stove, her back to me. She's wearing a tank top with thin straps and a pair of loose gray sweats. Nothing special, but for fuck's sake, a paper bag would look hot on that body. I don't know if I've ever seen such a perfect ass in my life.

Her hair is up and there is just so much skin showing right now. Her shoulders, arms, upper back. I'm still trying to wake up, but my dick is already way ahead of me.

"Hi, Daddy!" Charlotte says.

Oh my god, I didn't even notice my daughter was in the kitchen. This is so bad.

"Morning, Bug." I scoop her up and she gives me a big squeeze around my neck. I hold her for another moment and breathe in the strawberry scent of her hair. I love this little girl so much. "How'd you sleep?"

"Good," she says. "Linnea is making pancakes."

I set her back down. "Yum."

Linnea looks at me over her shoulder. "I hope that's okay."

"Yeah, definitely," I say. "This is your home too, now. Help yourself to anything."

She smiles. "Thanks. Do you want some?"

God, that smile. "Sure, sounds great."

Charlotte and I carry plates and silverware to the table while Linnea finishes cooking. She brings over a plate with a tall stack of pancakes and we all sit down. I get up again to grab the butter and when I get back, Linnea is already helping Charlotte cut a pancake into bite sized pieces.

"Thanks," I say.

"Sure," she says with a smile.

She's leaning forward to help Charlotte and my eyes are drawn to those amazing boobs. I used to think a word like *luscious* when applied to tits was stupid, but that was before I was faced with the amazingness that is Linnea. She sits up straighter and grabs the syrup. I tear my eyes away, hoping she didn't catch me staring at her chest. Great, she hasn't even been here twenty-four hours, and I'm almost sexually harassing her.

I distract myself with breakfast. Pancakes aren't my first choice for a breakfast food—I'm more of an eggs and hash browns kind of guy—but these are really good. I can't remember the last time someone else cooked me breakfast. There's something comforting about sitting at the table, quietly eating pancakes that I didn't have to make myself.

"I know I just got here, so there's no hurry, but I wanted to talk to you about your work schedule," Linnea says. "I'd like to teach piano lessons a couple times a week. But I'm here for Charlotte first, so if that doesn't work, it's okay."

"I'm sure we can figure it out," I say. "Worst case scenario, my sister Kendra can watch Charlotte if I absolutely have to go in and you aren't here. Where will you teach? Here?"

"No, at a music store," she says. "That's what I was doing back home. Henley's Music isn't far from here, and they offer lessons. I'll go talk to the manager this week and see if I can get one of the lesson rooms. Just let me know what days are best for you, and I can work around that."

"Sure," I say. "How will you get around? Do you drive?"

"I have a license, but I'll use the bus," she says. "I'm used to it and I already looked up the routes. There's a stop just two blocks away, so I'll be fine."

"Okay." I guess she's got things pretty well figured out already. "You know, I obviously don't have a piano. Are you going to need somewhere to practice?"

"Oh, no, I have an electric piano that's being delivered in a few days," she says.

"Does that work as well as a regular piano for you?"

"Yeah, it's fine," she says. "I have a very nice one. The keys are weighted, so it feels right. It just takes up less space."

"Can I play your piano?" Charlotte asks.

"Of course," Linnea says. "I'll teach you to play all kinds of fun things."

"Are your parents shipping the piano?" I ask.

"Yeah." She puts her fork down. "Speaking of my parents, I'm... well, I'm sorry if this was kind of sprung on you."

I feel a little pang of guilt for how much I was complaining to Alex about her. "It's fine. Honestly, I've had such a hard time finding someone to watch Charlotte. My schedule can be erratic, so they have to be willing to be here late into the night sometimes, and a lot of nannies only want to work days. We had one girl who we both liked, but she got engaged and moved out of state. The rest have been… well, let's just say they didn't work out."

"You said Brittany was a twit," Charlotte says.

I wince. "I was upset when I said that, Bug. That wasn't a nice thing for me to say."

Linnea stifles a soft laugh.

"My point is, you living here makes it a lot easier," I say. "And you already knowing Charlotte is a big deal too."

"I like Linnea," Charlotte says.

"I like you too, Bug," Linnea says.

Charlotte beams at her and my heart swells with affection for both of them.

"So, you teach piano," I say. "Are you looking to do anything else in terms of a career in music?"

"Well, the plan is to land a spot with a symphony," she says.

"Wow, that sounds like it would be amazing," I say. "Would you be looking to do that here?"

"If it worked out," she says. "But I don't think there's much chance of getting on with the Seattle Symphony. Their pianists are amazing, and I don't think they'll have any openings for a while."

"Oh, so where would you go?" I ask.

She shrugs. "Depends. Most major cities have a symphony, but I'm more likely to get on with a smaller one until I have more experience. When an opening comes up, I'll have to go audition."

I'm hit with a surge of disappointment at the thought of her leaving. Which is crazy. She doesn't want to be a nanny for the rest of her life. She's a musician. Of course she's going to pursue her career.

We finish up breakfast and I turn on the TV for Charlotte. Linnea and I both head upstairs to shower and get dressed. There's an awkward moment when I come out of my bedroom to find her wrapped in nothing but a towel, going between the bathroom and her bedroom. Her long, wet hair hangs down her back and her skin has a hint of pink from the hot water. She gives me a shy smile and slips into her bedroom, shutting the door behind her.

Downstairs, I play a few games of go-fish with Charlotte—she wins two to my one—until Linnea comes downstairs.

"Can Linnea take me to the park?" Charlotte asks.

"Well, honey, Linnea isn't really watching you today, because I'm off work."

"Oh, I don't mind," Linnea says. "Is the park close?"

"Yeah, it's up the street," I say. "But really, you don't have to."

"I can take her for a little while," she says. "I bet you don't get breaks very often on your days off."

She's right, I don't. I never ask anyone to watch Charlotte on my days off. Mostly, I want to spend time with her. But I've also had to call in too many favors to make sure I have someone to take care of her while I'm working. It's been months since I had even a few hours to myself when she wasn't asleep.

"Actually, that's true," I say. "If you're sure."

"I'd be happy to," she says. "You ready, Bug?"

"I need shoes, but I can tie them myself," she says.

"Wow, you are a big girl," Linnea says with a smile. She meets my eyes and winks.

For fuck's sake, she's killing me.

After I give Linnea directions, she and Charlotte head to the park. I watch them for a moment as they walk up the sidewalk, hand-in-hand. It's amazing how animated Charlotte has been since Linnea arrived. It usually takes her a long time to warm up to people.

It's such a relief. I've been getting increasingly worried about Charlotte's shyness. Not because there's anything inherently wrong with being shy or quiet, but she's having such a tough time at school. She started first grade a few weeks ago, and it hasn't gone smoothly. I want my little girl to be happy and thriving, and it's hard to see her struggle.

I wander into the kitchen—Linnea already cleaned up breakfast—and glance around. I should probably unpack some more boxes, but instead, I sit down on the couch. I'm running on empty a lot, and having even an hour where no one needs me to do anything is nice.

A little while later, there's a knock at the door. I wonder if I accidentally locked them out—I need to get an extra key for Linnea. I answer, but it's my brother-in-law, Weston. He glances behind him, almost like he's worried someone is watching, and comes inside.

"Hey, man."

He nods to me and checks his phone, pocketing it again with a look that I can only describe as relief. We go into the living room and he takes a seat on the couch.

"You seem really tense," I say. "Is everything okay?"

He blows out a breath and leans back. "Yeah. I just need to hide out from Kendra for a little bit."

I laugh. "Why?"

"We're trying to get pregnant," he says. "And she's treating me like her own personal sperm factory."

I'm so surprised, I cough a few times before I can respond. "She's... wow. Uh, okay. I didn't realize you guys wanted kids right away."

"Yeah," he says with a shrug. "Kendra was basically made to be a mom; I knew she'd want a family. Plus, you have Charlotte and she's pretty great."

That makes me smile. Weston's never struck me as a kid person, but he and Charlotte took to each other immediately. Now they have a really cute little bond.

"She is. But I don't get why you're hiding."

"I'm fucking exhausted," he says. "I can't perform on command just because her temperature is right. It's like she doesn't care whether or not I'm in the mood, she just wants me to give it up whenever she snaps her fingers. At first I thought trying to make a baby would be great. Extra sex? Sign me up. But this is getting ridiculous. Does she want me to come home for lunch every day because she misses me? No, she just wants another sperm injection. Same with early mornings, after work, and don't get me started on weekends. She got in the shower, so I made a break for it."

I really don't want to hear about my sister having sex with her husband, but this is kind of hilarious. "So, you're telling me that you, Weston Reid, found a limit to how much sex you can have?"

"It's not that." He shoots me a glare and I think I touched a nerve. "I *can* as often as she wants. But would it kill her to put in a little effort for me? It's so clinical. I'm not a piece of meat."

I can't help but laugh and he glares at me again. "I'm sorry."

"I'm being serious," he says.

"I know, I know." I stop laughing, but there's no way this isn't funny. "Yeah, I bet that's rough."

"You have no idea," he says. "When a woman gets it in her head that she wants to get knocked up, there's no stopping her. I'm just a dick and a couple of testicles to her lately."

It's awful of me, but seeing Weston with bruised feelings is rather amusing. The guy used to be, in Kendra's words, a total man-whore. I don't think I want to know how many women he used for sex before he decided to settle down with my sister. It's funny to see the tables turned on him a little bit.

His phone dings and he groans while he pulls it out. "Oh, great."

"What?"

"Her cervical fluid is the right consistency," he says.

I put a hand to my forehead. "I am *so* sorry I asked."

He starts typing. "I'm telling her to come here."

"Uh, you're not getting your wife pregnant here," I say.

He glares at me again. "No, I need to distract her for a little while. She hasn't seen Bug recently anyway." He looks around as if suddenly noticing the absence of Charlotte. "Where is she?"

"She's at the park with Linnea, the new nanny. They'll be home soon."

Weston nods, then looks at his phone again. "Yeah, she's coming by. Don't tell her what I said, though."

"Don't worry, that's not a conversation I want to repeat."

The front door opens and Linnea and Charlotte come in. Charlotte sees Weston and her eyes light up.

"Uncle Weston!" She rushes over and jumps in his lap.

"Hey, kiddo," he says.

Linnea comes into the living room. "Oh, hi."

I introduce Linnea to Weston and she gives him a shy smile.

"I think my sister is coming over too," I say. "Sorry to inundate you with people so soon."

"That's okay," she says. "But it was hot outside. I'm going to run upstairs and change."

"Sure, take your time."

"I'm going to change too," Charlotte says.

I'm about to tell her she doesn't need to when I stop myself. There's no reason to tell her not to change her clothes, and it's cute to see her copying Linnea.

The girls head upstairs and Weston looks at me with raised eyebrows.

"What?" I ask.

"She's your new nanny?"

"Yeah," I say. "She's Melanie's sister, actually."

"Wow," Weston says. "Well, you're fucked, aren't you?"

"Excuse me?"

"You know what I mean," he says.

"No, it's not like that," I say. "She's just here to help me with Charlotte."

"Right," Weston says. "Where's she staying?"

I hesitate because I know exactly what he's going to think. "Here."

He laughs. "Yeah. Good luck with that."

"I don't need luck, because there's nothing going on," I say. "I've always had nannies for Charlotte. I don't have issues keeping my dick to myself."

He stands and pats me on the shoulder. "Of course not. And she's just another nanny."

4

LINNEA

Charlotte's school is walking distance from their house—one of the reasons Caleb bought it, I think, which of course makes me a little melty. I shake my head and try to stop thinking about him. I have a job to do, but I keep getting lost in little daydreams about him. It's ridiculous, really. I figured I'd get over my insta-crush right away, but here I am, weeks later, and I still find myself thinking about his smile.

Okay, so I'm thinking about more than his smile. But damn it, he has so many things to daydream about.

Most of the other people waiting for the first graders to get out are moms. Several have toddlers in strollers or clinging to their legs. One little girl, who always has the cutest little pigtails, claps and squeals when her big sister comes out. It's the sweetest thing.

I bet Charlotte would love to be a big sister.

Not for the first time since I moved here, I think about my own sister. I still feel guilty, like I've never been sad enough over losing her. I *was* sad when she died. I cried and felt that crushing sense of loss that makes the world feel like it's dull and gray—like you aren't sure if you'll ever be happy again.

But after a while, I got on with my life. Or maybe it's more accurate to say, I went back to trying to survive the hell that was high school. Maybe I shouldn't be so hard on myself. My teen years weren't exactly smooth sailing, and losing my sister in the midst of it didn't make things easier.

I was so shy, I had a hard time functioning at school. Luckily, I didn't get bullied—I was too invisible for that. No one noticed me. But it's a strange thing to walk through crowded hallways, constantly surrounded by people, and feel as if they can see right through you. As if nothing would change if you weren't there.

I came out of my shell a little more in college. Being away from home helped. My parents were always critical and it was impossible to live up to Melanie. She was so perfect. And when she was gone, all their hopes and dreams came to rest squarely on my shoulders.

But I was such a strange, quiet thing. My family didn't understand me—not my love of music, nor my soft-spoken demeanor. There was a time, when I was about eleven, when I became quite convinced I must have been adopted. I don't even look like my parents. Apparently I take after my paternal grandmother. But it was hard being the odd one in the family. All I ever wanted was to feel normal.

Being the nanny among what I'm pretty sure are mostly mothers is a little strange, but I won't let it get to me. Although I'm not nearly as shy as I used to be, I still have a hard time striking up conversations with strangers. There's one mom who makes eye contact with me and smiles most days. I've been trying to work up the courage to say hi to her and introduce myself, but so far, I haven't quite done it. Soon. Maybe I'll be brave enough soon.

The door opens, the pigtail girl claps and bounces up and down on her toes, and the kids start coming out. The teacher makes sure there's a parent or other adult waiting before she lets each child go. I wait as Charlotte's classmates are all released to their respective adults.

Kids stop coming out, but I don't see Charlotte. The teacher, Ms. Peterson, glances back a few times, then makes eye contact with me. "Hold on one second."

She disappears from the doorway, and I step forward to peek inside. Charlotte is still sitting at one of the tables. I can see her name tag, decorated with pink flowers: *Charlotte Lawson.* Caleb did her hair this morning, and it's still in a ponytail with a pink clip holding the wisps of hair that tend to fall around her face.

She's staring at the table, her expression blank. Her hands are limp in her lap and her backpack is propped up against one of the table legs.

"Charlotte," Ms. Peterson says. "It's time to go. Your nanny is here to pick you up."

Charlotte's eyes lift, meeting mine, and I burst into the classroom. She looks terrified, her brown eyes pleading with me to help her.

"Bug." I crouch down next to her chair. "Sweetie, what's wrong?"

Her lower lip trembles, but her eyes stay dry. She doesn't say anything.

I gently brush a little tendril of hair away from her forehead. "You ready to go?"

She nods.

"Okay, Bug. Let's get your backpack. Do you want me to carry it for you?"

She nods again.

I grab her backpack by the top strap and stand, but she still doesn't move. Ms. Peterson crosses her arms and sighs. My eyes snap to her.

"She just needs a minute," I say.

Ms. Peterson doesn't say anything, but her impatience is like a cheap perfume, saturating the air with its odor.

I lean down enough to grab Charlotte's hand and gently coax her out of her chair. "Do you think we should make popcorn when we get home? I've been thinking about popcorn all day, but I didn't make any. I think we should make some together."

She slides her hand in mine and squeezes it tight. I don't know why she's so scared, but I cast another glance back at Ms. Peterson. Did she say something to upset Charlotte? I'm angry at the very thought of it, but I don't think Charlotte will tell me anything here. I need to get her home.

"Do you like butter on your popcorn, Bug?" I ask, leading her toward the still-open door. She's holding my hand so tight, it almost hurts. She has quite a grip.

We get outside and Charlotte stops. The door closes behind us and I can't help but shoot a glare that Ms. Peterson won't see. I can tell she's frustrated with Charlotte, and it makes me not like her very much. I crouch down again so I can look Charlotte in the eyes.

"Bug, can you talk to me? Can you tell me what's wrong?"

She looks down at the ground, keeping my hand in a death grip. "You didn't forget."

"I didn't forget what, sweetie?"

"Me."

"Of course I didn't forget you," I say. "Were you afraid I would?"

She nods, but doesn't look up.

"Why would you be afraid I'd forget you?"

"It's the seventeenth day," she says.

"I don't understand."

"Brittany forgot me on the seventeenth day."

"Your old nanny? Do you mean she forgot to pick you up at

school? But what does the seventeenth day mean? The seventeenth day of what?"

"The seventeenth day of being my nanny."

"Oh," I say, understanding dawning on me. "Is today my seventeenth day?"

Her voice is so tiny. "Yes."

I pull her forward and wrap my arms around her. "Oh, Bug. I'm not going to forget you. Not on the seventeenth day. Not on any day."

She nods against me and I can feel her little body shake as she starts to cry.

"You were worried about that all day, weren't you?" I ask.

"Uh huh."

I rub her back slowly and let her cry into my shoulder. I want to cry along with her. It breaks my heart to think of her fretting all day long, worried that I wouldn't be here to pick her up.

"Listen," I say, and pull back a little so I can look at her. I wipe the tears from beneath her eyes. "I'm going to make you a promise, right now. Do you understand what promise means?"

"Yes," she says. "It's like an oath."

"It is like an oath," I say. "And that's a great word. I'll make you an oath, okay? I promise I will never forget you. If I'm supposed to be here, I'll be here. I will always be here for you."

"Every time?" she asks.

"Every single time," I say. "No matter what."

She sniffs and I wipe away her last tear. "Did you say popcorn?"

I laugh. "I sure did. Let's go home."

We walk home, hand-in-hand, and she's no longer holding onto me with a death grip. When we get there, I make a big tub of popcorn with lots of salt and butter. She might not be hungry for dinner now, but I figure sometimes a girl needs to ruin her appetite.

Caleb comes home just before her bedtime. She runs to greet him at the door as soon as she hears his keys. Like always, he scoops her up and holds her for long moments.

The whole thing is really not fair. He's so gorgeous he makes my breath catch every time I look at him. He's smart and funny. He's a genuinely nice guy in a world where so many of them aren't. And he loves his daughter so much. I didn't think they made men like him. Maybe in books or movies, but not in real life. And yet, there he is, standing by the front door, as real as can be.

And completely unattainable for someone like me.

I let out a long breath and smile when Caleb comes into the living room, still carrying Charlotte. She has her head resting on his shoulder.

"I'll get her to bed," he says.

"There's dinner in there for you," I say. "I put it away, so you can just heat it up or save it if you're not hungry."

He holds my eyes and I wish I knew what he was thinking. It's almost like he's spellbound. By what, I can't imagine. But he just stands there for a long moment, rubbing slow circles across Charlotte's back, his gaze locked with mine.

He blinks and clears his throat. "Thank you. I'm starving, actually. I'll be down in a little bit."

"Okay."

Charlotte murmurs a goodnight as he takes her upstairs. I watch them go, feeling a little ache in my chest.

5

CALEB

My phone buzzes in my pocket just as I'm walking out of room 305. It's been a quiet morning, which is a welcome respite after last night's chaos. They haven't needed me in the OR yet today, so I've been busy checking on patients.

Linnea: I'm stopping at the store. Need anything?

Me: Maybe more of those condoms.

Me: WAIT. NO.

Me: Cookies. I swear I meant cookies. The lemon ones. God, never mind.

Linnea: It's fine! Yeah, I can get those.

Me: Charlotte is out of school early today, right?

Linnea: Yep. 11:30.

Me: Want to come by the hospital after? We can get some boobs.

Me: NO

Me: BOOBS

Me: OMG

Me: F O O D

Me: I'm so sorry. Stupid autocorrect. Lunch. We can get lunch.

Linnea: That's OK. Yeah, sounds good. I'm lesbian soon so I'll see you then.

Linnea: OMG, no!

Linnea: I'm LESBIAN soon.

Linnea: Why, autocorrect? Is it contagious? No, I'm leaving soon. LEAVING.

Linnea: I think we should quit now. I'll see you at lunch.

I shake my head and put my phone back in my pocket. Well that was mortifying. Condoms? Boobs? You have got to be kidding me, autocorrect. I'm glad Linnea has a good sense of humor or I could be in trouble.

My pager beeps, sending a familiar surge of adrenaline through me. I've been wakened from a fitful half-sleep by that sound so many times, it always makes me feel like I have to jump out of bed, no matter what I'm doing.

I'm needed in the ER for a surgical consult, so I head downstairs. The attending and I decide to admit the patient for overnight observation before resorting to surgery. The rest of my morning goes by quickly. I have more patients to check up on. The intestinal perforation is stable and doing well, and the cholecystectomy looks like he'll be ready to be discharged in the morning. His wife is with him, so I spend some time answering her questions.

Seeing the gratitude in her eyes reminds me why I got into this field in the first place. Sometimes I wonder if I chose the right specialty. Being a trauma surgeon can be intense and stressful, and the hours aren't great. I look at Weston with his cushy office and flexible schedule and wonder if I should be doing something else.

But trauma surgery is so rewarding. It's like a puzzle. If a patient comes to me, they're in bad shape, and it's my job to figure out what's wrong with them. Time seems to slow and all my senses sharpen. I have to think fast and act quickly. Very often the patient's life is in my hands. I don't get that kind of a rush from anything else, and I have to admit, it's addictive.

And I'm good at what I do. I've always been cool-headed under pressure. I'm able to stay calm, assess the damage, and take decisive action.

I know I wouldn't be as happy doing something else. But I always have to consider my family. Before Linnea came, I was seriously thinking about finding a different job. My schedule made it so hard to find good childcare, and I couldn't keep relying on my sister. But with Linnea, everything seemed to fall into place.

My pager beeps again, but it's just a question about a patient. I walk over to an empty nurse's station and use the phone to call downstairs and answer.

Kyle, the on-call anesthesiologist, wanders over to the station. "How's the appendectomy doing?"

"Acceptable," I say. "I discharged him."

"I wasn't happy with his oxygen levels," he says. "I included that in my notes to the attending. I hope he gets that sleep apnea under control, or we'll have him back in here before too long."

"Yeah." My phone buzzes again. It's probably Linnea. "Just a sec, Kyle, I need to check this."

Linnea: We're downstairs. Can you still get away for lunch?

Me: Yep. Meet you in the main lobby.

I pocket my phone. "I'm heading downstairs for lunch. My daughter is here."

"Nice," he says. "Who's bringing her? Your sister?"

"No, Linnea," I say. "Her nanny."

He nods. "I'm heading that way too. I'll ride down with you."

Kyle and I take the elevator downstairs. Hopefully I won't get called out on an emergency, although that's more likely to happen at night. Days tend to be quieter in an ER.

The elevator doors open and I spot Charlotte standing near

the front entrance. I glance at Linnea and almost stop in my tracks. She's wearing a pale green sleeveless shirt, form-fitting black pants, and tan wedge heels. Her wavy blond hair is down and she tucks it behind her ear as she smiles at me.

And yes, her boobs look amazing.

"Whoa," Kyle says under his breath. "That's your nanny?"

"Eyes on her face, Kyle."

He clears his throat.

"Hi, Daddy," Charlotte says when we approach.

"Hi, Bug." I pick her up and nod to Kyle as he heads down the hall. I can practically feel him trying not to stare at Linnea.

"I'm glad you could get away for a little bit," Linnea says. "It's good to see you."

"Yeah, it's good to see you too."

Her face flushes, and I think I might have just done a very unmanly thing and blushed a little bit too. Shit.

"I can't go very far when I'm on call, but there's a deli just across the street," I say.

"That sounds great," Linnea says.

"Can I have mac and cheese?" Charlotte asks.

"Let's go see what they have," I say.

We head outside and across the street. The deli is busy, but there are a few open tables. I help Charlotte find what she wants —they do have mac and cheese—and we all order at the counter. The guy gives us a number to take to our table and says our food will be out soon.

Just as we sit down, Charlotte announces she has to go to the bathroom. Linnea grabs her purse and starts to get up, but I put a hand on her arm to stop her.

The feel of her skin sends a jolt of electricity racing through me. I try not to let it show on my face.

"I can take her."

"You sure?" she asks.

"Yeah, happy to. Come on, Bug."

The bathrooms are single occupant, so it's no big deal to take her in the men's room. She chats with me as she goes potty—telling me all about their bus ride downtown. When we come out, there's a guy sitting at our table, directly across from Linnea.

I'm instantly angry. Who the fuck is this guy? I roll my eyes at his hipster-stache. Dude, if you can't grow real facial hair, just shave.

He nods to something Linnea is saying—I can't see her face —but the smile he gives her makes my back stiffen. I know that smile—every guy does. Predatory. I scoop up Charlotte so we can move faster and walk across the deli.

I stop next to the table and glance at Linnea before leveling the guy with a stare. "Hi."

He looks up at me, blinking in surprise. "Oh. Is this your table?"

"Yeah."

"Uh, sorry." He doesn't look at Linnea again, just gets up.

I keep my eyes on him until he leaves out the front door, then set Charlotte down.

"Who was that?" Charlotte asks.

Linnea starts to answer, but I speak first. "Someone who had the wrong table."

"Oh," Charlotte says.

Linnea bites her lower lip and glances away.

Shit. Maybe she wanted to talk to him. She doesn't know many people yet. I know she's met a few people at the music store where she started teaching piano but that's about it. My schedule makes it hard for her to get out and have much of a life. I just acted like kind of a dick, chasing that guy off. It's not like I have any say in who Linnea talks to.

And why should I let it bother me? She's Charlotte's nanny. That's all. It's not like I could date her, even if I wanted to.

Who am I kidding? I want to. I've been entranced by her since the moment she came down that escalator in the airport. But it's just not an option.

"Sorry about that," I say. "I, um, assumed he was bothering you."

She lifts her eyes to meet mine. "It's okay."

"Are you sure?"

"Yeah, it's fine. He kind of invited himself to sit down and then asked me if I drink milk."

"If you drink milk? What's that supposed to mean?" I ask.

Linnea smiles and rolls her eyes. "He said it did my body good."

That makes me laugh. "You're kidding. That's a terrible line."

"It was pretty bad," she says.

The waitress brings our lunches, setting our plates down in front of each of us. I need to get a handle on myself. It's inevitable that Linnea is going to meet people—start dating. She should be dating. She's beautiful and fun, and she'll make some lucky asshole one hell of a girlfriend. Some really lucky asshole one hell of a wife someday.

I've never been a jealous guy, but every time I think of her with someone else, it pisses me off.

We eat lunch and I glance up at her a few times. Keeping things professional with her is more difficult than I thought. But I guess that just means I have to try harder.

6

LINNEA

A little rush of nerves hits me as I stand outside the bar. It's nondescript from the outside, wedged between a nail salon and a tattoo shop. My eyes linger on the tattoo shop for a few seconds. I've been thinking a lot about getting a tattoo, but I haven't mustered the courage to go through with it yet.

Chloe, a girl who works at Henley's Music, invited me out tonight. I met her my first day teaching piano lessons, and she always says hi and chats with me when I'm there. I told her how I'm new in town and working as a nanny for my niece. She invited me out once before, but Caleb had one of his overnight shifts, so I had to be home with Charlotte.

When I told Caleb that Chloe had invited me out tonight, he seemed thrilled that it was on his night off so I could go. Honestly, I think he was more excited than I am. I was waffling over whether or not I wanted to accept, but he told me I really should.

It's not that I don't want to hang out with Chloe. She's really friendly and I bet she's fun. But I'm so nervous. I'm meeting her and some of her other friends at a bar where a local band is playing. I don't know the bar, I don't know the band, and I don't know the other people who'll be here. I don't really know Chloe that well either. Clearly I haven't outgrown all my shyness, because this situation is the type of thing that makes me anxious.

But Caleb is right. I should take a chance and make some friends.

I pull open the door and noise spills out like smoke billowing into the night air. Electric guitar, drums, and an undercurrent of heavy bass notes. A man's voice carries above the melody—raspy and rough with a depth that makes him sound like he's attempting to be both soulful and edgy.

The lights are dim and conversation buzzes beneath the music. I take a few tentative steps inside and the door closes behind me. It feels like I've stepped into another world—one where the atmosphere is too thick, the air pressing at me from all directions. My face flushes from the heat of all the bodies. The bar is packed and the scent of cheap beer mingles with hints of dozens of different perfumes and colognes.

I loosen my grip on my purse; I was clutching it like someone was trying to rip it out of my hands. My shoulders are tight, hunched up near my ears, so I consciously relax them. I must look like a terrified little kid, standing just inside the door, my wide eyes sweeping the crowd.

Deep breath, Linnea. You can do this.

I spot Chloe at a table that's packed with people. She's the epitome of a rock and roll girl, with a short pixie cut dyed pink, piercings in her lip and nose—and who knows where else—and several colorful tattoos. Her ripped jean shorts are *so* short, but she has great legs, so why not. A loose black shirt hangs off one shoulder, showing a bright red bra strap, and I wonder how she can walk in those studded platform heels.

I'm suddenly overcome with self-consciousness at my own outfit. If I was going to the theater or the symphony, I'd be dressed well, but my cream blouse and herringbone pencil skirt make me feel like a stuffy librarian compared to Chloe. I love my red heels, and they do add a pop of color. But I don't know if they're enough to offset the painfully *proper* look I always wear.

Maybe I should just go.

Chloe spots me and waves, so I squeeze through the crowded tables. Her face lights up with a bright smile.

"There she is!" She raises her voice to be heard above the music. "Guys, this is Linnea. Linnea, this is... well, this is everybody."

I smile and wave at the sea of faces in front of me; the table is bar-height, so everyone is standing. I'm glad she didn't throw all their names at me, because I'd never remember. Not with the music pounding in my ears and the press of people around me. I try to keep my face casual and friendly, but inside I'm all knotted.

Somehow the table occupants are managing to carry on a conversation amid the noise. It's hard to follow, so I stay quiet and try to pay attention in case someone talks to me directly. I think they're talking about the band, but I'm not sure.

Chloe nudges me with her elbow and leans in. "So, what do you think? Great place, huh?"

"Yeah." I should follow that with something else—maybe comment on why this bar is great—but I can't think of anything to say. I hesitate too long, but manage to spit out, "Thanks for inviting me."

"No problem. If you want a drink, you have to fight your way to the bar." She nods in the direction of the far side where the bar is almost entirely obscured by people.

There's no way I'm shoving my way through all that to get a drink, but I don't want her to think I'm boring, so I just nod. "Okay."

The band begins another song—it sounds exactly like the

last one—and I can't decide if I should be paying attention to the band or the conversation at the table that I can barely hear. The D string on the guitar is slightly out of tune, making every chord a little discordant to my ears. I know I can hear things other people can't, so I doubt most people are bothered by it. But now that I've noticed, it's hard to focus on anything but the one wave of sound that doesn't fit, its tone slightly flat.

"So, Linnea, where are you from?" a guy next to me asks.

"Michigan," I say.

He nods, the motion of his head slowing, like he's waiting for me to say something else. But I answered his question. What else does he want to know?

"What about you?" I ask, fumbling for something to say.

"I grew up here," he says.

I nod back and feel my cheeks warm again. I wish I was better at this, but I have no idea how to make small talk—especially not with people I don't know. He turns away from me and takes a sip of his beer. I try not to pick at the zipper on my purse.

The people around the table erupt with laughter, but I must have missed the joke.

"This is why I love you guys," Chloe says, still laughing. She turns to me. "I gotta pee. Need to go?"

"No thanks."

"I'll be back," she says and disappears into the crowd.

Time drags on and I stand next to the table, feeling increasingly awkward. Everyone else seems to be having such a great time. They drink, talk, laugh, slap each other on the back, or point to other people around the bar.

I keep trying to think of something to say that might contribute to the conversation, but I don't come up with anything. The flat string on the guitar twangs in my ear, making my back clench, and I start to wonder how it's not bothering anyone but me.

Chloe comes back, but stops to talk to a guy across the table. Her eyes flick over to me once or twice, as do his. I'm pretty sure they're talking about me. I shouldn't stare, but I watch his mouth and make out the words, *does she ever talk?* Chloe shrugs and keeps talking, but I look away.

I wish I wasn't like this. I wish I understood how to make friends like normal people do. It's not that I have no self-esteem, or feel badly about myself all the time; I don't. But I get so tongue-tied and anxious when I'm around people I don't know. I worry I'm going to say the wrong thing, or my mind goes blank and I can't think of anything to say. Getting to know people in college was a little easier; a lot of the students in the music program were quiet like me. But it still took me most of my first year to make even a single friend.

This scene—hanging out in a bar with a bunch of people who I'm sure are perfectly nice and fun—should be fine. But every minute I'm here, the knot in my stomach tightens. My throat is so dry I'm not sure if I'll be able to make a sound if I do speak. I feel myself fading into the background, people's gazes passing over me like I'm not here. Like I'm invisible.

I force myself to stay a while longer, hoping it gets better. Maybe Chloe will come stand next to me again and I can think of something to talk to her about. But she doesn't. She makes eye contact with me a few times and smiles, but she's wrapped up in a very animated conversation with a guy and another girl across the table. I think they're talking about their tattoos, because Chloe lifts her shirt, revealing a wreath of flowers encircling her belly button.

The guitarist really needs to take a break between songs and tune his guitar. I glance over at the bar, wondering if it's thinned out enough that I can go get a drink, but if anything, the crowd is thicker. The noise feels heavy, like it's weighing me down. The guy who asked me where I'm from glances at me again, but he's not looking at my face. His eyes are on my chest—typical—and after a moment, he looks away.

The band rolls into yet another song and I sigh. Not only is the guitar slightly out of tune, but every song is depressing. They seem to be going for an angsty grunge sound, but after the fifth or sixth song, it starts to sound monotone and whiny.

I lose track of Chloe; maybe she went to the bar, or back to the bathroom. I want to go, but I don't want to leave without saying goodbye. It's bad enough that I showed up and just stood here, not talking to anyone. I wait about five more minutes, but she doesn't appear.

I've had about all I can take, so I slip away from the table. When I glance back over my shoulder before leaving, I can't see any sign that anyone noticed I'm gone.

Outside on the sidewalk, I take a deep breath of the fresh night air. Traffic whizzes by, but the sound of engines and wheels on pavement is melodic compared to the oppressive weight of noise in the bar.

I pull out my phone and send a text to Chloe, thanking her for inviting me, and letting her know I have to get up early for work tomorrow. Which is true, I do. Charlotte has school, and even though Caleb will be home, mornings are better for everyone when I help them get ready for the day.

Rather than waiting for the bus, I order an Uber. It isn't far, so it won't cost much, and I just want to get home. I only have to wait a few minutes and my ride pulls up to the curb.

When I get back to Caleb's house, I'm greeted by the soft glow of lights in the downstairs windows. Charlotte should be in bed by now, but it looks like he's still up. I'm careful to be quiet when I come inside, just in case he went to bed and left the lights on for me.

I find him on the couch with a laptop in his lap, the TV on

but muted. He looks up and his smile melts away some of the anxiety I was feeling.

"Hey," he says. "You're back early."

I sink down into an armchair and let my shoes slide off my feet. "Yeah, I guess."

"How was it?"

What do I say? I hated it because it made me feel invisible again? I'm worried he's going to be disappointed in me if I tell him the truth.

"It was fun," I say. "The band wasn't really my style, but live music is nice anyway."

"Good," he says. "Was it just... what was her name?"

"Chloe," I say. "And no, there were a lot of people. The place was packed and Chloe was there with a big group. They were nice."

He nods a little, his eyes lingering on my face with that expression I can't read. "That's great. I'm glad you had fun. I hope you didn't come home early on my account. I know Charlotte has school tomorrow, but I can take her if you want to sleep in."

"Oh, no, that's okay. I was ready to come home." I tuck my feet up under me and gesture at his laptop. "Are you working?"

"No." He closes it and moves it to the coffee table. "No, I was just looking a few things up." He grabs the remote and holds it out to me. "If you want to watch TV or something, feel free. Or, maybe you're ready for bed."

I take the remote. "Thanks. I'm not all that tired."

He smiles again and it makes me all tingly inside. "Me neither. So, what should we do?"

Make out on the couch?

My cheeks warm and I turn my attention to the TV, hoping he doesn't notice. I bring up Netflix and scroll through the options. "Is there anything you like to watch?"

"I'm up for whatever. I don't have any shows I watch regularly or anything."

"Really? None?"

"Nope. Not unless you count *My Little Pony*."

"Well, at least that show isn't too terrible."

"I have learned that friendship is magic, so I have that going for me."

I laugh. "It's a good lesson. What about *Supernatural*?"

"No, haven't watched it."

I raise my eyebrows. "You're kidding."

"Not in the least."

I scroll through and find *Supernatural*, then bring up the first season. "Okay, we definitely have to remedy that. I can't believe you don't know Sam and Dean."

"Sounds like I'm missing out."

"You have no idea," I say. "This is my favorite show."

"I'm excited to watch it with you, then," he says.

Our eyes meet and there's that expression again—the one I can't read. We stare at each other for a few heartbeats too long. But instead of making me feel anxious and uncomfortable, the prolonged eye contact is pleasant. True, it makes my tummy swirl with a little flutter of nerves. But it's a feeling of excitement, rather than dread.

I like it.

I bring up the first episode and press play. I don't know what it says about me that I'm so much more comfortable here, hanging out with Caleb—who, let's not forget, is my employer—rather than at a bar with a bunch of people my own age. That thought is a little unsettling, and I'm reminded once again of how abnormal I am. But instead of dwelling on it, I snuggle down into the soft armchair to watch my show.

7

CALEB

The parking lot is packed, but that's no surprise. We're in the midst of a random September heat wave, and when the sun comes out in Seattle, people come out of the woodwork. Probably because it's cloudy and gray for so much of the year.

Charlotte reads a book while I circle around, looking for a spot. I happen to have a Saturday off and Kendra suggested we all meet at Alki Beach for the day. Charlotte lit up like a tiny little star when I said the word *beach*, so come hell or high water, I'm finding a damn parking spot.

Linnea points. "Over there. Someone's leaving."

"Thanks." I turn and stop while the other person backs up.

It occurred to me when we got about halfway here that I didn't need to bring Linnea. I never used to bring Charlotte's nannies with me to hang out with my family. They've always just watched Charlotte while I'm at work, but never when I'm off. I try to tell myself Linnea is different because she lives with us. She didn't have plans today, so why not invite her along?

It has nothing to do with wanting to see her in a swimsuit. That would be completely inappropriate.

But really, it would have been strange not to bring her. She's hung out with my family a few times. We get together pretty often, and Linnea always comes along. No one has questioned it, which makes me wonder where the line is between us. It's feeling a little blurry lately. She's not *just* the nanny.

Although, of course she's not; she's Charlotte's aunt. But it feels like more than that. We've become friends. Maybe even *good* friends.

I pull into the parking spot and Linnea helps me grab our gear for the day. You'd think with just one child, I wouldn't have to bring half of what we own, but that's what it feels like. Charlotte carries her backpack, stuffed with books, a beach towel, hairbrush, change of clothes, and her own bottle of sunscreen. Between me and Linnea, we have a cooler, a bag with more towels and sunscreen, a beach blanket, Charlotte's sand toys, and another bag of snacks.

Everyone else is already here; I chalk it up to being the only one with a kid. They have towels spread out on the sand, a little way up from the edge of the water. The parking lot was full, but down on the beach, there's plenty of space.

Kendra is laying with her head on Weston's thigh. She's dressed in a blue and purple floral bikini and a sun hat obscures her face. Weston has on blue board shorts and sunglasses.

To the surprise of no one, Mia is reading a book. She's also wearing a bikini—hers is black with green and blue stripes—and she's leaning back against Alex. He's dressed like Weston—board shorts and sunglasses.

Everyone says hi as we approach and Kendra gets up to help us get settled. Charlotte gives everyone hugs and fishes a picture out of her backpack that she drew for Weston. Kendra watches Charlotte give it to him with her hand covering her mouth like she's trying not to cry. It makes me wonder if they've had any luck getting pregnant. They haven't said anything; I'm certainly not going to ask.

Charlotte wastes no time pulling off the t-shirt and shorts I insisted she wear in the car, and Linnea immediately starts putting sunscreen on her.

"Thanks," I say.

"Sure." She smiles at me and goddammit, she's beautiful.

We get our big blanket spread out and our stuff situated. I take off my shirt so I can soak up some sun. The heat feels great. Linnea pulls off her tank top and skirt, revealing her swimsuit underneath. If I didn't think she looked like a pinup before—which I did—she certainly does now. She's wearing a vintage-style navy and white polka-dot one-piece that frames her ridiculous tits beautifully. I have to tear my eyes away from her, but I know Weston saw me staring. Damn it.

"Kendra, see my new swimsuit," Charlotte says. She fluffs out the little ruffle around the waist. "My old one was too small."

"That's so pretty, Bug," Kendra says.

Charlotte looks from Kendra to Mia, then to Linnea. "Linnea, why doesn't your swimsuit show your tummy?"

Mia snorts. "Bug, I don't think a bikini exists that could contain Linnea's... I mean... it's probably just..."

"Contain Linnea's what?" Charlotte asks.

"You know what happened?" Linnea cuts in, totally nonplussed. "I tried on a whole bunch of swimsuits, and this one was my favorite. Even though it doesn't show my tummy."

"Why is it your favorite?" Charlotte asks.

"It's comfortable," Linnea said. "And I think the polka dots are pretty."

"It is pretty," Charlotte says.

"Thank you," Linnea says. "Yours is pretty too."

"Wow, that was a good answer," Mia says.

"Can I go play in the water?" Charlotte asks.

I'm grateful for the change of subject. "Sure, Bug."

I start to get up, but Linnea takes her hand.

"That's okay, I'll take her."

"Thanks."

Linnea holds her hand as they walk down to the water. Charlotte has a little plastic bucket and shovel. They stop at the edge of the water where the waves lap lazily up the sand.

Kendra stretches out on the towel again, leaning against Weston, her face obscured by her sun hat. Mia fusses with a pair of sunglasses that she's trying to wear over her regular glasses; Alex expertly ducks out of the way of her flying elbow.

"How's the new nanny working out, Affleck?" Weston asks.

I glance over at him. "What?"

Mia laughs. "I get it. Because Ben was banging the nanny."

"He was what?" I ask. "Wait, was that ever confirmed?"

"He was *so* hitting that," Weston says.

"Yeah, well, it made the news because he was married," I say. "I'm not."

"So you're hitting that?" Weston asks.

"No, that's not what I... Fuck off, Reid."

"Whatever you say, Affleck."

"Stop calling me that, asshole."

Mia gasps, putting a hand to her mouth.

"You okay, babe?" Alex asks her.

"I can't believe I didn't see it before," she says.

"See what?" Alex asks.

"Linnea is the nanny."

I furrow my brow at her. I have a feeling I don't want her to finish this train of thought, but maybe it's better if she does it before Linnea comes back. "Yes, she's Charlotte's nanny. You already knew that."

"No, that's not what I mean," Mia says. "You're the hot single dad, and she's the nanny. K-Law, back me up here."

Kendra lifts her sun hat. "Oh my god, Mia, you're right."

"See? Kendra knows what I'm talking about."

"Maybe someone could clue me in, because I have no idea," I say.

Mia sighs, like she's having to explain something simple to a person who should know better. "That's a thing, Caleb—the hot single dad falling for the nanny."

"A thing?"

"Yeah," she says. "So, are you?"

"Am I what?" I ask.

"Falling for her."

For fuck's sake. I shake my head and try to act like I'm blowing off her comment as utter nonsense. "I don't know what you're talking about."

"Sure you don't," Mia says, her voice thick with sarcasm. She tilts her head, and I think she's watching Linnea down by the water's edge. "Man, I'm off my game. I should have picked up on that a lot sooner."

"You and me both," Kendra says.

"You think?" Alex asks.

I groan. Of course my brother—the man who writes romance novels—speaks their language.

"Oh yeah," Mia says. "I mean, Linnea is awesome and Caleb is a total DILF. It works."

"He's what?" Alex asks, his voice flat. "Did you just say my brother is a dad you'd like to fuck?"

I look over at them in alarm, my eyes wide.

"Yeah," Mia says. "I don't mean that I literally want to fuck your brother. It's just an expression."

Alex glowers a little and Mia laughs.

"Come on, he looks just like you," Mia says. "He's a good-looking guy. I'm sure lots of women want to fuck him."

I put my hand over my eyes and shake my head. "Oh my god."

"Yeah, some girls are into the dad bod," Weston says.

"What?" I ask.

He shrugs. "Some girls like their guy cuddly. Maybe that's why they go for the DILFs."

I gape at him.

Kendra peeks at me from beneath her hat. "He doesn't have a dad bod. He has a six pack."

I glance down at myself, feeling oddly self-conscious. I work out six days a week, even on days when I have a long shift.

"You do have a cute little roll underneath, though," Kendra says.

"What the fuck, Kendra," I say.

She laughs. "I'm just teasing. Besides, I'm sure Linnea doesn't mind."

"You guys, stop," I say. Linnea is still far enough away that she can't hear us, but I have to put an end to this nonsense right now. "Nothing is going on."

"Yet," Mia says, the word snapping in her mouth like gum popping.

"No, *yet* has nothing to do with it," I say. "Seriously, you guys need to shut up. You're going to embarrass her."

"I would never," Mia says.

"Well, you wouldn't on purpose," Kendra says.

Mia scrunches up her nose. "Okay, that's fair. But if this happens, let the record show, I called it." She looks at me and points at Kendra and Weston. "And I called it with them, too."

Linnea brings Charlotte back and we all break out food for lunch. Weston keeps sneaking Charlotte cookies—like I can't see him—but I let him get away with it. We hang out and eat, and thankfully the conversation doesn't return to things like dads falling for nannies, DILFs, or dad bods.

I take Charlotte on a walk down the beach and we find a few seashells. Then Linnea and I help her build a sandcastle. It's more like a sand mound, but Linnea finds a few sticks to poke in the tops of the so-called towers, like flags, and we use the seashells we picked up as decoration.

Charlotte has to use the bathroom, and Linnea volunteers to take her. I head back to our stuff and sit on the blanket.

"Okay, what about those?" Mia asks.

"What are you guys doing?" I ask.

"Playing real or not real," Mia says. She points to a woman in a black and gold bikini. "So, her? I say real."

Weston pulls his sunglasses down and glances at the woman. "Not real."

"What?" Mia says. "Yes they are."

"Nope," Weston says.

"They don't look fake at all," she says.

"Wait," I say. "Real or not real, meaning boobs?"

"Yeah," Mia says, sounding dejected. "I swear, those look totally natural. How can you tell?"

"Too round and too much lift for her size," Weston says. "They're not bad. Although they're not good enough to be a set of mine."

Mia sticks her chest out and looks down. "I'm pretty round, aren't I?"

Weston looks her up and down. "Yeah, your breasts have an excellent shape." He reaches over and lightly cups a hand beneath one of her boobs. "Good lift, too."

"Dude, hands off," Alex says.

"He's a doctor," Mia says. "It's fine."

"He won't be if I break his fingers," Alex says.

Weston doesn't seem the least bit fazed, and Kendra laughs softly from beneath her hat.

"Okay, before she comes back, what about Linnea?" Mia asks, ignoring Alex. "Real or not real?"

"Is this a game you guys play often?" I ask.

"Sometimes," Mia says. "I never beat him, though. I shouldn't play against a plastic surgeon. Come on, Weston. Are hers real?"

"Real," he says.

"How can you tell?" Mia asks. "I know they are, but let's be honest, they're amazing. They could be fake, right?"

"Yeah, women pay a lot of money to look like her," Weston says. "I can tell because they have a slight teardrop shape." He turns to me. "You should tell her to make sure she always wears a supportive bra. Gravity isn't going to be on her side when she gets older. Especially if she has kids."

I gape at him.

"Yeah, but then she can just go see you, right?" Mia asks.

"Yeah, I'll fix her," Weston says, totally matter of fact.

"Oh my god, can we stop talking about Linnea's boobs, please?" I ask. This is almost worse than the DILF conversation.

Thankfully, they drop the subject before Linnea and Charlotte come back. My family is so weird.

After we hang out a while longer, we decide it's time to go. Linnea helps me pack our things. We say goodbye to everyone and head back to the car.

The three of us are warm and tired from a day spent in the sun. I glance over at Linnea and she smiles. There's a comfort between us that surprises me. It's a pleasant, contented feeling. I enjoyed this day so much more than I would have without her. I'm not sure what that means, but I'm starting to wonder if what I'm feeling is more than just physical attraction.

There's no denying she's beautiful—and my god, so fucking sexy. But if I was only interested in her body, I think it would be easier to get over this infatuation. Instead, the longer she's here, the worse it gets.

I take a deep breath. It must be the sun. Or the heat. Or spending an afternoon looking at her in a swimsuit. I think back on what Mia said. Am I falling for her?

I know what a bad idea that is, but I'm not sure I can stop.

8

LINNEA

The sun makes me squint, so I pull my sunglasses out of my purse. It's a short walk to Charlotte's school, and it's such a nice day. The air is cool—a refreshing change after the heat we had a few weeks ago. Now it feels like fall. Maybe I'll see if Charlotte wants to go to the park before we go home. We don't have anything planned this afternoon.

A few of the moms stand in a little half-circle near the classroom door. They glance at me when I approach. The looks they give me aren't exactly friendly, so I usually keep my distance. I don't know why they look at me that way. They don't know me. In fact, they've never tried to talk to me. Granted, I don't try to talk to them either, but who can blame me? It's not even shyness at this point; some of them just don't seem very friendly.

I lean against the short fence that runs around the small courtyard in front of the classrooms. A few more moms wander over, a couple of them pushing strollers. I glance up at the small group by the door and I see one of them say the word *nanny*.

Wow, I think they're talking about me.

I got good at reading lips when I was little. Being quiet doesn't mean you aren't paying attention—quite the opposite—

and I noticed *everything*. It became a habit to watch people's mouths to see what they were saying. I didn't realize until I was older that in a lot of situations, it's rude.

This time, I don't care if I'm basically eavesdropping from across the courtyard. They're not trying very hard to hide that they're discussing me. Maybe because I have sunglasses on and it looks like I'm not paying attention to them.

It's obvious why he hired her, one woman says. Another woman leans closer to her. *Do you think he sleeps with all of them?* The first woman nods. *Why do you think he goes through so many nannies?*

I get a sick feeling in the pit of my stomach. Is that what they think of me? What they think of Caleb? It's not his fault he went through so many nannies; it wasn't because he was sleeping with them. And he's certainly not sleeping with me.

Not that I would object if he wanted to...

Cool it, Linnea. Calm those traitor hormones. Do I have to remind myself—again—of all the reasons Caleb is off limits?

The friendly mom, as I've been calling her in my head, arrives. She's super cute in a gray cardigan over a pink t-shirt and jeans. Her dark hair is cut short, and like usual, she's wearing a brightly colored cloth headband. Today's is pink and orange paisley.

She stands close enough that I could start a conversation if I wanted. I've thought about it so many times, but I've never been good at making the first move—not with men, or potential friends. But maybe I should just suck it up. I glance at the women who were talking about me, but they aren't looking in my direction anymore.

I slip off my sunglasses and make eye contact. My heart starts to beat faster, but I take a deep breath. "Hi. Sorry, I see you all the time and I've never introduced myself. I'm Linnea."

She smiles. "Megan. It's nice to meet you. Your little girl is...?"

"Charlotte," I say. "But I'm her nanny."

"Oh, I see," she says. "My son is Noah."

I get a little tongue-tied at that point because I'm not quite sure what to say next. I want to explain that I'm not just Charlotte's nanny—I'm her aunt—but now it seems strange to say it. Just when the silence is about to get awkward, Megan leans closer and lowers her voice.

"You know, I've noticed that Charlotte and Noah seem to have a little something in common," she says.

"What's that?"

"Don't take this the wrong way, because I'm in the same boat," she says. "But the other kids come out laughing and run to their moms. But Charlotte always looks so serious. I only noticed it because Noah is the same way."

"Charlotte's shy," I say. "I think some people assume she's mad or pouting, but she's actually feeling anxious and scared."

"Oh, poor sweetie," Megan says. "Noah's his dad's mini-me, which means he's stoic and grumpy."

I laugh and Megan laughs along with me. We glance over as Ms. Peterson opens the door.

One by one, the first graders come out. Megan is right, most of them run, hop, or skip to their parent. There's a pause, and a little dark-haired boy comes out. He's wearing a blue t-shirt and his green backpack looks enormous on him.

"Hey, kiddo," Megan says.

Noah shuffles over to her, and he does look a little sullen. He leans against her and she gives him a hug.

Charlotte is a few seconds behind him. She comes out with her eyes locked on the ground, her back stiff and straight. I always get a pang of sadness when she comes out of the classroom. I wish she didn't struggle so much.

"Hi, Bug," I say softly and crouch down. She slips her arms around my neck and I snuggle her for a long moment, feeling her relax. I don't ask her if she's okay anymore. It's always on the tip of my tongue, but I know if there's something bothering her, she won't tell me about it yet. I have to give her a little time.

I stand and smooth her hair down.

"Hey, what do you think about bringing Charlotte over for a playdate?" Megan asks.

I get a little ping of excitement at the idea. Maybe this would help Charlotte make a friend. That would be so amazing. I glance down at her. "What do you think? Would you like to go have a playdate at Noah's house?"

She tucks her hand in mine, but her grip stays light. It takes her a second to respond, but I can tell this isn't making her nervous; if it was, she'd be holding onto me with her death grip. She meets my eyes and nods.

It's such a little thing, but I'm flooded with happiness. "Okay, good. Yeah, we'd love to."

"If you don't mind being spontaneous, and the very high possibility of a messy house, you guys could come over now," she says. "If you don't have other plans, obviously."

"Sure," I say. "We don't have any plans today."

"Awesome. We live just up the street," Megan says with a smile.

Megan's house is lovely. It's set back from the street with a trim front yard. Hanging baskets spill dark green ivy near the door. Inside is small, but cozy. The front area has a living room with a couch facing a TV, and a fireplace on the side wall. Further in is a kitchen with pretty white cabinets and yellow walls. She sets her things down on the kitchen table and asks Charlotte and Noah what they want for a snack.

While she busies herself in the kitchen, I coax Charlotte into a chair at the table. Noah sits across from her, but he doesn't say anything. A few minutes later, Megan brings over a plate of apple slices and a bowl of pretzels.

"Can I make you some coffee or something?" Megan asks once the kids are busy eating.

"Tea would be nice, thanks."

She makes us both a mug of tea, and when the kids are finished snacking, Noah asks Charlotte if she wants to go play. To my relief, Charlotte nods—she even smiles—and follows him down the hallway.

"Wow," Megan says. "That was easy."

"Yeah it was," I say. "This is so nice. Charlotte has a hard time making friends."

"Noah does too," she says. "I worry about him, but my husband always assures me he'll be fine. James was the same way when he was little, and he turned out okay. He's still a serious guy, but I was able to teach him how to smile, at least."

I laugh, a vision of breezy, colorful Megan with a stiff and stoic husband flashing through my mind. "Sounds like you complement each other."

"We do." She takes sip of her tea. "You know, it's surprising to me that you're Charlotte's nanny."

"Why?"

"You seem closer to her than that," she says. "She was in Noah's class last year, and there were a few different girls who picked her up. I could tell they were nannies. They acted like babysitters. But I really thought you might be her mom. I wondered if maybe you worked before and your schedule changed or something."

"Well, I'm more than her nanny," I say. "I'm her aunt. She's my sister's daughter. But my sister was killed in a car accident when Charlotte was a baby."

"Oh my god," Megan says. "I'm so sorry."

"Thanks." I tuck my hair behind my ear, suddenly thinking

about Caleb. About how hard it must have been to lose his wife. It reminds me that I'm just his wife's little sister—and how ridiculous this crush really is. "It was hard. But Charlotte's dad is an amazing father, so that helps."

"That's good," she says.

She asks a little more about me, so I tell her that I play piano, and about getting my music degree. When she asks about becoming a nanny, I find myself spilling the whole story: how my parents made the decision without me, and probably pushed Caleb into it too. But also how great it's been since I moved out here—how much I love what I'm doing now.

"You're so good with her," Megan says. "You're always so gentle."

"I was a lot like her," I say. "I understand what she feels like, I guess."

Megan smiles. "She's lucky to have you. Definitely have kids someday. You're a natural."

"Thanks," I say with a laugh. "I'm not really in a position where that's going to happen any time soon. But I'd love to."

Megan pauses and lifts her eyebrows. "Do I hear laughing?"

The sound of Charlotte's giggle mingled with Noah's laughter drifts down the hall. "I think you do. It sounds like they're having fun."

"Okay, it's official," Megan says. "I'm adopting you. You're nice, easy to talk to, you don't seem to be judging my messy house, and our kids are having fun. We have to do this again."

"I would love that," I say. "How about we have you over next time?"

"Done," she says. "Anytime. Just let me know."

I chat with Megan for a little while longer, then round up Charlotte to go home. She's reluctant to leave, and Noah is reluctant to let her go, which makes both Megan and me almost squeal with glee. We promise both kids they'll see each other at school tomorrow, and we'll have another playdate very soon.

Caleb's car is already in the driveway when we walk up to the house. I check my phone, worried he might have texted to see where we are, but I don't have any messages. We go inside and I hear Caleb talking. I pause just inside the door while Charlotte takes her shoes off.

"Sure, that sounds great," Caleb says. He must be on the phone. "I'm looking forward to it... All right, perfect. I'll see you soon."

I hesitate, even after Charlotte runs in to find him. Who was he talking to? It sounded like he was making plans. That couldn't have been a date, could it? There was something in his voice that makes me wonder—a note of affection, maybe?

"There's my favorite girl!"

What am I thinking? It's none of my business. He could have been talking to Kendra, or his dad. And even if he was making plans with a woman, it doesn't have anything to do with me. I certainly don't have the right to an opinion on what he does in his free time—or who he spends it with. He's a single adult—there's nothing wrong with him dating.

Pushing aside the unease in my tummy, I head to the kitchen to see what he wants to do for dinner.

9

CALEB

Coming off an overnight shift usually leaves me in one of two states—either dead tired and wishing I could sleep for a week, or so wide awake I wonder if I'll ever sleep again.

Today is the latter.

That's a good thing, as long as I can hold out until at least Charlotte's bedtime before I crash. I have to be at the hospital at seven tomorrow morning, so the best thing for me to do is stay awake until tonight. The way I'm feeling, it shouldn't be too much of a problem, provided I stay busy.

I park in the driveway and head for the front door. Charlotte is still at school, and I'm not sure if Linnea is home. I find myself hoping she's here, and just as quickly squashing that hope down. Hard as I try to bury my attraction to her, it rears its ugly head at just the thought of seeing her. And the promise of a few hours alone with her before it's time to pick up Charlotte from school is tempting in all kinds of ways. That surge of temptation almost makes me turn around and go back to my car.

But then I hear it. Music. Is that Linnea playing?

I've heard her play a little, but never like this. Very carefully, I slip my key in the lock and open the front door—slow, so I don't disturb her. I know she needs to practice and I'd hate to break her concentration.

That's what I tell myself, at least. Really, I just don't want her to stop playing.

I stand just inside the front door and quietly shut it. From the entryway, I can see her sitting at her piano. Her back is to me, and she doesn't pause or look over her shoulder. I don't think she heard me come in.

Her hands caress the keys with such fluid dexterity, it's mesmerizing to watch. She sways to the rhythm of her song, as if the music fills her body. Her head tilts, leans to one side, then the other. Hands stretch out to reach the keys at each end.

I don't recognize the piece, but the music is breathtaking. Intense and dramatic. She hits the keys with authority, as if she has no doubt about which notes to play. I've never seen this side of her. She's sweet and soft-spoken, but this music is powerful and passionate. Her whole body moves as music fills the air, and I stare at her, captivated.

The song winds down and she stops, her hands still resting lightly on the keys.

"Wow," I say. "That was amazing."

She gasps and turns around. "Oh, I didn't hear you come in."

"Sorry," I say. "I didn't want to disturb you."

"It's okay." She glances down, and tucks her hair behind her ear. "I just didn't realize someone was listening."

"It was absolutely beautiful." *Just like you.*

Her eyes lift to meet mine. "Thank you." She tucks her hair again, on the same side, although it didn't need it. "Sorry, I knew you'd be home this morning, but I wasn't paying attention to the time."

"It's okay. I'm glad I got to hear you play." I've got heat and tension growing where they shouldn't, so I break eye contact and walk toward the kitchen. I hear her following me. "So, what are you up to today?"

"Well... actually..."

I pause and glance back at her. She's standing just outside the kitchen, where the carpet meets hardwood, plucking at her hair like she's nervous.

"Is everything okay?" I ask.

A knot of dread forms in the pit of my stomach. I bet she has an audition. I bet she's trying to figure out how to tell me she's going to leave.

I swallow hard, alarmed at the rush of emotion that thought elicits. I know it's coming at some point, but I don't want it to be now. Charlotte is going to be devastated.

Let's not talk about how I'm going to feel.

"Yes, everything is fine." She takes a deep breath, like she needs it to be brave enough to talk, and then the words come out fast, in a rush. "I have an appointment to get a tattoo and I'm kind of scared and I was wondering if you'd come with me."

I blink at her. What did she just say? I didn't hear *audition* or *symphony*. I think she just said *tattoo*.

"I'm sorry," she says. "I shouldn't have asked you. It's fine. I can go by myself. I planned on it anyway."

"No," I say, hurrying to get the word out. "No, that just wasn't what I thought you were going to say. When's your appointment? I'd love to come with you."

Her face brightens. "It's, well, it's in an hour."

"Great," I say. "I need something to keep me awake until tonight anyway."

~

THE TATTOO SHOP is on Roosevelt in a strip-mall style building. There isn't any parking out front, so we circle the block and find a spot. It's a short walk, so we get out and head down the sidewalk.

"Is this, um..." I falter, because as far as I know, Linnea doesn't have any tattoos. I've seen her in a swimsuit, so if she does, they must be... well-hidden. "Is this your first tattoo?"

"Yeah," she says. "I think that's why I'm so nervous."

"What made you decide to get one?"

"Well, I've thought about it for a long time," she says. "I just think they can be really beautiful. It's art you wear on your body, you know?"

"Yeah."

"Do you have any?" she asks.

"No," I say. "I've thought about it a few times. I might get something that represents Charlotte someday."

"That would be so sweet," she says.

"How did you find the shop?" I ask, suddenly wondering if she's done any research. Is this place going to be clean?

"Oh, Mia knows the artist," she says.

"Mia?" I ask. "Alex's Mia? How does she know a tattoo artist?"

"He's someone she grew up with," she says. "They went to school together or something. I was talking with her and Kendra and told them I was thinking about doing this, so Mia gave me his number."

"Do you know what you're going to get?"

"Yep," she says. "I already met with him last week. He's going to have some designs for me to choose from today, but it will be a treble clef and some music notes."

"That's perfect," I say.

"Yeah, I think so," she says.

Before I can ask her where she's planning to get her tattoo, we're at the shop. I open the door for her and we both go inside.

There's a large L-shaped front counter with every kind of

piercing jewelry imaginable displayed in the glass case. I'm actually not sure where some of them are designed to go. A woman with tattoos covering most of her arms and several piercings in her face greets us.

"Hi, can I help you?"

"I have an appointment with Dex," Linnea says.

"Great, I'll tell him you're here," she says.

Linnea fiddles with her hair and I glance around at the samples on the walls. There are posters and prints with hundreds of different tattoo designs.

"Hey, Linnea, good to see you again."

The guy who approaches is tall, with thickly muscled arms covered in ink. He's wearing a faded gray t-shirt and jeans, and I have no doubt women find this guy attractive. Dark hair. Blue eyes. Square jaw covered in rough stubble.

Linnea holds her hand out and he takes it gently. "Nice to see you too," she says.

"So are you ready for this?" he asks.

"I think so."

"You're going to do great," he says, flashing her a smile.

Linnea nibbles her bottom lip.

I can't decide if I appreciate his friendly demeanor—it's obvious he cares about making her feel comfortable—or if I'm annoyed at the way she's looking at him.

"So, you brought someone?" Dex asks.

"Yeah, I hope that's okay," she says. "This is Caleb."

"Yeah, it's fine," he says. "You can both come on back."

He leads us behind the front counter and past several tattoo stations where artists are busy working on clients. One has a woman stretched out on a table, lying face down. He's working on a design on the back of her calf. Another has a man seated in a chair while he tattoos something on his forearm. That artist has a long silver beard that hangs down to his beer belly. Why couldn't Linnea have picked that guy to do her tattoo?

Dex's station is at the back of the shop. It's full of posters and stickers, most of them black. Lots of skulls. There's a colorful sign near a few coat hooks that says *I believe in unicorns*. I'm not sure what to think about that one.

He pulls up a stool and gestures for me to sit, then has Linnea sit in the chair. He brings out some drawings with several variations on the music theme.

"Okay, here's what I came up with," he says, showing the drawings to Linnea. "What do you think? Any of these what you were hoping for?"

"That one," she says without hesitation, pointing to a drawing of a treble clef with a swirl of music notes. "That's exactly what I was thinking."

"Awesome," he says. "Any changes, or just like this?"

"Just like that," she says.

"Great. Give me just a second and I'll get the stencil ready."

He goes to a flat area, almost like a desk, on one side of his station. Linnea bites her lip again and twists her hands in her lap.

"Nervous?" I ask.

She nods. "A little."

I'm close enough to touch her, so I reach out and squeeze her hand. "You'll be fine."

Before I take my hand away, she squeezes mine back. "Thanks for coming."

"Okay, Linnea, we're going to try this on," Dex says. "Is this your boyfriend, or...?"

"Oh, um... no," she says, her face flushing. "But it's okay if he stays. I'll just turn."

I'm a little stunned at hearing the word *boyfriend*, and before I can say anything, he drops a fucking bomb.

"Cool, then go ahead and take off your shirt and bra and we'll make sure of the placement."

My eyes almost bug out of my head and it's all I can do to keep from choking. Take off her what, now?

She stands up and turns her back to me, then lifts her shirt over her head. I keep my eyes directly on the back wall.

Okay, so I peek. Once. Fine, twice. I'm only human.

"You can just hold your shirt up to keep your boobs covered," Dex says and I clench my jaw when he says *boobs*. "Caleb, can you give her a hand with her bra? Or I can in a second."

Oh, for fuck's sake. Is he kidding? Has he *seen* her? But hell no, this dude is not taking her bra off. "Yeah, sure."

She's holding her shirt over her chest and gives me a quick glance over her shoulder before turning away again. My eyes lock on the clasp of her pale pink bra and I swallow hard.

Okay, let's just get this over with.

Her hair hangs down her back, so I move it aside. It feels like silk between my fingers. I unfasten the clasps and her bra comes loose. I open it so the straps slip down her shoulders. All I can think about is how much I want to run my hands all over her skin and reach around to cup those magnificent tits. My heart pounds too hard, the blood rushing in my ears. She shrugs out of one strap, letting it slide off her arm while still holding her shirt up against her chest. I help her get the other one off, guiding the strap down her arm so her bra doesn't fall on the floor.

"You can just hang onto that for her," Dex says, totally nonchalant, as if the woman with the most amazing boobs in the history of breasts isn't standing there almost topless. "Or you can hang it up."

Somehow holding her bra sounds like a better option than hanging it on a hook where anyone can see it. Although anyone can see *her* right now, which is freaking me the hell out. I glance around, but no one is paying attention.

What can I do about it, anyway? And why do I even care? Dex certainly doesn't seem to think this is a big deal. I suppose he tattoos beautiful women with amazing boobs all the time, and Linnea is just another client.

Dex has Linnea hold up her arm while he places the stencil along her rib cage, just behind the side of her left boob. She clutches her shirt to her chest with her other hand and I'm not sure whether I should look or avert my eyes. God, why didn't she tell me where she was getting this damn tattoo?

"Take a look in the mirror," Dex says. "Let me know if that looks right. I can still make changes."

Linnea steps in front of the full-length mirror and turns to the side, lifting her arm out of the way. "Yes, that's perfect."

"Great." Dex works the hydraulics on the chair, turning it into a flat table. "I'm going to have you lie down, facing Caleb. Just relax for now. It'll take me a minute to finish setting up."

She gets on the table and lies on her side, holding her shirt over her chest. Her eyes meet mine for a split second, but we both look away. I'm probably not helping her feel less nervous, considering I'm the furthest thing from relaxed I can imagine.

I take a deep breath. "Don't worry. You've got this."

"My parents will kill me if they find out," she says.

There's just enough concern in her voice that I can tell she isn't kidding. "Is it their business? It's not like you're still a kid."

She meets my eyes. "You're right. I'm not."

Dex gets to work on her and I'm amazed at how tough she is. She's being stabbed with a tiny needle, but she barely flinches. I chat with her to help keep her mind off any pain she might be feeling. We start talking about Charlotte and the time seems to fly. A little over an hour later, Dex sits back and declares that he's finished.

She gets up and checks her new tattoo in the mirror. The lines are delicate and flowing. It's gorgeous. And it looks sexy as fuck on her. I'm back to swallowing hard and trying to keep my eyes elsewhere.

Dex puts a bandage over the tattoo and gives her a sheet with care instructions. She puts her shirt back on, but tucks her bra in her purse.

Nothing about that is helping.

She pays and thanks Dex. He gives her a gentle hug and we both say goodbye.

"So, was it as bad as you thought?" I ask as we walk back to my car.

"Not at all," she says. "It hurt, but it wasn't unbearable. Now it just feels warm, kind of like a sunburn."

"You did great," I say. "I'm impressed."

"Thanks," she says. "And thanks for coming with me. Sorry if it was, um... uncomfortable."

"Nah, it was fine," I say. That's almost true. I handled it at least. "I'm glad I could come."

"I'm glad too." She bites her lip. "I kind of can't believe I just did that. A tattoo is so unlike me."

"I don't know about that," I say. "I think it's perfect for you."

She smiles again and her eyes sparkle. God, this woman is going to be the death of me.

10

LINNEA

Charlotte slips into my lap and leans her head against my shoulder. "Can I sit with you?"

"Of course." I adjust so she can get comfortable and put my arms gently around her.

We spent the afternoon at her grandad's house and just finished up dinner. Kendra cooked—it was amazing, as usual—and now Caleb and Alex are in the kitchen cleaning up. I offered to help, but they insisted they had it handled. Kendra and Weston had to leave right after dinner. Weston has a conference in Reno and Kendra's going with him; their flight is early, so they didn't want to stay too late.

I can tell we shouldn't stay much longer either. Charlotte's eyes are droopy, and although she's not the type of kid who is always running around, curling up with me on the couch definitely means she's tired.

Charlotte's grandad, Ken, smiles at me from his recliner. "She wore herself out."

"She sure did. I think her uncles had something to do with it." Alex and Weston played with her out in the backyard before dinner.

"True," he says. "How's school going for the little miss?"

"It's fine," I say.

"She talk much when she's there?" he asks.

I glance down; her eyes are closed and her breathing even, but I lower my voice anyway. "Some days. We've been having playdates with a little boy in her class. They have fun together, and I think it's helping a little."

He nods. "She'll come out of her shell. We just need to be patient with her."

That makes me smile. "I think so too. She's so comfortable here, and Caleb said she wasn't at first. Maybe that will happen with school too."

"Well, she should be comfortable here," he says. "It's her family."

Charlotte's lucky in that respect. I don't remember ever feeling comfortable with my family. Not even in my own home.

"I'm glad she does," I say.

"How's life here treating you?" he asks.

"I love it here," I say.

"Piano lessons going well for everyone?"

"Very well," I say with another smile. I'm glad it's worked out for me to continue teaching. I love sharing my passion for music with kids. "I have a great group of students. And I've been teaching Charlotte at home. She's a natural."

"Of course she is," he says with a proud smile.

It's strange, but I don't remember Melanie ever talking about her in-laws. Ken is one of the sweetest men I've ever met. He has his gruff moments, but he's never unkind. He always asks me how I'm doing—and not just in a generic way. Like he's genuinely interested. He's wonderful with Charlotte, and I can see why she's so at ease here. Maybe Melanie didn't spend much time with him. She and Caleb didn't live here, although I know they visited. But I was taken with him the first time we met. If he was my father-in-law, I'd be gushing about how great he is.

"Do I remember you saying you're planning to audition with a symphony?" he asks.

I resist the urge to let out a heavy sigh. I talked to my mother earlier and she wouldn't stop drilling me about how much I've been practicing. I had to remind her that sending me to be Charlotte's nanny was her idea. I can't spend eight hours a day practicing *and* do my job. Somehow that hadn't been an acceptable excuse.

"That's the idea," I say.

He nods slowly, watching me like he's figuring something out. "Well, if that's what you really want, I'm sure the right opportunity will come along."

"Yeah, it will," I say.

He tips his head to one side. "Although sometimes the right thing surprises us."

I'm not sure what he means, and I'm just about to ask when Caleb walks in. He looks at Charlotte, sleeping soundly in my lap, and puts a hand to his chest. The look on his face makes me all melty.

"Sweet girl. We should get her home."

"Yeah."

He scoops her up and takes her to the car while I gather our things and say goodbye. She wakes up when he straps her in, but falls asleep again once we're moving. I notice Caleb glancing back at her in the rear-view mirror, a little smile playing on his lips. It makes my heart squeeze and I have to force myself to stop staring at him.

When we get home, Caleb carries her upstairs. Her eyes flutter open and I blow her a kiss.

Since Caleb's getting her to bed, I settle in on the couch. I'm hoping he'll come down and join me once she's settled. He usually does. If he's home, and not so exhausted he falls asleep shortly after Charlotte does, we spend our evenings hanging out together.

Nights with him are such a contradiction for me. In some ways, it's my favorite time. Charlotte is sleeping peacefully and the house is quiet, so it's just the two of us. We watch TV or just sit and talk, and it's so easy. So comfortable.

But it's also a little bit like torture. I've lived here for months now, and my stupid crush is not going away. I feel such a deep ache when I'm with him—so much longing.

It's ridiculous, but no matter how often I tell myself he's just a friend—not to mention, my boss—there's something inside me that refuses to listen. That wants him anyway.

Wants him so badly.

He comes downstairs and I train my face to stillness. I think I'm doing a good job of hiding how I feel. I certainly can't let him see. It would be so humiliating if he found out—especially if he rejected me. And of course he would. Just because we get along doesn't mean he's interested in me.

Remember Linnea, he's older. He's your boss. He was married to your sister. Calm your hormones.

My hormones don't generally listen to me. Especially where Caleb is concerned.

"Hey." He smiles and sits on the other side of the couch. God, that smile.

"Hey," I say, hoping he can't hear how hard my heart is beating. He's way over there, but it's possible. "She asleep?"

"Yeah, she's out." He rubs his jaw and I wonder what that stubble would feel like against my skin.

Damn it, I'm still doing it.

I should suggest we watch TV so I have something else to hold my attention. But all I do is cast glances at him from the corner of my eyes. He has his phone out and he's flicking through what might be his email. Even sitting there in a t-shirt and flannel pants, he looks perfect. Despite his busy schedule, he keeps himself in great shape; his body is gorgeous. He's muscular and lean, with well-defined arms and a broad chest. I've seen him shirtless a few times and it's just not fair. I want to lick my way up those abs, and I've never had that thought about a man before. Not even my last boyfriend.

He looks up at me and one corner of his mouth turns up in a smile. "You know, I don't think I've thanked you lately."

"For what?"

"Everything," he says. "You've gone above and beyond what any of Charlotte's nannies have ever done."

I smile to cover the little dip in my tummy at the reminder of the reality of our relationship. I'm just the nanny. "You're welcome. It's why I'm here."

"It's just been such a load off my shoulders," he says. "I don't know if I realized how stressed I was before."

The sincere relief in his voice stirs up my stupid feelings all over again. "I'm glad I can help. I'm sure being on your own hasn't been easy."

"No, it's tough." He puts his phone down. "I figured it would be, but it's one of those things you don't realize until you live it. And I feel like there are so many things I miss. No matter how hard I try to be everything she needs, I know I'm not enough."

"Caleb, you're the most incredible father I've ever met," I say. "I mean that. I've been around kids a lot and I've seen all sorts of parents. Some are sweet and attentive, some seem more interested in their phones than their kids. I don't always know what's going on behind the scenes, but you can tell when a parent has a good relationship with their child. It shows. And I've never seen a relationship that's as wonderful as the one you have with Charlotte."

He stares at me for a long moment, his lips parted. Finally, he clears his throat. "Thank you. That means a lot to me."

"It's true."

He shifts in his seat. "There are still things I'm not good at, though. Even just little things."

"Like what?" I ask.

"Like doing her hair," he says. "If it isn't a ponytail, I'm out of my league. Lately she's been asking me to do a ballet bun, but I don't even know what that means."

"That's not hard. You just need a hair donut."

"I'm assuming that's not a sugar-glazed pastry that somehow goes on your head," he says.

"No, dork," I say with a smile. "I have one, I'll show you."

I run upstairs and grab my hair donut along with a couple hair ties and some bobby pins. "This is a hair donut," I say when I get back, holding up the round spongy accessory that does look a lot like a donut. I put the rest of the stuff on the coffee table.

"I have no idea what you do with that."

"Well, you start with a ponytail. You know how to do that. Then the ponytail goes through the center of the donut, and you wrap the hair around it to make a bun."

He looks worried.

"Come on, you can practice on me," I say. Oh god, I shouldn't have said that. He's going to say it's not appropriate. I can already feel a blush creeping up my neck.

"Actually, that would be great, if you don't mind."

Deep breath, Linnea. You're fine. "Not at all. I'll just sit there, I guess." I gesture to the floor in front of him and lower myself so I'm sitting with his legs on either side of me. He scoots forward to the edge of the couch. God, he's so close I can smell him—clean and warm, with a hint of something spicy.

"Okay, so what do I do?" he asks.

"Well, start with a high ponytail," I say. "I can do that if you want."

"No, I've got it."

I swallow hard as he runs his fingers through my hair. He begins at the bottom, sliding his hands up my neck, gently pulling my hair up as he goes. He keeps it in one hand and uses the other to brush the hair from the top of my head backward. His fingers run along my scalp, sending sparks through my whole body. Even after he has my hair all gathered in one hand, he keeps sliding his fingers through it, softly pulling out the tangles.

Since he can't see my face, I let my eyes drift closed. It feels so good, I bite my lower lip to keep from moaning. My body relaxes, and he continues. I'm turning to water at his touch, melting into a pool on the floor. I don't know why he's still pulling his fingers through my hair; he has it where it needs to be for a ponytail. But I don't care.

Finally, he loops the hair tie around and tightens it. I blink my eyes open, trying to get my brain to work again.

"So, um..." he says, his voice so soft. "What's next?"

"Oh," I say. "Right. My ponytail goes through the center of the donut and then you pull my hair around it so it's covered. The ends get wound around the bottom, and you pin everything in place."

"Okay."

I feel the gentle tugs as he finishes the bun. My heart feels fluttery and I'm desperately hoping my face isn't bright red—even as I wonder if I can teach him more hairstyles just to feel his hands in my hair again.

Bad idea, Linnea.

He slides in another bobby pin. "There. Did I do it right?"

I touch my hair, and it feels like a perfect bun. "Yeah, I think so. Nice job." I twist around so I'm facing him. "How does it look?"

"It's really pretty on you."

Now I know I'm blushing. Did he just call me pretty? "Thanks."

His eyes hold mine and I start to feel like I can't quite breathe. There's something in the air—tiny pings of tension that make my skin prickle. My heart races. All kinds of things below the waist start tingling. And he still doesn't look away.

"Daddy?" Charlotte's voice carries from upstairs. She sounds like she's crying.

The spell is instantly broken. Caleb is up and rushing to her bedroom before I can blink twice.

With my hand on my chest, I take a trembling breath. I don't know what just happened there. Was he looking at me like… like I was looking at him? He couldn't have been. Because I'm certain I forgot myself just now, and looked at him with all my feelings plain on my face, my silly crush right there for him to see.

I should go upstairs and see if he needs help with Charlotte —she probably had a bad dream. After all, I'm the nanny. That's why I'm here.

11

LINNEA

Glancing at the clock in the kitchen—again—I drum my fingers on the table. Charlotte is having a snack, and I'm going to be late.

It's my day to teach piano lessons. So far, we haven't had any problems making it work, even with Caleb's hectic schedule. But he was supposed to be home half an hour ago. He hasn't called or texted to say he'll be late, or that someone else is coming over to watch Charlotte for the afternoon. I check the calendar on the fridge again—Caleb and I keep it updated with our schedules—but it doesn't say I'm supposed to take her to her grandad's house or over to Kendra's. Little jolts of nervousness ping through me. I'm worried I forgot something.

I'll give him five more minutes. Then I'm either going to have to call my first student and cancel, or pack up Charlotte and bring her with me.

"You haven't told me how your day was," I say to Charlotte.

She twists her little mouth and looks pensive. "I don't know."

"Hmm." I smooth a piece of hair back from her forehead. "What kind of stuff did you do today?"

"Math stations," she says. "And reading time."

"That's good," I say. "Reading time is your favorite."

She nods.

"Did something happen to make you sad today?" I ask.

She doesn't answer, just rolls a green grape around her plate with one finger. My heart sinks a little. She still has good days and bad days at school. I can tell today wasn't one of the good ones.

"You can tell me about it, Bug," I say. "Maybe I can help."

"Noah wasn't at school today."

"Oh, that's too bad," I say. "Did you miss him?"

She nods.

"Are you worried about him?"

She nods again.

"How about I text Miss Megan and see if he's okay," I say. "Would that make you feel better?"

"Okay," she says, her voice brightening.

I send Megan a quick text, letting her know Charlotte missed Noah, and asking if everything is all right. Charlotte goes back to her snack and seems to relax. Another minute ticks by, and I get more tense.

Megan texts me back, thanking me for checking in and letting me know that Noah is fine. He had a tummy ache this morning, so she kept him home.

"See, Noah is fine," I say. "He'll be back tomorrow."

Charlotte nods. "Are you sure he's coming back?"

"Yes, I'm sure." I smooth her hair back again. She has so much anxiety over people leaving and not returning, as well as her fear of being forgotten or left behind. I wonder if it has something to do with losing her mom. It's hard to know—she was just a baby when Mel died, so she doesn't have any memories of her. But maybe that's where some of her deepest worries come from.

The front door opens and Charlotte's eyes light up, like they always do when her dad gets home. She hops off her chair and starts running for the front door. Caleb comes in, a smile on his face, but then he turns and says something, as if he's talking to someone behind him.

Charlotte stops dead in her tracks as a woman walks in the door behind Caleb.

It feels like the floor just dropped out from under me. I have a momentary sensation of falling, like I left my stomach behind.

She's beautiful. Her clothes are sophisticated and stylish—a cream blouse and slacks with expensive looking shoes. A curtain of shiny dark hair hangs around her shoulders, and her makeup is flawless.

Oh my god, is she...?

"Hi, Bug," Caleb says. He motions for the woman to come in, and crosses the distance to Charlotte. "It's okay. I brought someone to meet you. This is Daddy's friend Abigail."

Abigail. Daddy's friend. I know it's possible that Caleb is dating. He's never mentioned going out with someone, but maybe he was just being discreet. That seems like something he would do. There are plenty of nights he comes home late, and I always assume he's working. I guess I was wrong.

And if he's bringing her home to meet Charlotte, it must be serious. He wouldn't introduce just anyone to his daughter—that much I know for sure.

I swallow hard, trying to bury the crushing disappointment that washes over me. I'm going to miss the next bus, and I'll be late if I do, so I quickly grab my things. Caleb has Charlotte in his arms and Abigail is speaking softly to her. I tear my eyes away; I don't want them to see me staring.

Glaring, more like.

"Sorry, I'm going to be late," I say, brushing past them. I'm proud of myself for how calm my voice sounds. It's completely at odds with the mess inside me. "I'll be back later."

"Oh god, Linnea, I'm so sorry, I forgot today was—"

I close the door behind me without waiting to hear the rest of what Caleb was going to say.

My stomach is in knots as I walk to the bus stop. Caleb has a girlfriend. I knew I was wrong about all those little moments—when I thought he looked at me like there might be something else there. This confirms it. He likes me fine—even cares about me, as a friend and as the person who watches his daughter—but that's all. I've never been anything else to him, so I shouldn't be so upset about this.

The bus picks me up and it's a short ride to the music store. I can't get the image out of my mind—the three of them standing together. Caleb holding Charlotte. Abigail smiling at her, saying hello. I don't know who I feel more territorial over, Caleb or Charlotte. I think about the time Megan said she thought I was Charlotte's mom. She thought Charlotte was mine.

I wish she *was* mine.

Sniffing a little, I swallow back the tears that are trying very hard to well up in my eyes. She's not mine. Not like that. She's my niece, and I'll always have that relationship with her, no matter what Caleb does. Even if someday Charlotte is calling someone else *Mom*. Someone like Abigail.

By the time I get to the store, I've forced the worst of my stupid heartache down where it can't touch me. I still feel a bit sick, and wish I could go home and curl up under the covers by myself. But I take a few calming breaths, and get on with my afternoon.

I have four students today, and the first three lessons pass quickly. I can tell my first student has been practicing—her scales are coming along nicely and I'm teaching her to play *Ode to Joy*.

My next student is a little less enthusiastic, so I suggest we try something new. After asking him some questions about what he likes, I find the sheet music to the theme from *Star Wars* in my folder. He's thrilled, and when he leaves, I hear him telling his mom how excited he is to play when he gets home.

The third student is a six-year-old girl, who of course reminds me of Charlotte. I work with her on some simple scales and we play *Twinkle, Twinkle, Little Star.*

By the time my last student arrives, I'm exhausted from the effort of staying focused and keeping thoughts about Caleb out of my mind. My student's dad, Nate, smiles at me when he ushers his son into the little practice room.

"Work hard, Jax," he says. He meets my eyes again. "Listen to your teacher."

I do my best to smile back, then get to work with Jax. He's a little squirmy, but boys often are. He's ready for a new song, and asks if he can learn to play *Happy Birthday*. I get that request a lot, so I already have the sheet music handy. We work on it for a little while, and go over a few more things in his music theory book.

"Okay, Jax, that's it for today." I help him gather up his books and new music. He shoves everything into his backpack and I try not to wince at how he's crinkling and bending his music. Hopefully his dad will help him smooth it out when it's time for him to practice at home.

Nate opens the door and peeks in. "You about ready, sport?"

"Yeah, Dad," Jax says.

Nate smiles at me again, and something about his expression makes me pause. His eye contact is prolonged, and one corner of his mouth turns up in a smile.

"Hey Jax, why don't you grab your stuff and wait right out there," he says. "I need to talk to Miss Linnea for a second."

Jax puts on his backpack and goes out to the waiting area outside the practice rooms. The door is glass, so I see him plop down in a chair.

"So, Linnea..." Nate clears his throat and licks his lips. He's a nice-looking guy, probably in his thirties. Blond hair, blue eyes. Jax looks a lot like him. "Jax is with his mom this weekend, so if you don't have any plans on Friday, I'd love to take you to dinner. What do you think?"

I'm completely unprepared for what he just said and it takes me a few seconds to recover. Did he just ask me out? "Oh, um, I'm not sure." I grab my phone and open my calendar. Not so much to see if I'm free—I know I am, and Caleb is off Friday afternoon through Sunday—but to give myself a second to think.

Should I accept? I'm not sure if I should go out with the parent of one of my students. But Nate seems like a nice guy. Maybe he's not my age, but my boyfriend in college was my age and that didn't turn out so well. Caleb is always telling me I should get out and meet more people. Of course he is—he has a girlfriend, so he'd be fine with me dating.

If Caleb is dating, I suppose I should make more of an effort to put myself out there, too. It's not like I can keep harboring my stupid crush.

"Yes, I'm free," I say. "That sounds nice."

He smiles again, showing a dimple in one cheek. "Great. I'll pick you up at seven. You can just text me your address."

"Okay, seven," I say. I'm about to suggest that maybe I should meet him somewhere rather than have him pick me up, but he doesn't give me a chance.

"Perfect," he says. "I'll see you Friday."

He leaves with Jax, and I'm left sitting in the practice room, wondering what just happened. Did I just agree to a date?

Yes, yes I did. And it's fine. I *should* go on a date. I haven't been out with anyone in months—not since before I moved to Seattle. I went out with a guy a couple of times when I was living with my parents. But my mother was so judgmental about it, always muttering about men making you *lose focus*. I hadn't been all that interested in him anyway; he was nice, but there was absolutely zero chemistry between us. So letting it fizzle out hadn't been a disappointment.

Since moving, I've been so wrapped up in Charlotte, and Caleb and his family, I haven't branched out and made many other friends. I haven't hung out with Chloe or anyone else from Henley's again. I do have Megan. But I'm friends with her because of Charlotte, mostly.

Maybe it's time I start carving out my own life, apart from the Lawsons. I'll be Charlotte's nanny for as long as it works out, but I need to stop holding onto the secret hope that maybe Caleb will notice me. That ship hasn't sailed; it never existed in the first place.

I gather up the rest of my things and go outside to the bus stop. I try not to think about Caleb and Abigail spending the afternoon with Charlotte. Although I do wonder if they'll be home when I get there. Thinking about that makes me change my plans.

Regardless of whether I have a date—and regardless of my awareness that Caleb was *never* an option—I don't think I can cope with seeing the three of them together.

Instead of catching the bus, I walk up the street to a café and order a pastry and some hot tea. After taking a seat at a little table in the corner, I text Caleb to let him know I'll be home late. I'll let the three of them have their time and I'll slip in later, when I can go straight to bed.

Getting over my ridiculous crush isn't going to be easy, but maybe my date on Friday will help.

12

CALEB

After a remarkably stressful night at the hospital, I get off work and head to the gym. I'm tired, but I want to blow off some steam on the court. I'm running later than usual, and Alex is already here when I arrive.

"No Reid today?" I changed before I left work, so I just take off my sweatshirt and toss my wallet, keys, and phone on top.

"No, he had something come up." He passes the ball to me.

I nod and dribble a few times. Our weekly basketball sessions are pretty casual. If we can make it, we show up. If not, it's no big deal.

Alex and I shoot around for a little while to warm up, then play a game of twenty-one. I beat him—barely. When we were kids I could never take him; he had that big brother power over me. I'll never forget the first time I won. I don't know which one of us was more shocked. Now we're pretty evenly matched.

After our game, we sit on the floor, courtside, while we catch our breath. I take a drink of my water and wipe the sweat from my forehead.

"Okay, I have a question for you." I'm not sure if I should bring it up, but this thing with Linnea has been killing me. I trust Alex more than anyone. He'll give it to me straight if I'm out of my mind. "Scale of one to ten, how bad would it be if a guy had a thing for his nanny? Theoretically speaking."

Alex raises his eyebrows at me. "So, we're pretending this isn't you?"

"I never said it was me."

"Are we also pretending the nanny isn't the guy's former sister-in-law?"

"That's... okay, there are additional circumstances that make this guy's situation complicated, how about that?"

"I guess I'd have to give that a five, maybe a six," he says. "There is the issue of you being her boss."

"Didn't say it was me."

Alex gives me a quick eye roll. "Sure. Anyway, *he's* her boss, which makes it a little complicated. I can see why he'd hesitate."

"Plus, if he goes for it and it goes bad later, he doesn't just lose a girlfriend," I say. "His daughter loses her nanny. And his daughter loves her."

"Yeah, that takes it up to a solid seven," he says.

"And she's so much younger," I say. "She's twenty-two. What girl her age wants to be with a guy who has a kid already? Shouldn't she be out dating? Hanging out with friends?"

"Are we still pretending this isn't Linnea?" he asks.

"No," I say, grudgingly.

"I'll be honest, the age thing doesn't seem like a huge problem," he says. "Linnea gets along so well with all of us. It's not like we have nothing in common with her. I don't even think of her as being really young. She's just... Linnea."

"Yeah, that's true." I hadn't thought about it that way before. But even though she's mature, it doesn't mean she's in a place in her life where it makes sense for her to be with a guy like me.

"The sister-in-law thing is a little awkward, though," he says. "Would her family have issues with that?"

"Undoubtedly," I say. "They weren't happy when I married Melanie. I can't imagine they'd be excited for me to start dating their other daughter."

"That's tough," he says. "But is that a good reason not to give it a shot with someone?"

"It's not a deal-breaker. Just a factor," I say. "How do you get along with your in-laws?"

He shrugs. "They're nice people. They kind of look at Mia like she's some kind of anomaly though. I don't think they understand her, or really try to, and it rubs me wrong."

"I think Linnea gets the same thing from Steve and Margo," I say. "She's different, and they don't really know what to do with that."

"She is a lot different than Melanie was," he says. "I'm actually kind of surprised you're into Linnea enough that you're thinking about it. She seems like Melanie's opposite. I figured if you ever took a chance with someone again, it would be with someone more like Mel."

I look away for a moment. It's hard to be honest about Melanie—feels like I'm dishonoring her memory. "Yeah, I can see why you'd think so. But the truth is, if Mel was alive, I don't know if we would have lasted."

"What makes you think that? I thought you guys were good together."

"We were," I say. "And don't get me wrong, I loved her. When we met, I was attracted to her drive. She was so self-assured. Knew exactly what she wanted. She was really dedicated to medicine, and I was too, so we had that passion in common. But you know, I think she was too much like Mom."

Alex winces. "But she wouldn't have walked out on Charlotte."

"No, she wouldn't have," I say. "Not the way Mom walked out on us. But I think ultimately that drive would have been a wedge between us. Knowing what it's like to raise a child, it would have been hard to balance everything. I've had to make compromises in my career in favor of being a father. I don't know if she would have been willing to do that for her family. I think her career would have come first, and that would have become a big problem for me."

"God, why did we both do that?" Alex asks.

"What?"

"Marry women so much like Mom," he says. "Janine was practically Mom's clone. I don't know how I didn't see it at the time."

"You were young," I say. "You got caught up in Janine's decisiveness. That's kind of how it was with Mel. Although I will say, Mel had a heart that was actually beating. I'm not convinced Janine did."

"Me neither," Alex said. "It worked out in the end, though."

"Yeah, you and Mia, man..." I laugh softly and shake my head. "You guys are so good together, sometimes I wonder if you're hiding something. But I don't think Mia could pull off a double life. She'd blurt out the truth."

"She doesn't blurt out that my alter ego is a woman who writes romance novels," he says.

"Good point," I say. "How's that going, by the way?"

"Great," he says. "I'm even branching out. Next month I'm releasing the first in a sci-fi series under my own name."

"No shit?"

He grins. "Yeah. I learned a lot writing as Lexi, so I took that and restarted my sci-fi series. It sucked to start from scratch after all the time I'd spent on it. But it's a thousand times better, and I actually finished it. Kendra's editing it now, and I'm halfway done with the second book. The Lexi-train is still going strong, so I can take some time to write other stuff. It's pretty cool."

"That's really cool," I say. "Good for you."

"Thanks." He takes another drink of his water. "You know, I think you should go for it with Linnea."

"Really?"

"Yeah," he says. "You wouldn't be thinking about it seriously if you didn't really like her."

"I just don't want to fuck things up," I say. "Dating her would be complicated."

"You just have to decide if it's worth the risk," he says. "Look, this is going to sound like I'm making shit up for a Lexi book, but I mean it: If it's real—if there's something there—you aren't going to be able to deny it forever. And if she feels it too, well..." He shrugs.

"Yeah, I think you're right," I say. "Maybe I need to give it a shot. Take her out. Talk to her. See if she's even interested. Because that's the other obstacle; I don't know if she is."

"She is," he says, completely matter-of-fact.

"How could you possibly know that?"

He raises an eyebrow at me. "You guys both have a thing for each other and I think you're the only ones who don't realize it."

"What do you mean?"

"I mean, we can all tell," he says, casting me a sidelong glance like I'm a dumbass. "We see the way you look at her. How have you not seen the way she looks at you? I don't know, man. It's hard to believe you're that blind."

I have seen the way she looks at me. Maybe. I wasn't sure if it meant anything. But I think Alex is right. If there's something between us, we won't be able to deny it forever.

"All right, well, thanks." I grab the ball and stand up. "Ready for another game?"

"Sure," he says, getting to his feet.

"And Alex?"

"Yeah?"

I tuck the ball under my arm. "Don't say anything—especially to Mia. Or Kendra. I'm not sure what I'm going to do yet, or how she's going to react. I can't come on too strong. If she says no, I don't want to make her feel like she has to quit. I can't let Charlotte lose her. No matter what."

"Of course not," he says. "And I have a feeling you guys are all going to be fine."

I nod and dribble the ball back out onto the court. Taking a chance with Linnea might be a huge mistake. But maybe at this point it's a mistake not to.

13

LINNEA

Caleb is home most of Friday, and I find myself avoiding him. I know he notices. We always hang out together, the three of us, when he's off. Usually we would have taken Charlotte to the park, or the library. Or maybe played board games with her. But I stay in my room for most of the afternoon.

I come downstairs to rinse out my mug and toss my tea bag in the garbage. Caleb wanders into the kitchen.

"Hey," he says. "You feeling okay?"

"Yeah, I'm fine," I say, hoping that sounds believable. Seeing him stirs up all those stupid emotions yet again. "I just needed some time to relax."

"Good," he says. "I was a little worried about you."

Damn it, Caleb, stop being so sweet. It's not fair. "No need. I'm okay."

"What do you have going on tonight?" he asks. "Charlotte and I have a riveting movie to watch. It's Disney, so it should be good. Want to join us?"

"Oh," I say, tucking my hair behind my ear. "Actually, um, I have plans tonight."

He blinks and a look of surprise crosses his features. "Oh,

yeah, of course. That's great." He hesitates for a second, his mouth partially open. "Are you hanging out with Chloe again, or do you mean like, a date?"

"A date."

"Right, good," he says, stepping away. "That's good. Of course you have a date. That's awesome."

"It is?"

"Yeah," he says. "You can't just hang out with us boring old people all the time."

"Oh, no, you guys are great to hang out with."

"But you should meet people your own age," he says. "I'm glad you're dating."

He's glad I'm dating. Of course he's glad. He doesn't want me making puppy eyes at him all the time. And people my own age? God, why does he think I'm a child? Sure, I'm still young, but I'm not a little kid who needs to be set up on playdates.

"Okay, well, good," I say. "Although I think he's closer to your age than mine."

"He's what?" Caleb asks. "I mean, oh, okay. How did you meet him?"

"His son is one of my piano students," I say.

"One of your..." He looks away and rubs the back of his neck. "Wow, are you sure that's a good idea? To date someone like that?"

"Someone like what?" I ask.

"Well... if he's older than you, and he has a kid," he says. "And that kid is one of your students. It seems like that could get awkward."

"Yeah, I thought about that," I say. "But he seems really nice. And it's just dinner."

"Right... just dinner... yeah, that's great."

"I mean, if you need me..." I fumble over the words, because I'm not sure what I want to say. Or what I want him to say. Why is this conversation so awkward? "That is, if you need me here tonight for anything, I can cancel."

"No," he says quickly. "No, you don't need to cancel your date."

"Are you sure?"

"Yeah," he says. "Go out. Have fun. That's what you should be doing in your free time."

"Okay," I say. "Well, I'm going to go get ready."

"Yeah. Have fun tonight."

"Thanks. I will."

I go upstairs but my feet feel heavy. I'm flooded with disappointment. But what did I want him to do? Tell me to cancel? Why would he do that? Caleb doesn't see me that way.

I *should* be dating. Getting out there. Meeting more people. As it is, my social life consists of a six-year-old girl, her dad, and his married, mostly-thirty-something siblings.

I'm not really sure what's wrong with that, but I guess it's not normal. I let out a heavy sigh as I shut my bedroom door. I'm never normal.

An hour later, the doorbell rings and I'm hit with a rush of nervousness. It's Nate. I should be excited and looking forward to this, but all I feel is a knot of anxiety in the pit of my stomach.

I check my reflection one last time. My floral dress is pretty. Between my boobs and my hips, it's hard to find clothes that fit right. Everything is either way too revealing, or way too frumpy. But I found a pretty wrap dress that minimizes my chest nicely without making me look like I'm wearing my grandma's clothes. My hair is down and when I let it drape over my shoulders, it hides my curves a little more. I rub my lips together to make sure my lipstick is even and step into my heels.

Here we go.

I walk down the stairs to find two men watching me. One is

Nate, dressed in a button-down shirt and slacks. His hands are in his pockets, and one corner of his mouth turns up in a smile.

Caleb's eyes are wide and his lips part. His gaze follows me as I walk the rest of the way down, and I feel my cheeks flush.

"Hi," I say to Nate.

"Wow, you look stunning." Nate steps in and puts a hand on my arm, then leans in to give me a quick peck on the cheek.

I try not to shy away, but it catches me off guard. "Oh, thank you."

Nate holds a hand out to Caleb. "Nate Ingram."

"Caleb Lawson." He shakes hands with Nate.

"Caleb is my..." How do I introduce him? My boss? My brother-in-law? *Is* he still my brother-in-law? "Well, I'm his daughter's nanny."

"Nice to meet you," Nate says.

Caleb nods, but I don't get the sense that the feeling is mutual.

I slip my phone in my little purse with a glance at Caleb. "Um, so, I'll be home later."

"Right," Caleb says, stepping away. "Yeah. Have a good time."

"Don't worry, Dad, I'll have her home before curfew," Nate says.

Caleb's expression hardens, but Nate laughs.

"I'm sorry, man, I'm just kidding," he says. "I get it, I'm the same way. Hard to turn off the dad thing."

"Yeah," Caleb says with a brief laugh, but I can tell he didn't find that the least bit funny.

Nate puts his hand on my back. "Shall we?"

"Sure."

I don't look at Caleb again, just let Nate lead me outside to his car.

We head downtown and Nate pulls up in front of the Hyatt. The valet opens my door and Nate comes around from the other side. He offers his arm and I tuck my hand into the crook of his elbow.

"Is there a restaurant here?" I ask.

"Yeah, it's nice," Nate says. "I thought it would be a good choice."

We walk through the lobby; everything is so sleek and modern. This place looks expensive. I was picturing something different when he asked me to have dinner—something more low-key. Maybe that's because I just got out of school; most college students don't have the money for expensive dates, so I haven't really been on one. Still, this all feels so fancy.

He leads us to the restaurant, Urbane. It also looks very modern, with exposed bulb light fixtures and dark wood tables. There's a long white marble bar fronted by white barstools, and large windows face the street.

The host walks us past the bar and around a corner to a small table by the window. Nate pulls out my chair and I thank him as I take my seat. A waiter walks by with a tray of cocktails, and I don't think I could name a single one. Electric blue, bright yellow, the glasses rimmed with sugar.

Anxiety tingles through me. What should I order in a place like this? I'm going to look like an inexperienced kid.

The menu doesn't help. I glance at the choices, but suddenly it seems like such a big decision. Should I have a drink? If I do, should I try one of these specialty cocktails? I don't drink a lot, but I know I like white wine. Maybe I should just order that. But is this the kind of place where you order wine? I glance around at the other tables, trying to get a feel for what people are drinking. I see a lot of those colorful cocktails in fancy glasses.

Nate puts his menu down and closes it. I guess he knows what he wants. I look at the food, trying not to get so fixated on the drinks. Maybe I'll let him order first and follow his lead. Or I can always ask the waiter for suggestions.

My tummy swirls with more nerves. Most of the entrees are expensive. I don't know if he's trying to impress me with a fancy dinner or what, but it's not working. I'd be much more comfortable in a place where one dinner didn't cost more than I spent on an entire meal for me and Charlotte the other day.

The waiter returns for our drink orders.

"I'll have a Burgundy Lush, and the lovely lady here will have an Urbane Daiquiri."

I blink at Nate, my lips parting. Did he just order for me?

"Would you like any appetizers to start?" the waiter asks.

"Yes, we'll have the crab cakes," Nate says.

"Excellent. I'll get your drinks and be back shortly to take your dinner order."

I'm still staring at Nate, about to ask him why he ordered without asking me, but he starts talking before I can start.

"I hope you don't mind," he says. "The daiquiri is one of their specialties; I know you'll enjoy it. And the crab cakes are excellent. It's their best appetizer by far."

Well, I guess he's just trying to show me what's good here. "Sure, that's fine. They both sound good."

"They are," he says. "I think you'll really enjoy them."

The intense look in his eyes and the way his voice has gone kind of low is not helping me relax. I go back to the menu and decide on lemon brined chicken. It seems like a safe choice.

"How long have you been playing piano?" Nate asks.

"Since I was four," I say.

"Impressive," he says. "Do you enjoy teaching?"

"I really do," I say. "I think, no matter what else I do, I'd like to keep teaching."

"That's great," he says. "Jax has been making a lot of progress."

"He's doing very well," I say, grateful to be able to talk about his son. It feels like neutral territory.

"My ex started him on lessons with someone else, but he was really unhappy. She was too rigid. Kind of like my ex." He grins. "Anyway, we're lucky to have found you."

The waiter comes back and asks if we're ready. He looks at me, but Nate speaks up.

"She'll have the pork tenderloin," he says. "And I'll have the center cut ribeye. On the rare side, red is fine, but warm throughout."

"Perfect," the waiter says. He takes our menus and leaves.

"You didn't need to order for me," I say.

"I know what's good here," he says. "Trust me. You'll love it."

Our drinks arrive and I nod at the waiter. I don't want to be rude, but I'm so annoyed that Nate ordered for me. Twice. I'm perfectly capable of choosing my own meal.

"Try the daiquiri," Nate says.

I glance up at him, trying not to get ruffled by the fact that now he's telling me what to do. Maybe he's just excited for me to try it. He obviously likes this restaurant and wants to share that with me.

I take a sip and it's hideously sweet. I'm not the most experienced drinker, especially when it comes to fancy cocktails, but this is awful.

"Wow," I say. "It's, um... very sweet."

"See, I knew you'd love it," he says. He takes a sip of his.

I don't bother to correct him. I'll just take little sips once the food gets here.

We make more small talk until our food arrives. The appetizer is fine, but my dinner isn't what I would have chosen. It's not terrible, but I would have enjoyed the chicken a lot more. I'm just not a pork person. I pick at my meal and try to maintain my side of the conversation, but Nate does a lot of the talking.

"Needless to say, that trip to Tokyo wasn't what I expected," he says.

He keeps telling stories about places he's been, implying that surprising or interesting things happened, but never quite getting into the actual details.

"Sounds like it," I say.

"Is your dinner all right?" he asks.

"It's fine," I say. "I don't usually eat pork, but this is good for what it is."

"Yeah, they have great food here," he says. "How about dessert?"

"No, I don't think so," I say. I'm so over this date. Even if he hadn't ordered me a drink and a dinner I don't like, I'm getting such a weird vibe from him. He hasn't said anything specific to make me uncomfortable, but my anxiety hasn't dissipated. In fact, I feel a little sick.

He smiles and the waiter appears. He asks for the check and hands over a credit card. I'm so glad this is almost over. The waiter comes back with his card and a receipt. Nate signs it and leaves it in the black folder, but he doesn't get up.

"So, I suppose we should go," he says. A little smile plays on his lips and he pulls something out of his wallet. He slides a card across the table toward me and raises an eyebrow.

I look down at the card. It has the hotel logo on the front. For a second, I don't understand what I'm looking at, but then it dawns on me. Oh my god, it's a room key.

"Oh, Nate." I pause, trying to figure out what to say. "That's not—"

"The rooms are beautiful here," he says.

"I'm sure they are, but—"

"Listen," he says, cutting me off again, "let's just go upstairs. Order a bottle of wine. Talk. See where this goes."

"I don't think—"

"It's not complicated, Linnea," he says. "You're a beautiful girl. I'd really like to spend more time with you. Haven't I made that clear?" He gestures to our surroundings. "Great restaurant. Nice atmosphere. I didn't exactly hold back."

"I realize that, and it's very nice, but I don't think that's a good idea."

He presses his lips together and taps his finger on the card a few times. "This is a suite. I'm not suggesting we go to a place that rents rooms by the hour. This is an upscale hotel."

I feel sick to my stomach. I want to get out of here, but Nate drove me. "A fancy hotel isn't really the point, though."

"It's not?" He sits back in his seat and crosses his arms. "So an expensive dinner and a suite at the Hyatt don't do it for you? Maybe I should have taken you out to a club. Grabbed your ass on the dance floor. Gotten you drunk and hauled you outside to fuck you in the back seat of my car?"

"God, Nate, what the hell?" I ask.

"No, really?" he asks. "What would it take? I didn't think you were one of those girls, but I guess I was wrong."

"What girls?"

"Just looking to take advantage," he says. "You want men to take you out to nice places, but you're not interested in doing anything in return."

I gape at him. He can't be serious. "Excuse me? I didn't ask for any of this. You asked me out. You picked the restaurant. You even ordered my dinner. I don't know why you think I owe you anything."

He shakes his head with a quiet laugh. "Figures. Women like you always think they can get away with this."

"Get away with..." I sputter a little, aghast. What is he talking about? I clutch my purse into my lap. "Nate, you need to take me home."

He tilts his head, his expression softening, and uncrosses his arms. "Linnea, I'm so sorry. I have a little bit of a temper. I didn't mean to upset you. It's just, you know, the pressures of being a single father and everything. It's hard."

Oh my god, I can't believe he's trying to use his kid as an excuse for being an ass. "Still. I'm ready to go."

"Just come up and see the room," he says, his voice soothing. "I promise, you'll love it."

"I need to go to the restroom." I stand, still clutching my purse.

Nate stands and grabs my wrist before I can walk away. He leans in close and his voice is hard. "Hurry back, and then I'm taking you upstairs." He squeezes my arm so tight it hurts.

I wrench my hand from his grasp. I'm nauseated with fear. My hands tremble as I walk to the bathroom. I slip into a stall and lock the door, then take a few deep breaths. There are red marks on my arm where he grabbed me.

I pull out my phone and before I even think about it, I have Caleb's number on the screen. But it's late. Charlotte is in bed by now. He can't just leave to come get me.

The easiest thing to do is order an Uber. Seven minutes. Damn. Is that really the closest driver? I wish Uber had a secret code for *girl in trouble* and they'd get here faster. Maybe send someone big and intimidating. How am I going to get through the next seven minutes? That's a long time to be in a bathroom. Nate might come looking.

The Uber will arrive faster than Caleb could get here anyway, but I bring up his number again. I shouldn't bother him. I'll be home in no time. But I'm scared.

I hit the call button.

"Linnea? Are you okay?"

"No." Any thought I had of pretending I'm fine dissipates as soon as I hear the concern in his voice. "No, I'm hiding in the bathroom at the Hyatt downtown."

"The Hyatt? What's going on?"

"We had dinner at the restaurant, but Nate has a room key," I say. "He's trying to convince me to go upstairs with him and he won't take no for an answer."

"I'll be right there."

"No, no, don't," I say. "I have a ride coming. It's just... Caleb, I'm scared. Can you stay on the phone with me until my ride gets here?"

"Yeah, of course," he says. "You're going to be fine. Just stay in the bathroom."

"Okay, but I have at least six more minutes," I say. "What if he comes looking for me?"

"Tell him you don't feel well," he says.

I take a shaky breath. "Okay."

"And don't hang up," he says. "Don't hang up until you're here, okay?"

"I won't."

"You'll be fine," he says and I cling to the confidence in his voice.

The door opens and I gasp.

"What's going on?" he asks. "Linnea?"

I hear the click of shoes on the tile and glance under the door. High heels. "It's nothing," I whisper.

"Okay, how much longer for your ride?"

I check the time. "Six minutes."

"Here's what I want you to do," he says. "Go out of the bathroom and walk straight to the front desk. If there are other guests there, interrupt. Don't worry about being rude. Tell them you need help—you need someone to walk you outside. Just be honest, tell them you're scared."

"Okay." Deep breath. I leave the stall and open the bathroom door.

"Are you going?" Caleb asks.

"Yes. I don't know if he's looking for me."

"Keep walking."

I walk out of the restaurant, my back tight with strain, and head to the front desk. There's no line, so I go straight to the first person I see.

"Excuse me, I'm sorry, but I need help," I say, amazed that my voice is so clear. "I was on a date and he's being very aggressive. My ride is coming, but is there someone who can walk me outside?"

"Oh honey," the woman says, full of sympathy. "Yes, of course. Ricardo?"

"Linnea, you're amazing," Caleb says.

My heart thumps. "Thank you."

A tall man with jet black hair and a hotel uniform comes out. "Yeah?"

The front desk woman steps close and talks to him in a quiet voice, gesturing to me. I glance over my shoulder and see Nate coming into the lobby. He's looking around, but doesn't seem to have spotted me.

"Let's go," Ricardo says.

"He's over there, by the entrance to the restaurant."

"Are you with someone now?" Caleb asks.

"Yes."

"Good."

Ricardo comes around the desk and stands behind me, like he's trying to block Nate's view. My hands are shaking so much I'm having a hard time holding the phone to my ear; my wrist still hurts where he grabbed me. I don't look back as we walk out the front doors. Ricardo gestures to the left, so I walk a short distance down the street. He stays behind me the whole time.

"You have a cab coming?" Ricardo asks. "Or do you need me to get you one?"

"Uber," I say. I move the phone away from my ear to check the time. "Any minute now."

He crosses his arms over his chest and nods.

A car pulls up, the window already down. "Are you Linnea?"

"Yes. Hang on, Caleb, my ride is here." I turn to Ricardo. "Thank you so much."

Ricardo opens the door for me. "No problem, miss."

"Linnea!" Nate's angry voice makes me jump.

"Get in the car," Caleb says in my ear.

"Go on," Ricardo says.

The car door shuts and I lock it as quickly as I can. I'm afraid to look back. "I'm in the car."

Caleb lets out a breath. "Don't hang up. Stay with me, okay?"

"I won't."

"You all right?" the driver asks as he pulls out onto the street.

"I am now," I say. "Thank you. I just need to get home."

He nods to me and keeps driving.

I don't say much to Caleb on the drive home, but just knowing he's there makes me feel better. He asks a few times if I'm okay, and where I am. I let him know when we pull onto his street. The driver parks in front of his house and I look out to see Caleb standing in the open doorway, still holding the phone to his ear.

14

CALEB

Relief floods through me when I see Linnea get out of the car. I'm breathing hard, my body raging with adrenaline. She shuts the door behind her and takes a couple steps, still holding her phone to her ear.

In an instant, she runs and crashes into me. My phone drops to the ground and I wrap my arms around her. I kiss her hair, holding her tight, crushing her against me.

I pull back and cup her cheeks. I need to see her face. I kiss one cheek, then the other. "Oh my god, Linnea." Kiss her forehead. "Are you okay?" Kiss her left temple, then her right. "I'm so sorry that happened to you." I keep kissing her, all over her face. "I wanted to come get you." Plant a hard kiss on her lips.

We look at each other for half a second, shocked. Then I surge in, still holding her face in my hands, and kiss her. *Really* kiss her. My mouth is soft, moving against her lips in a slow caress. Her hands slip around my waist and she presses her body against me. I delve in with my tongue, just a taste, and hers is there to meet mine. Heat races through me as the tips of our tongues brush.

I tilt my head to take the kiss deeper and she welcomes me

in. Her mouth opens and her tongue slides against mine. We move together, our mouths tangled in a slow dance. A warm, wet kiss that goes on and on, well past when I should have stopped. I shouldn't be kissing her at all—especially not like this—but she feels so fucking good, I can't stop.

I'm suddenly aware of Linnea's body. Her arms around me. Her tits pressed against my chest. I'm a heartbeat away from pushing her up against the wall. Ripping this fucking dress off her. But rational thought floods back. I can't do that. Especially not after the night she just had.

But because she isn't stopping me, I kiss her a little longer.

Gradually, I take the kiss from deep to shallow. I pull my tongue back and kiss her lips a few more times before I gently separate.

Her eyes are dazed and she blinks at me, her lips still parted.

"Sorry," I say quietly. I drop my hands. "I, um... I didn't mean to..."

"It's okay," she says.

The taste of her lingers on my lips; it's making it very hard to stay in control. "Are you sure you're all right?"

"Yeah," she says. "I'm fine now. That was just... it was awful. I never should have gone out with him."

"It's not your fault," I say. "You had no idea he'd be like that."

"I guess not." Her eyes linger on me for a moment and she takes a deep breath. "Tonight was... I'm really overwhelmed. I should probably..." She gestures to the stairs.

"Yeah," I say.

"Thank you," she says. "For everything."

"You're welcome."

She steps in to hug me and I wrap my arms around her. It's brief, just a squeeze before she steps back. She touches her hand to my chest and gives me a tired smile.

"Goodnight."

I watch her walk up the stairs, my heart racing. Holy shit, what did I do? I just kissed the fuck out of Linnea—right after she was on the brink of being date-raped. God, I'm an asshole.

Waiting for her to get home was the worst. I was losing my mind with worry from the moment she called. Actually, I started worrying about her as soon as she walked out the door with that douchecanoe. The way he looked at her made me want to rip his face off. But what was I supposed to do? Linnea's a grownup. She can decide who she wants to date.

But him? If I had to guess, he was mid-thirties. He was way too old for her—probably older than me. And she teaches his son? That's a clusterfuck now. There's no way she can keep the guy's kid as a student. What an ass. He screwed his own kid over. I can't imagine doing something like that to Charlotte.

Of course, I wouldn't try to force a woman to come up to a hotel room with me either.

I shut and lock the front door, then grab my phone. Luckily it didn't crack when I dropped it. I'm way too keyed up to go to bed, so I go sit on the couch and turn on the TV.

I'm going to have to talk to Linnea about that kiss tomorrow. But what do I say? I wasn't trying to take advantage of her when she was vulnerable. When she ran to me, I was overwhelmed with relief. I shouldn't have started kissing her in the first place, but I didn't even think about it.

The real kiss, though? I thought about that. Only for a split second. But I looked at her and I knew I had to have that gorgeous mouth. I can't claim that was an accident. It's not like I tripped and our lips happened to crash together.

I lick my lips again, still tasting her. That's really the worst part. Now that I've had a taste, my whole body aches for her. I want to kiss her again. And again. I want to kiss her *everywhere.*

What if... what if I went upstairs to talk to her now? Nothing would have to happen. I could check on her, make sure she's really okay.

Don't kid yourself, Caleb. There's only one reason you want to go to her right now. And it's not to have an innocent chat.

Fuck, I shouldn't have kissed her like that. This isn't how I meant for things to happen. I wanted to talk to her, maybe over dinner. Approach this carefully. I have more than just me to consider; this impacts Charlotte too.

Of course, Linnea did kiss me back.

She *really* kissed me back. It was as if she wanted it as much as I did. Although she did say she was overwhelmed. Maybe that's all it was—just relief at being home. She was caught up in the moment.

I rub my hands up and down my face and let out a long breath. God, I really made a mess of things. And I'm not sure what I'm going to do about it.

~

AFTER A VERY RESTLESS NIGHT—I might have slept a few hours, but I'm not sure—I get up. I don't have to be back at the hospital again until Sunday evening and I've been looking forward to having an entire weekend off. But the biggest thing on my mind is what happened with Linnea.

I shower and get dressed. When I come downstairs, the girls are already there. Charlotte is still in pajamas and her hair is messy. She comes over to give me a good morning hug, then goes back to the couch with her book.

Linnea is at the dining table with a mug of tea. She smiles but looks away quickly. Damn it, I was hoping things wouldn't be awkward between us this morning.

I try to talk to her a few times, but Charlotte appears out of nowhere whenever I open my mouth. She needs help with breakfast. Then she wants to know if she can have more milk. There's an opportunity when Linnea is putting her dishes away, but before I can get a word out, Charlotte is suddenly next to me. When did my kid learn to freaking teleport?

"Daddy, I forgot my vitamin," Charlotte says.

I smooth down her hair. "Sure, sweetie."

Linnea already has the jar of children's vitamins out. She opens it and hands one to her. Charlotte takes it, pops it in her mouth, and goes back to the living room.

I glance back at Charlotte to make sure she's staying put. "Linnea, I think we should talk about last night."

She sets the vitamins back on the counter. "Yeah, okay."

"Daddy?" Charlotte's voice behind me makes me jump. Oh my god, again? "Can I turn on the TV?"

"Yes, Bug, that's a great idea. Go turn on the TV." I grab Linnea's hand as Charlotte scampers off again. I only mean to lead her out of the kitchen, but I twine our fingers together. "Let's go upstairs."

The *My Little Pony* theme song comes on as Linnea and I walk upstairs, our hands clasped together. Her closeness and the feel of her skin makes my heart beat harder. We just need a few minutes alone, so I pull her into my bedroom and close the door behind us.

I should let go of her hand, but I don't—I adjust my grip so I can turn and face her.

"Look, I'm sorry about last night," I say. "I wasn't trying to take advantage of you."

"I know," she says. "But... Caleb, I really can't."

She pulls her hand away and it feels like my heart sinks straight into my stomach. Damn it. I shouldn't have entertained the thought that this conversation would turn out any other way. I'm about to tell her it's fine, but she's not finished.

"Especially if you're already seeing someone, it wouldn't be right."

I blink at her. Seeing someone? What is she talking about? "What? I'm not... You think I'm seeing someone?"

Her lips part and she hesitates for a beat. "Well, yeah. You brought Abigail home to meet Charlotte. It must be getting serious if you wanted her to meet Bug."

"Abigail?" I shake my head. "I'm not dating Abigail."

"You're not?"

"No, she was Mel's friend when we were residents. She was in town with her husband for a few days and got in touch to see how Charlotte and I are doing. I invited her to come see Bug; she hadn't seen her since she was a baby. They didn't rent a car, so I picked her up, and I brought her here because it's better for Charlotte. She's more comfortable at home."

She touches her hand to her lips. "Oh my god, I thought..."

"Linnea, I haven't dated anyone in quite a while," I say. "Certainly not since you've been here. I'm sorry, I should have explained who Abigail was, but you had to leave and I didn't see you again that night. Then I forgot all about it."

"I'm sorry Caleb, I feel so stupid."

"No, don't. I can see why you thought that." I want to tell her that no other woman has existed for me since the moment I saw her on that escalator at the airport. That I wonder if any woman will ever exist for me again. But I should cut my losses and make sure we're okay. The last thing I want to do is screw this up for Charlotte. "Like I said, I'm sorry about last night. I was really worried about you and I got carried away. I hope we can move past it. Charlotte loves you so much. We can't lose you."

"No, you won't," she says. "I'm not going anywhere."

Relief mixes with my disappointment. "Good. Thank you." I rub the back of my neck. I'm damn lucky she's such a good person, or she might have been out the door before morning. "Okay, so we're good, then?"

"Of course we are," she says.

I nod and start to step past her. There's no sense in making this more awkward than it already is.

She puts a hand on my arm. "But, Caleb?"

I stop and look at her. "Yeah?"

"Why are you sorry?"

"What?"

"Well, I'm just wondering... are you sorry because it wasn't the right time? Or are you sorry that you kissed me at all?"

Oh god, how do I answer that? I'm not sorry I kissed her—not really. I probably should be. I'm doing this all wrong, and it feels like things between us are spinning out of control.

"Which do you want it to be?" I ask, my voice quiet.

"Neither."

That sends a jolt of electricity racing through me. I step closer. "There are a lot of reasons this is complicated."

"I know."

Closer. She tilts her face up and our noses almost touch.

"I want to kiss you again," I say. "But I'm not sure if I should."

"You should," she breathes.

And I'm done.

I lean in and slant my mouth over hers, slipping my hands around her waist. She moves her arms around my neck and presses herself close. I kiss her long and slow and deep, savoring the feel of her mouth. Her soft lips. Her tongue tangled with mine. I kiss her like I can. Like I have a right to. And in the midst of this kiss that is setting me on fire and making my cock achingly hard, I'm hit with the realization that she *did* want this.

Holy shit.

Gradually, I pull away. I brush her soft hair back from her face and she gazes up at me with those beautiful blue eyes.

"Did you just kiss me again?" she asks.

"I did."

"I'm sorry, I think my brain is stuck back five minutes ago when I thought you were dating someone else and you'd never see me this way."

I laugh. I guess there's no sense in holding my feelings back now. "God, Linnea, I've wanted to do that since I picked you up at the airport."

"Are you serious?"

"Yeah," I say. "I saw you come down that elevator and it was like being hit by a freight train."

"Me too," she says.

"What?"

She nibbles on her bottom lip. "I've had this silly crush on you since I got here."

"Aren't we a pair?" I say. "But I don't think it's silly."

"I guess not, if it wasn't just me," she says. "So... what happens now?"

I stare at her for a long moment. We're steps away from my bed. The door is closed. But as much as I want her, I shouldn't. Not yet. This isn't just about me wanting her body—although, god, that body. But this means more; *she* means more.

Plus, Charlotte is downstairs and bound to come looking for us any minute. When I do have Linnea, I don't want to rush. I want to be able to enjoy every second.

"How about I take you out," I say. "I know we see each other all the time, but I want to do this right. Can I take you out on a date?"

"I would love that so much," she says. "But who'll watch Bug?"

I touch her cheek and kiss her again, gently. I love that her first thought is Charlotte. "I'll take care of it. Does tonight work if I can find someone last-minute?"

"Yeah, tonight works," she says.

I'm still holding her close and I smile at her, taking her in—feeling the relief of finally letting this out. Alex was right, this was inevitable. I try to push aside my concerns—what people will think. What will happen down the road. For now, I'll focus on this. On her. On giving us a chance.

15

CALEB

As the day goes on, I find it almost impossible to keep my hands off Linnea. But we're with Charlotte, and this isn't the kind of thing we can spring on her. Not until we know for sure what's happening between us. Sharing a kiss—even a kiss like *that*—and confessing we both feel something only means more is possible. I want to tread carefully where my daughter is concerned.

I've never been serious enough about a woman to introduce her to Charlotte. As far as she knows, Daddy has always been alone. And that's not far from the truth. Between the demands of school, and now my job—and doing it all while raising her—I haven't had a lot of time for relationships. It took a long time after losing Melanie before dating was even a possibility. Since then, I've dated a little. But I haven't met anyone who made me want to put in the effort. Not until Linnea.

So we make eye contact and smile, like we're sharing a secret. We take Charlotte to the park, then the library. I'm in a pretty great mood, so I suggest we all go out for ice cream too. Charlotte eats her pink bubble gum cone and alternates between sitting in my lap and sitting in Linnea's.

When we get home, Linnea pulls out her phone and looks at the screen. Her eyebrows draw in and she takes a deep breath.

"Is everything okay?" I ask.

"Nate keeps texting," she says. "I answered him once, only to say I won't be teaching his son anymore. But he won't stop sending me messages."

I hold out my hand. "I'll take care of it."

She hesitates, but gives me her phone. "What are you going to do?"

"Just block him for you," I say, not mentioning the fact that I'm memorizing his number. I tap a few things and make sure he can't call or text her phone anymore, then hand it back. "There. Problem solved."

She smiles. "Thanks."

"Of course." I place a quick kiss on her forehead. "I think Bug got ice cream on my shirt. I'm going to change."

I go upstairs and slip into my bedroom, closing the door behind me. I type Nate's number and hit call. The asshole better answer.

"Nate Ingram," he says.

"This is Caleb Lawson," I say, keeping my voice low. "We met last night when you picked up Linnea."

"Right..."

"Listen, you piece of shit. Do not text, call, or contact her again in any way. Keep texting her and I'll break your thumbs. And if you go anywhere near Henley's Music while she's there, I'll gut you like a fucking fish."

"Hey man, I—"

"Don't. Stay away from her, or I'll cut you open and harvest your goddamn organs. Are we clear?"

He coughs. "Uh, yeah. Clear."

"Good." I hang up.

Now the problem is solved.

While I'm alone, I finalize my plans for our date night. I make a couple of calls, and then text Kendra to see if she and Weston can watch Bug.

Me: Hey, are you guys busy tonight? Can you watch Charlotte for a few hours?

Kendra: For sure. What's up? Work issues?

Me: No. I have a date.

Kendra: !!!!!!!!

I shake my head and wait, because I know she's going to keep asking questions.

Kendra: Who is she?

Kendra: How did you meet her?

Kendra: Is it a first date?

Kendra: Wait. Why can't Linnea watch her? Does she have plans? Is something wrong?

I hesitate another minute, waiting to see if she'll keep going. My phone stays quiet, so I take a deep breath and answer. This is going to send Kendra off the deep end.

Me: My date is Linnea.

Kendra: OMG!

Kendra: Are you serious?

Kendra: YES! FINALLY!

Kendra: Okay, yeah. We can be there around 7.

Me: Perfect. Thanks.

Kendra: Anytime.

I'm sure by the time my phone is back in my pocket, Kendra has already texted Mia. There's not much I can do about that. I'll make sure Kendra knows to be subtle about it with Charlotte. We won't lie to her—we'll just tell her Daddy and Linnea are going to have dinner. With little kids, the simplest explanation is usually best.

~

Kendra and Weston arrive and Charlotte is so excited to see them, she's not the least bit worried about me and Linnea leaving. We say goodbye, and as soon as the front door closes behind us, I grab Linnea and pull her in for a kiss.

"Sorry," I say. "I've been wanting to do that again all day."

"No need to apologize," she says. "Me too."

We get in the car and she asks me what we're doing. I keep my cards close and tell her—again—that it's a surprise. She's already confused because I told her to dress casually, and when she came downstairs wearing what was admittedly a very cute skirt, I had her change into jeans.

At our first stop, she waits in the car while I run in. I'm just picking up our dinner. It's not fancy, but it's good food, and it will be easy to eat where I'm taking her. The second stop is a convenience store, and I try to get my purchase into the trunk before she can see what I'm doing.

I drive us out to Golden Gardens Park in Ballard, up in the northwest corner of Seattle. It's a long stretch of sandy beach on Puget Sound. It's also one of only two parks in the city that allow bonfires.

We get out and I hand her the bags with our dinner. "Can you carry these?"

"Sure," she says. "But what are—"

I touch a finger to her lips. "You'll see."

In the trunk, I have the small bundle of firewood I bought at the convenience store, plus the blanket I keep for beach trips with Charlotte. I tuck the blanket under my arm and grab the firewood by the plastic strap holding it together.

"Are we having a beach picnic?" she asks.

"Yeah, I thought this would be nice. We can build a fire in one of the fire pits and watch the sun set." I wait for her reaction, but she just stares at me, her lips parted. Suddenly I wonder if I screwed up. Maybe I should have tried to get reservations at a nice restaurant. "Unless that doesn't sound good and you'd rather we do something else?"

"No," she says quickly. "This is perfect."

We don't have to walk too far before we find a fire pit that's open. It's a large metal container right on the sand. The sun is still up, and the breeze is mild, but I get straight to work building a fire. In just a few minutes, I have a little blaze crackling.

Linnea lays the blanket out on the sand next to the fire. We get out our dinner—sandwiches from my favorite deli—and sit close together, facing the water.

"I figured it would be nice to be somewhere quiet. And I don't think you've seen the sun set over the water—at least not here."

"I never have," she says, her voice soft.

"So this is good?" I ask. "Are you warm enough?"

She meets my eyes. "Yes, I'm fine. And this is so good. I like this so much more than dinner at some expensive restaurant."

I know she's referring to her date with that asshole. It's hard to believe that was just last night.

"Good." I reach over and touch her chin, bringing her mouth to mine. Her lips are so soft, her mouth warm and yielding.

We sit and eat next to the crackling fire, talking and laughing like we usually do when we're together. The sun dips low toward the horizon, igniting the sky with a blaze of orange and red. The water sparkles and Linnea leans in and rests her head on my shoulder while we watch the sun go down.

After the sun sets, I wrap my arms around her—just because I can. I breathe in the scent of her hair as she relaxes against me. We're quiet for a while, gazing out at the water while the last bit of light fades and stars wink to life in the dark sky.

Eventually we both start to get cold, so we douse the fire, pack up, and head to the car. We get home to find Kendra and Weston snuggled up on the couch watching TV, and a certain little girl nestled in her bed upstairs. I can tell Kendra is about ready to burst—she probably wants to know all the details of our evening—but Weston herds her toward the front door. I walk them out, thanking them for watching Charlotte. Kendra goes out to their car, and Weston pauses just outside the front door.

"Here." He reaches into the inside pocket of his jacket. "I figure if you have any, they're old as shit." With a glance toward Kendra, as if to make sure she's not looking, he hands me something.

It's a bunch of condoms. I close my fist around them quickly and look over my shoulder to make sure Linnea isn't within earshot.

"Dude, what the fuck?"

"I'm just trying to do you a favor," Weston says.

I shove them in my pocket. "Thanks, I guess? But I don't think—"

"Whatever, Lawson." He shakes his head and walks out to his car before I can say anything else.

I go back inside and Linnea is standing in the kitchen. Her hair is a little windblown and her cheeks are still pink from the night air. Suddenly these condoms are burning a hole in my pocket. But Linnea has such an air of innocence about her. I'm reminded that she's a lot younger than me, and I'm not sure what she's ready for.

"Thank you again for tonight," she says. "I think it was the best date I've ever been on."

"Wow." I step closer and run my hand down her arm. "That's really good to hear."

She pops up on her tiptoes, and this time she initiates a kiss. At first I mean to hold back, but she slides her tongue across my lips, and I surge in. I grab her by the waist and pull her against me. Kissing her deeply, I let my hands move over her round hips to her ass. She makes a little noise in her throat and her hands clutch my shirt. I've wanted my hands on this ass for so long. I squeeze her and she presses her hips closer, rubbing against my erection.

The feel of her body pressing against my hard cock is intoxicating. I'm starting to lose control, my mind taken over by need. I back her up against the counter and lift one of her legs so she's partially straddling me. She moans into my mouth, the heat of our kiss growing. I hold her tight against me and she shifts her hips, grinding against my thigh.

I leave her mouth and kiss down her neck. She tilts her head back and her skin tastes so sweet. This isn't enough. I need more of her. All of her.

My hand dips under her shirt and finds the soft skin of her back while my other hand keeps her leg up. I press my thigh between her legs and she gasps. Her sharp intake of breath makes me pause, my mouth next to her ear. I should probably slow down, but god, I want her so bad.

"Yes, Caleb," she says, her voice breathy.

My heart thunders in my chest and it's hard to focus on anything but the aching pressure in my groin. "What?"

She shifts so she can meet my gaze. Her eyes are hooded, her lips full and red. "I'm telling you yes. Take me upstairs."

I lower her leg until her foot hits the floor, my hand running up her thigh. Stepping back, I let her move in front of me, then follow her up the stairs. I'm in a daze, hypnotized by the swish of her hair, the sway of her hips. And that ass—fuck. She's already driving me out of my mind and she's not even undressed yet.

Oh fuck. Linnea's about to get naked.

I quietly shut the door behind us and pull my shirt off as I move in toward her. She bites her bottom lip and touches my chest, sliding her delicate hands down my abs. I grab the hem of her shirt and she lifts her arms while I slip it over her head.

She's wearing a sheer black lace bra that shows the outline of her nipples. I swallow hard and I can't stop staring.

Oh my god, her boobs. I get to touch those magnificent boobs.

She unbuttons her jeans and slides them down her curvy hips to reveal matching black panties. I take my pants and underwear off, and the way she licks her lips when she looks at my dick makes me crazy.

She looks up at me shyly through her eyelashes as she reaches behind to unfasten her bra clasp. My hands actually tremble as I slide her bra straps down her shoulders and the cups fall away, revealing the most beautiful set of tits I've ever seen.

They're as perfect as they seem when she's dressed. Round. Firm. Creamy skin. Erect pink nipples. I run my hands up her rib cage to cup her tits in both hands. My brain is short-circuiting at the sight of her gorgeous curves, the feel of her skin, her nipples pebbling against my palms.

"Do you know how beautiful you are?" I brush her hair back from her face and kiss her, then nudge her onto the bed.

I lean over her, propped up on one elbow, and run my hand up her thigh, past her hip, up her ribs. Cupping her breast, I slide my tongue over the hard nub of her nipple.

She gasps, her body twitching. "Oh god, Caleb, they're really sensitive."

I groan, squeezing it gently. "Do you want me to stop?" I run my tongue around her nipple in a lazy circle.

Her voice comes out in a whimper. "No."

"Good." I lick her again, then take her breast in my mouth and suck.

Her back arches, and she moans. It's the sexiest fucking thing. My cock is so hard it almost hurts, but these tits—I can't pull myself away from them. I lick and suck and squeeze her, moving from one side to the other, while she shudders and gasps. Driving her crazy is making me absolutely insane.

Leaning over, I find the lines of her tattoo. I've fantasized about running my tongue along the design more times than I can count. I kiss and lick her, grazing my teeth over the delicate treble clef, the little swirl of music notes.

I slip my hand into her panties and she moans again. Searching gently with my fingers, I feel her respond. I rub her clit and slide my tongue across her nipple again. "You're so wet."

She moves her hips against my hand and I give her more, sliding my fingers inside her. I suck on her breast while I play with her pussy, enjoying her slick heat. Her hips move faster and I work my fingers, exploring, finding her most sensitive places.

The steady rhythm of my fingers on her clit and my mouth on her tits has her panting, her body writhing. She puts her hand over mine to give herself pressure where she needs it. The sight of our hands between her legs is so damn sexy. I want to make her come like this.

"That's it, beautiful." I suck on her nipple again and she moans. "Let go. Let me make you come. Then I'll put my cock inside you and do it again."

"Oh god, Caleb," she breathes. "That feels so good... just like that... yes..."

Her body convulses as her orgasm takes her. I love seeing her so uninhibited, trusting me with her body. Watching her come sends a shock wave of desire through me. I have to be inside her. I pull her panties off and reach over the edge of the bed to get one of the condoms out of my pants pocket. I almost hate to admit it, but I'm going to have to thank Weston for that. He was right—if I have any around, they're probably too old to be trusted.

Linnea watches me roll the condom down over my erection. Her cheeks are flushed and her tongue flicks across her lips. I climb on top of her, feeling her soft skin and the heat of her body. Lowering my hips between her legs, I let my cock rest against her opening.

Her tits press against my chest as I lean down to kiss her mouth and spread her open with the tip of my cock. She whimpers again, a strangled, desperate sound.

"Yes?" I ask.

"Yes."

All at once, I thrust inside her. She lifts her hips to meet me and leans her head back, a moan escaping her lips. I groan into her neck, the feel of her pussy overtaking me.

She clutches my back as I start to move, slowly at first. If I go any faster, I'll come in her too soon. She feels too fucking good.

"Linnea, you feel amazing," I say, my voice low in her ear.

Her pussy is so hot, and I slide through her wetness easily. I lift up so I can kiss her tits again. Her skin tastes so good and the feel of her firm nipple in my mouth sends bursts of heat straight to my groin.

"Harder," she breathes.

Sliding my hand down, I cup her ass and drive my cock in.

"Yes, harder," she says.

"I don't want to hurt you."

Her eyes are clouded over, her lips full and swollen. "You won't. Fuck me harder."

The word *fuck* coming from her mouth is like a lightning strike. My fingers dig into her ass while I pump my hips. I'm intoxicated by her scent and the feel of her body. She yields to me completely, her legs open wide, her arms around me. We move together, driving, grinding, thrusting, our skin glistening with sweat. Soft whimpers escape her lips with every thrust of my cock.

God, it's been so long since I've felt this—something more than the quick thrill of sex. So long since I felt consumed by a woman—connected to her. I want to touch her, kiss her, love every inch of her.

I completely let go, growling and groaning as I fuck the life out of her. The feel of her nipples dragging across my chest and the pressure in my groin as my balls tighten is maddening. Her eyes roll back and her pussy clenches, tightening around my cock as she starts to come again.

It makes me lose my fucking mind. I explode inside her, the orgasm rocking through my body. My back stiffens, my hips thrust, and my cock pulses over and over. I can't think, can't breathe. I ride out the climax with her, driven only by instinct—the primal need to mark her, claim her as mine.

I hold her close as we both catch our breath, and place soft kisses on her neck and jaw. My lips find hers and I kiss her mouth in a slow caress, savoring her taste.

"That was unbelievable," she says.

I smile and kiss her lips again. "You're unbelievable."

She stays in my bed while I get rid of the condom. I climb back in and pull the sheets up over us. She settles into my arms, her body molding to mine—soft curves against my hard edges. I'm completely relaxed, drifting in a pleasant haze. I can't remember the last time I felt so *good*—the last time everything felt so right.

16

LINNEA

I wake to the weight of Caleb's arm over me. I'm curled up against him, my back to his front, my ass nestled against his thighs. His hand cups one of my breasts and his breath is warm against my neck.

The ache between my legs is pleasant and the feel of his body against mine makes me wish we never had to move. I can't see the clock, so I'm not sure what time it is, but I think it's early. Unfortunately, I do need to move. I should go to my bedroom before Charlotte wakes up and finds us here.

But it feels so good to lie in his arms. I close my eyes and shift a little, snuggling closer against him. His hand squeezes my breast, sending a jolt of sensation through me. My back arches, almost involuntarily, and I feel his cock harden against my ass.

He takes a deep breath, his muscular chest expanding against my back, and makes a low noise in his throat. The gentle pressure of his hand on my breast is waking me up in an entirely different way.

"Good morning, beautiful." He kisses my shoulder and the back of my neck.

"Morning," I say. "What time is it?"

He kisses my shoulder again. "Don't want to know."

His hand moves down to grab my hip and he presses his hard length against me. Oh my god, he feels so good. I arch into him and he keeps planting soft kisses on my neck.

I still can't quite believe last night happened. Our date was perfect—so romantic. When we came home, all I could think about was how much I wanted him. I've never felt that way before, not about anyone. I was desperate for him.

And when he took me, it was unlike anything I've ever experienced. I'm still a little giddy from the way he touched and kissed me—from the way his cock filled me. Was all that sensation—all that hot, blissful pleasure—real?

The jolts of electricity racing across my skin as he caresses and kisses me again tell me it was.

I'm just about to reach behind and grab his cock—I want to feel it in my hand—when a noise makes us both freeze.

"The door," he whispers in my ear so quietly I can barely hear him. "Stay here."

The door squeaks again and he slowly moves away from me. I'm facing the other way, so I can't see what's happening. My eyes are wide and my heart is racing. Oh my god, Charlotte is coming in.

"Daddy?" Her sleepy voice comes from the doorway.

Caleb sits up and moves one of his pillows so it partially blocks me from view—hopefully. If she's not fully awake yet, she might not realize I'm here.

"Hey, Bug," he says. The bed moves as he gets up and it sounds like he's slipping underwear or pants on.

I hold as still as I can.

"Is it morning?" Charlotte asks.

"Yeah, but it's early," he says. "Let's go downstairs."

I wait until their voices disappear, then get up and grab my clothes before hurrying to my room. My door is still closed, so it doesn't look like Charlotte went to my room first. Hopefully she has no idea I slept in her daddy's bed last night. Obviously we'll need to tell her that we're dating now, but she doesn't need the details of our sleeping arrangements—or anything else that goes on in his bedroom.

It *is* early—before seven—but I'm awake, so I decide to throw on some clothes and go downstairs. I find them on the couch, Charlotte curled up in Caleb's lap. He smiles at me—a slow, sexy smile that makes my heart flutter and my core tingle. I smile back and go into the kitchen to make tea.

I'm hoping Caleb will talk to Charlotte about us, but as the day goes on, it's clear he's not going to. He doesn't kiss or touch me in front of her, and I don't hear him say anything about it. I'm a little disappointed—mostly because I'm so aware of the space between us. I want to be close—to feel his arms around me, his lips on mine. As it is, we steal a few kisses when Charlotte is in another room. And when he has to leave for the hospital that evening, he kisses my neck and whispers that he'll miss me.

Caleb is at the hospital overnight, so I sleep in my own bed. It was tempting to sleep in his, even alone, just so I could smell him. But I decided it would be better if I didn't. Just before I fall asleep, my phone vibrates with a text.

Caleb: I miss you, beautiful. I can't wait to kiss you again.

Me: Me too. Tomorrow can't come soon enough.

His message leaves me feeling dreamy and I drift off to sleep with a smile on my face.

AT SCHOOL DROP-OFF, I invite Megan and Noah to come over for an impromptu playdate this afternoon. Caleb won't be home until later, and Charlotte and Noah haven't played together in a couple of weeks. She agrees, and after school they walk home with us.

The weather is gray and drizzly, so we set the kids up with some toys and games in the living room after they have a snack. Megan and I settle in at the dining table with steaming mugs of tea.

We chat a little about how the kids are doing in school and she tells me her older sister just announced she's expecting a new baby.

"Now everyone is asking me when we're having another one," she says. "And we're thinking about it. We didn't really mean to wait so long after Noah, but it sort of happened that way. I just wish everyone would get off our backs."

"Yeah, that must be frustrating," I say.

"It is," she says. "But that's just my family for you."

I nibble on my bottom lip and stare into my tea. Are we good enough friends that I can talk to her about this? I guess I won't know unless I try. "So… can I talk to you about something?"

"Yeah, of course." She leans forward and sets her mug on the table.

"Well, something kind of happened between me and Caleb," I say.

She raises her eyebrows and her lips twitch in a smile. "Really? Something, like what?"

"Like, a lot of things," I say. "Like, he kissed me. And took me on a date. And…"

"And?" she asks.

My cheeks warm. "And I might have kind of slept with him the other night."

"Wow," she says. "This is a good thing, right? You wanted to sleep with him?"

"Yeah," I say with a little laugh. God, I must be bright red. "I did, and it's a good thing. I've had this crazy crush on him since pretty much the moment I got here."

"I figured you had a thing for him, but I didn't want to pry," she says.

"You could tell?"

"Sure," she says. "The couple of times I've met him, I could tell there was something between you two. I figured if you wanted to talk about it, you'd bring it up."

I shake my head. "And here I thought I was doing such a good job hiding my feelings."

"I don't think a stranger walking by would have noticed, but I've gotten to know you," she says. "So, how did this happen? Did one of you finally work up the nerve to confess your infatuation?"

"Sort of," I say, and I tell her about my crappy date—and how Caleb kissed me when I got home.

"Whoa," she says, her voice a little awed. "I bet that freaked you out."

"Kind of," I say. "I was so overwhelmed with everything that had happened. It wasn't until I was in bed that it really hit me. And then I thought maybe it hadn't been what I thought. Maybe he was just relieved that I got home safely."

"But obviously it was a lot more than that," she says.

"Yeah. We talked the next morning and it all came out—for both of us. Then that night he took me to the beach to watch the sun set."

"Aw," she says.

"It was wonderful," I say. "But I'm still not sure what to think. I didn't think he felt the way I did. And now that I know he does, it's hard not to worry about all the reasons this is complicated."

She shrugs. "You're both single adults. So, he's a little older than you, and he used to be married to your sister. And, well, you're his nanny."

I laugh. "God, it sounds pretty bad. My parents are going to lose their minds."

"Uh-oh, really?"

"It makes me kind of sick to my stomach to even think about telling them," I say.

"Do they not like him?" she asks.

"I'm not sure if they dislike *him*, or just dislike that he married my sister," I say. "My parents are so opinionated. They thought getting married was going to ruin her career or something. And now the same guy is sleeping with their other daughter?"

Megan bursts out laughing. "I'm sorry." She puts a hand to her chest and takes a few deep breaths. "I'm so sorry, I swear I'm not laughing at you. That's just... wow."

"I know. It's bad, isn't it?" I ask.

"No," she says, emphatic. "It's not *bad*. If he was the kind of guy to take advantage of you, or if he was pushing you into this, *that* would be bad. But crushing on a guy like him? Hard to blame you. Let's be honest, he's hot, he's a freaking doctor, and he's a great dad. What's not to love? And the fact that he likes you too is pretty damn cool."

"Yeah, I didn't stand a chance, did I? And he's not pushing me into anything. Kind of the opposite. He liked me right away too, but he didn't think he should do anything about it."

"Restraint and patience can be such sexy traits in a man," she says.

"Yeah. I'm just..."

"What?" she asks.

I take a deep breath. "Well, everything when we... well, you know... was great. Not just great. It was amazing. But now I'm a little intimidated. I don't have a lot of experience."

"You mean with sex?" she asks.

"Yeah."

"Like, how inexperienced are we talking?" she asks.

"Well, I wasn't a virgin," I say. "I dated a guy in college for a year and a half, and I slept with him. And there was a guy in high school before that, although... well, that was just bad all around."

"First times usually are," she says.

"No, it wasn't that kind of bad," I say. "He was just... he was awful to me."

"What happened?" she asks, her voice going soft.

"Boys didn't notice me in school," I say. "I was too shy to talk much, and I dressed in big sweatshirts and stuff. One day, this guy saw me take off my sweatshirt in front of my locker, and I guess he decided I had something he wanted. He started flirting with me and eventually he asked me out. I didn't want to sleep with him, but he pressured me pretty hard and I gave in. I regretted it so much afterward. When I wouldn't go out with him again, he got mad and told everyone at school that I was a slut. Then I wasn't just the weird quiet girl, I was the slutty weird quiet girl."

"Oh god, Linnea, that's awful," she says. "Fuck that guy."

"Yeah," I say. "I didn't want to have anything to do with boys after that. Not until college. The guy I dated then was nice, and he cared about me. Or at least, I think he did. He wasn't a very emotional person."

"Why did you break up?" she asks.

"He was leaving to go to a Master's program in New York," I say. "So that was that."

"Wait, he just broke up with you?" she asks. "Did you guys talk about whether to stay together or try to figure something out?"

"Not really," I say. "He was very... logic driven. I don't think he considered trying to have a long-distance relationship. He was moving away, so we were over."

"Ouch," she says. "Well, you're better off without that. James acts like he has no emotions, but even he wouldn't be that cold."

I laugh. The way Megan describes her husband always makes me giggle. "You're right, I am better off without him. It was just too bad he didn't care about me enough to try."

"What a dumbass," she says. "So, okay, you've only been with a couple guys, and let me guess, sex with Mr. I Have No Feelings wasn't exactly spectacular."

"No," I say. "To be honest, until the other night, I kind of didn't know any better. But now..."

She lifts her mug. "You go, girl."

I clink mine against hers. "But the problem is—please don't make fun of me—I'm not sure if I'm any good at it. Or if I know the right things to do. How do people figure this stuff out?"

"Of course I won't make fun of you," she says. "It's not like our mothers sit us down and tell us how to be good lovers."

"Oh god."

"I know," she says. "Can you imagine a conversation like that with your mother? Makes me shudder."

"Horrifying," I say.

"Exactly. This is why we need girlfriends." She shifts in her chair, like she's getting more comfortable. "Since you're concerned about your bedroom skills, let me first ask, did it seem like he enjoyed himself?"

I think back on the way Caleb drove into me. The way he groaned and growled into my neck. He was aggressive and unrestrained, like he was losing his mind. And when he came, it was unlike anything I've ever felt before. I cross my legs and take a sip of tea to cover the rush of heat that hits me. "Yeah, he... he was definitely enjoying himself."

"And you?"

"Oh my god, Megan," I say. "I've never... I don't even know what to say."

"That good?" she asks. "We're talking, *girl got her orgasm* good?"

"Twice."

"Marry him," she says, her expression serious.

I laugh. "But what do I do now? He obviously knows what he's doing. What if our first time was only good because it was our first?"

"In my experience, sex with someone who knows what they're doing can definitely be good," she says. "But that can't compare to sex that's good because you're both crazy about each other."

"So, you're saying you don't think it matters that I don't really know what I'm doing?"

"I'm saying if you guys have real feelings for each other, that's going to do more to make sex awesome than whether you have some tricks up your sleeve," she says. "Can I be really straightforward?"

"Yeah."

"Listen to your body," she says. "And feel for his reactions. Women have a lot of strength in our legs and hips. Use it. Move around, see what feels good. You'll know if it makes him feel good—believe me. And if you trust him enough to go all the way to fucktown, you should be able to talk to him. Ask him what he likes. Better yet, ask him to *show you* what he likes."

"Okay," I say. "I think I can do that."

"Besides, if a guy knows what he's doing, he'll play you like a fine instrument," she says. "Let him lead you."

I take another sip of my tea and set it down. "Thanks, Megan. It's nice to have someone to talk to."

"You bet, sweetie," she says. "Ditto. Have you guys said anything to Charlotte yet?"

"No," I say. "I thought he might yesterday, but maybe he just wasn't ready to bring it up yet."

"It is delicate," she says. "I can see why he might wait to explain it to her. I'm so grateful I don't have to juggle dating *and* parenthood. But at least you already know his daughter likes you."

"That's true," I say. "I'm crazy about that little girl."

Megan smiles. "I know you are. I'm happy for you."

"Thanks. I'm just trying not to get ahead of myself."

She reaches out and squeezes my hand. "You have a good head on your shoulders. I think you'll be fine."

17

LINNEA

The week is busy, and it goes by so fast, it almost seems like I miss it. In some ways, it feels like nothing has changed. Charlotte has school. I practice piano for hours every day. Caleb gets called in for extra shifts at the hospital, so he's gone more than usual.

We barely see each other until Thursday night. He comes home late and I can tell by his face and the way he walks in the door that he's exhausted. He still pulls me into his bedroom, murmuring in my ear how much he missed me.

I missed him too. But he's worth the wait. And this time, I set the alarm on my phone before I fall asleep. I don't want to give up sleeping wrapped in his arms, but I also don't want a certain little girl to find me in her daddy's bed.

He's stuck at the hospital late again on Friday, and I can tell Charlotte is starting to feel his absence. She's more withdrawn, even with me, and she only picks at her dinner. I read with her until her bedtime and a surprise call from Daddy perks her up quite a bit. He promises he'll be home tomorrow and he'll spend time with her then.

I keep Charlotte busy on Saturday morning so Caleb can sleep in. She helps me make pancakes and then I set her up at the table with paints and some big sheets of poster board. It's almost eleven before Caleb comes down, looking rumpled and sexy in plaid pajama pants and a t-shirt. Charlotte jumps down and runs to him and he scoops her up. It melts me every time I see the way he hugs her.

He brings her back to the table and she shows him her paintings. One is a garden with trees and lots of flowers. Another shows four stick figures next to a house.

"Who is this, Bug?" he asks, pointing to the first figure.

"That's you," she says, then points to the other figures. "This is Linnea, this is me, and this is Noah."

"And where are we?" he asks.

"We're home," she says. "That's our house, except Linnea planted pink flowers in the front."

"Did she?" He meets my eyes and winks. "That sounds very pretty. What's this one?"

She pulls out another picture. "This is me playing piano."

Caleb points to a bunch of circles lined up in rows at the bottom of the page. "What's this?"

"Those are people," she says.

"Are those people listening to you play?" he asks.

I stare at the picture. She painted herself playing in front of an audience. I meet Caleb's eyes, hoping he realizes what a step this is for her. His surprised expression tells me he does.

"Yes," she says.

"Where is this?" I ask.

"At school," she says.

Caleb and I make eye contact again, like we're both afraid to say the wrong thing and startle her tender little heart. Both hoping this means she's having some kind of breakthrough.

"Do you want to play piano at school?" I ask gently.

She tilts her head, looking at her picture, and twists her lips. "I think maybe yes. Ms. Peterson said if we want, we can do something for the parents at first grade parent night. Lily in my class is going to say a poem, and Nicholas is going to show some of his gymnastics." She purses her lips again, still staring at the painting, like she's imagining herself playing in front of an audience. "I think I can play *Twinkle, Twinkle, Little Star*."

I'm so excited, I think I might burst. I never would have thought she would decide to play in front of an audience so soon. Granted, she plays beautifully. I've called her a natural more than once, and I'm not exaggerating. She could play that song in her sleep and play it perfectly.

Caleb looks like he might actually have a tear in his eye. He kisses her head. "That sounds wonderful, Bug. I'm so proud of you."

"Thanks, Daddy."

I glance at the time. "Hey Bug, I think Grandma and Grandpa are going to call in a couple minutes."

"Do you mind helping her log on?" Caleb asks. "I'm going to make some coffee."

"Sure."

I get up and go to the desk next to the kitchen and boot up the laptop. When I lived with my parents I always talked to Charlotte on Skype when they did—and Caleb was never part of it. I knew he was around—sometimes we could hear him talk in the background—but he didn't join in the calls.

I didn't blame him for being distant. When Melanie died, my parents pushed Caleb—hard—to move to Michigan with Charlotte. His refusal left them furious, but he stood his ground. They said some awful things about him in those days—things I'm sure they never realized I heard.

To his credit, he always let them stay in Charlotte's life. He sent them pictures and videos when she was a baby, and welcomed them into his home when they wanted to fly out to visit. When she got a little older, they started doing Skype calls so she could see and talk to them. Caleb never got in the way of that, although he tended to stay off screen.

It's no surprise when he ducks into the kitchen and busies himself with making himself coffee and breakfast while I get Charlotte set up at the desk. She doesn't actually need my help; she knows how to do it all herself. But I sit with her anyway.

The call comes through and she clicks the mouse to answer. I adjust the webcam so it's focused on her and stay quiet while my parents gush over how big she's getting.

"How's school?" my mom asks.

"It's fine," Charlotte says. "We're working on how to write a sentence and using periods and question marks."

"That's excellent," Mom says. "What else have you been learning?"

"We have a butterfly habitat with caterpillars," Charlotte says.

"Are you learning about the life cycle of the butterfly?" my dad asks.

"Yes," Charlotte says. She explains the stages of butterfly development while my parents nod along.

"Good, I'm glad they're teaching you science," Mom says. "It's one of the most important disciplines."

"I'm playing piano too," Charlotte says. "I can play *Mary Had a Little Lamb*."

"That's nice," Mom says, and I try to ignore the disinterest in her voice at Charlotte's mention of music. "What else have you been up to?"

"Noah came to my house to play," Charlotte says. "And Linnea had a sleepover with Daddy."

I freeze and my face goes hot. Both my parents look at me and I desperately wish I hadn't pulled up a chair to sit next to Charlotte. I could be standing in the kitchen, watching from a distance. But I can't duck out of view now.

"Oh," Mom says. Her expression is in sharp detail on the screen—arched eyebrow, thin lips pressing together.

I glance back at Caleb. He sets down his mug and moves like he's going to come over and talk to them, but he pauses when I meet his eyes. I shake my head slightly and mouth, *No.*

"I wanted to have a sleepover in my room, but we just had a pajama party," Charlotte continues. "Miss Megan says I can spend the night at their house with Noah sometime. We might go to the park with Noah next week, if it isn't raining."

"Won't that be fun," Mom says with mock sweetness.

I try to head this off. "Mom, she doesn't mean—"

"We'll discuss this later, Linnea," Mom says, cutting me off. My dad hasn't said a word, but I can see the tightness in his jaw.

My eyes flick to Caleb again. His face is clouded with anger and I give him another tiny head shake. I really don't want him jumping in on this right now. Especially not in front of Charlotte.

I sit in tense discomfort while my parents talk to Charlotte for a few more minutes. I had no idea Charlotte knew I'd spent the night in Caleb's room. I've only done it twice, and both times I didn't think she'd noticed. I guess I underestimated her. She notices everything—just like I always did.

My parents don't say another word to me, nor do they ask to talk to Caleb. They tell Charlotte goodbye and when the call ends, Caleb comes over and kisses the top of her head.

"Why don't you go upstairs and play for a little while, Bug?"

"Okay, Daddy," she says.

He stands next to the desk, his coffee back in his hand. "Are you okay?"

I take a deep breath, but my stomach is already in a knot. *No, I'm not remotely okay.* "Yeah, I'm fine."

"Do you want me to call them?" he asks.

"What would you say?" I ask.

He shrugs. "That they don't have anything to worry about, and you're a capable adult who can make her own choices."

Yeah, that would go over well. "No, it's okay. You don't need to call them."

"Are you sure?" he asks.

"I'm sure."

My phone rings on the table behind me. I know it's her. I close my eyes for a second as a wave of anxiety rolls through me.

"You don't have to take that if you don't want to talk to her," he says. "What happens between us is private. It isn't anyone else's business."

It rings again and I stand.

"Linnea." He puts a hand on my arm. "You don't have to."

"She'll just keep calling if I don't answer. I'd rather get it over with." I grab my phone off the table and answer as I walk upstairs to my room. "Hello?"

"Linnea." My mom's voice is cold and unemotional. "What is going on in that house?"

I close the door and sink down on the edge of my bed, feeling like a little kid who got caught sneaking a cookie—which was about the worst thing I ever did as a child, although the way my parents treated me, you'd think I was born rebellious. "Nothing, Mom."

"I have a hard time believing that," she says.

"Mom, it's not—"

"I thought your father and I made it clear what we expect of you," she says. "We've done everything in our power to give you as many opportunities as we can. But you have to uphold your end of the bargain."

"Yes, I know—"

"Have you followed up with the Colorado Symphony yet?" she asks, cutting me off again. "I passed on the director's contact information to you weeks ago and you haven't told me what's going on. When is your audition?"

She's asking me about auditions? Now? "I didn't get an audition."

There's a heavy sigh on her end of the phone. "Linnea, we talked about this. You have to use the time Charlotte is in school for practicing. If you aren't putting in the time, what do you expect?"

"I practice every day."

"Then why didn't you get an audition in Colorado?"

"I don't know."

"You have to stay focused," she says. "That's the only way you're going to achieve your dreams. People who allow themselves to become distracted are the ones falling by the wayside in life. They don't amount to anything."

I put a hand over my forehead. "I'm not distracted."

"Clearly you are," she says. "I didn't expect this situation to carry on as long as it has."

"Mom, you told me to move here," I say.

"Until Caleb could find someone reliable for my granddaughter," she says.

"That's not what you said at the time," I say.

"That's precisely what I said. We didn't pay for a *very* expensive music degree for you to be a nanny."

"Then why—"

"Caleb needs to find someone else," she says. "As soon as possible."

"I don't think that's really up to you, Mom." I wince. I can't believe I just said that to her.

She's silent for a moment, and when she speaks again her

voice sends a chill up my spine. "Linnea, if there is something going on between you and that man, you are going to put an end to it. Immediately."

"Mom—"

"I'm going to assume my daughter is smarter than that," she says. "I raised you to be an intelligent, capable, independent woman. A woman who would not be lured in by an older man."

My throat is dry and my voice barely works. "Lured? That's not—"

"I think we're finished here," she says and I grind my teeth together in frustration. "You know what needs to be done. I expect you to do what's best for your future."

I mumble a reply that might sound like I'm agreeing with her.

"Good," she says. "I'll talk to you soon."

I drop my phone on the bed next to me and bury my face in my hands. My palms are sweaty, my heart racing, and I can't stop shaking. I hate how she does this to me. Every time. She makes me feel so helpless. My mind goes blank, my body trembles, and it's all I can do to choke out short replies. Forget trying to stand up for myself. I can't when she won't stop talking long enough to let me think.

In the aftermath of her phone call, a hundred comebacks race through my mind. All the things I should have said mock me. I'm so frustrated at how I freeze up when I talk to her. She's my mother; I shouldn't feel like I'm facing down a judge who might sentence me to life in prison. But the fear and anxiety that hits me when she lectures makes me feel like my life is in the balance. Like she has control and there's nothing I can do.

There's a soft knock on my door.

I take a deep breath. "Yeah?" I wish I wasn't so shaky.

Caleb comes in and closes the door behind him. Without a

word, he sits next to me. I lean against him and he wraps his arm around me, drawing me in close.

He kisses the top of my head. "You okay?"

The safety of his embrace and the warmth of his body melt away the worst of my anxiety. I relax against him, no longer trembling, and the sick feeling in my stomach starts to fade.

"Yeah, I'm okay." I take another deep breath. "She mostly just lectured me about practicing and auditions and staying focused."

"You practice all the time," he says.

"I know."

"I don't want to say anything bad about your mom, but..."

"It's okay. I know what she's like. Don't forget, I heard her end of a lot of your conversations with her."

"Then you know I'm not exactly her favorite person," he says.

I shrug. I don't particularly want to get into what my parents think of Caleb. Or what they'll think when—or if—I tell them I am indeed dating him.

"It's really not their business," he says, his voice soft. "This is about you and me, and no one else."

"Yeah." I sit up straighter and he gently rubs up and down my back. "It doesn't matter what she thinks anyway."

"No, it doesn't." He rubs my back a few more times. "Want to go get another tattoo? Maybe somewhere really visible on a webcam?"

That makes me laugh.

He touches my chin and leans in for a soft kiss.

"Thanks," I say.

"I was going to take Charlotte out for some daddy time, since I've barely seen her all week," he says. "But if you want us to stay home, we can."

"No," I say. "Don't. She needs that. I'm fine. My mom just... she does this to me. It's okay."

He places his hand alongside my cheek and looks me in the eyes. "Are you sure?"

"Yes," I say. "Go have a daddy-daughter day with Bug. I'll be here when you get back."

18

CALEB

Charlotte and I spend the afternoon at the children's museum. She loves exploring the hands-on exhibits. There's another family with a little girl—she must be around two—who seems to decide she likes Charlotte. She follows her around and it doesn't take long before Charlotte is talking to her and showing her things. They spend time in the big market play area, carrying shopping baskets and pretending to buy play food.

I get a little choked up seeing Charlotte interact with the toddler. For one, Charlotte's actually talking to another child. Granted, the girl is a lot smaller than she is, which might explain her ease. But I've never seen her this relaxed in a crowded place before. The other kids brushing past her don't seem to bother her at all.

But it also makes me wonder if Charlotte is always going to be an only child.

Melanie and I didn't plan on getting pregnant when we did. Our lives were so busy. I was nervous about being a father; I wasn't sure I was ready. But from the moment Charlotte was born, I was completely, totally, and utterly in love with her.

It's hard to explain how much your life changes the first time you see your child. She was this tiny, perfect little thing—completely innocent. And so fragile. It took me a few days to get over the fear that I was going to hurt her when I held her. But then I held her all the time. Every chance I got. Melanie never had to ask me to take the baby so she could have a break. I was always right there, ready to scoop her up. I couldn't get enough of her.

And then, all too soon, it was just the two of us.

Charlotte was what got me through those dark days after Melanie died. I knew I had to stay strong for her. I couldn't let grief overtake me. She gave me a reason to keep going.

There's an odd juxtaposition between my personal life and my career. Professionally, I'm exactly where I always planned to be. I knew in high school that I'd go into medicine, and by the end of my first year as an undergrad, I was set on trauma surgery. That part of my life went as planned.

My personal life, though? None of it is what I thought it would be. When I was dating in college, I always kept it casual. I didn't plan to put any energy into a serious relationship. I figured I'd save marriage and family for my thirties, when my career was established. Then Melanie swooped into my life, and a year later, I was married. We didn't plan to have kids right away, but next thing I knew, I had Charlotte. And I certainly didn't plan on being a single father, raising my baby girl on my own.

But here I am, a single dad with a six-year-old girl. I never would have guessed this would be where I'd end up.

I have no regrets about Charlotte. If I had to do it over again, I'd still get married. I'd live through the pain of losing Melanie if it meant I could have Charlotte in my life. I wouldn't give her up for anything.

Charlotte and the little girl wander over to an area with toy trains. I make eye contact with the toddler's parents and smile as we follow our kids. They smile back, and the mom rests her hand on her obviously pregnant belly. I stand off to the side, hands in my pockets, and watch while Charlotte plays.

My mind wanders and I imagine being here with Linnea. I know I'm crazy as soon as I think it, but I picture her rubbing a round belly. Pregnant with my baby.

I feel guilty for daydreaming about her that way. She has her own hopes and dreams for the future. Saddling her with a baby when she's still so young would change the course of her life. I know she likes kids, and she's such a natural with Charlotte. But she has her music career to think about. Sometimes I feel like Charlotte and I are only borrowing her for a little while.

And if things did go that far between us, and we did have a baby together, it would be both Charlotte's sibling and her cousin. God, we sound like hillbillies or something.

I'm questioning whether I should have let things happen between us the way they did. Is it selfish of me to want to be with her? I feel things when I'm with her that, quite honestly, I wasn't sure I'd ever feel again. My attempts at dating in the last couple of years left me convinced I'd never fall in love again. That I'd had my chance, and it was over. You don't get that twice.

But I'm falling for Linnea, hard and fast. And I still don't know if I should be.

The little girl's parents tell her it's time to go. She makes a pouty face, but complies when they tell her to thank Charlotte for playing. They thank me too, and we all say goodbye.

"You ready for a snack?" I ask.

Charlotte takes my hand. "Yep. I'm hungry."

There's a large food court with a variety of restaurants in the same building as the museum, so we head upstairs. We decide on bagels and take our snack to a table.

I need to talk to Charlotte about Linnea. I wasn't going to

right away—not because I want to hide it from her, but when I said dating Linnea would be complicated, I wasn't kidding. I haven't needed to have a conversation like this with my daughter before.

But Charlotte is nothing if not observant. She probably knows more than I realize, and she obviously noticed that Linnea spent the night in my room. She might not understand it —and there's only so much detail she needs at this age. The problem is, I'm not sure exactly what to tell her. Things between me and Linnea are so new—so unexplored. I feel like I'm rushing us into something serious because we're already close. Because in so many ways, Linnea is already a part of our little family. But that isn't fair to Linnea, and I don't want to give Charlotte the wrong idea.

"How's your bagel?" I ask.

"It's yummy," she says.

"Good," I say. "Bug, do you know what it means when people are dating?"

"Yes," she says.

"What does that mean?"

She puts her bagel down and purses her lips like she does when she's thinking. "That's when grown-ups like each other and they kiss each other."

I smile. "Yeah, that's about right. How would it make you feel if I said that Daddy and Linnea are dating?"

"Are you going to get married?" she asks.

There's a *yes* sitting right on the tip of my tongue. It should freak me the hell out that it would be so easy to say it. "I don't know. People usually need a long time to decide something big like that."

"Is she still going to take care of me when you're at work?" she asks.

"Yes."

She looks down at her half-eaten bagel and I can tell she's wrestling with something. I stay quiet and give her time to think.

"Did you love my mom?" she asks.

Her question catches me completely off guard. She rarely asks about Melanie. I've always been open about her mom—shown her pictures, and talked about how much Melanie loved her. About a year ago, she wanted to know how her mom died, and I told her about the car accident. Since then, she hasn't asked about her again.

"Yes, Bug. I loved your mom very much."

"Do you still love a person when they're dead?" she asks.

"Yes, you do," I say. "I still love your mom. I always will. Are you worried that if I love someone else, it will mean I don't love your mom anymore?"

"No," she says.

"Then what's bothering you?" I ask.

"Did you love my mom and me at the same time?" she asks.

"Yes, of course I did. I loved you as soon as you were born. That didn't change how I felt about your mom. It made me love her more because she gave me the best gift. She gave me you."

"Okay."

I brush a few tangles out of her hair. "Are you worried that if I love someone else, I won't love you as much?"

She nods without looking at me.

"Oh, Bug." I scoop her up out of her chair and into my lap. For a long moment, I just hold her. She wraps her arms around my neck and I rub slow circles across her back. "Nothing will ever change how much I love you. Nothing in the entire world."

I move her so she's sitting and I can look at her face. "Listen, sweetheart. Love doesn't have limits. It's as big as we want it to be. Do you remember the Grinch movie, when his heart grows bigger?"

"Yeah."

"Love is like that," I say. "Before I met your mom, I loved my family. Loving your mom didn't make me love them less, it just made my heart bigger. And when you were born it got so big, I wasn't sure it was going to fit inside my ribs anymore."

She pokes my chest and giggles.

"Loving someone new just makes your heart grow," I say. "So if I love someone else—someone like Linnea—it just means I have more love in my heart. And you still made my heart the biggest."

"I think you should marry Linnea and then I can have her as my mom," she says.

I hug her again to give me a second for the lump in my throat to go down. This kid is killing me today. "Well, it's too soon to think about that. Daddy and Linnea are... we're special friends now. Does that make sense?"

"Yeah," she says. "Can I finish my bagel?"

I kiss her forehead and scoot her back into her chair. "Yes, you can finish your bagel."

After we eat, we take a little walk. It's chilly outside, but we have coats, and it's not raining. Charlotte asks me questions, but they're the usual for her—things like why does that bird have a blue head and what makes some clouds gray and other clouds white. No more questions about her mom, or love, or Linnea.

I'm glad she doesn't seem to mind the idea of Linnea and me dating. Her comment about marrying her leaves me with a poignant mix of relief and sadness. I like knowing that it would make Charlotte happy to have Linnea be a permanent part of her life. But it's a reminder that she does indeed feel the loss of her mother.

I've never wanted to be with a woman just to replace Melanie for Charlotte. I certainly don't want to think of Linnea that way. If I do get married again, how Charlotte feels about her will of course be a consideration. But I'm not looking for a mom-substitute for my daughter. That kind of expectation wouldn't be fair to her, or to me.

But... would Linnea want that? I know she loves Charlotte. There's no question about that. But loving your niece and the little girl you watch almost every day is one thing. Marrying her father and taking on the role of mother is a much bigger deal.

I shouldn't be thinking about this so soon. I took Linnea out for the first time a week ago. But I guess any single parent is going to view a relationship in terms of its future potential. We have to. We've kind of been there, done that. There's not a lot of room for casual when there's a child involved.

It's good that I talked to Bug, but I'm still torn about Linnea. I guess the answer is to give it time. Let things unfold. I can't deny I'm falling in love with her. I just can't get over the feeling that our lives are on different paths, and it's inevitable that they're going to diverge.

19

CALEB

Recording a time of death is the worst part of my job.

I was supposed to be off at six, but ten minutes before I left, I got paged. Patient was male, mid-fifties. After a four-car pile-up on I-5, he was brought in unresponsive with numerous contusions, lacerations, possible broken bones, and suspected internal bleeding.

He was indeed bleeding. Profusely. One of the first things I have to do is determine the priority order of a person's injuries. Broken limbs can wait. Bleeding takes precedence, as do spinal and head injuries. This guy seemed to have a little bit of everything, but the thing that was killing him was the shit-show in his abdominal cavity.

I did everything in my power to save him. But in the end, it wasn't enough. His injuries were too severe. He went into cardiac arrest and we weren't able to revive him.

The exhaustion I didn't feel when I was in the OR hits me on the drive home. My limbs get heavy and my back aches. But more than that, I feel defeated. I go up against death all the time. I win some, I lose some.

The weight of tonight's loss is heavy.

Most surgeons have the ability to detach themselves from the emotional side of their job. We have to. If we felt something for every patient we operated on, we'd go crazy. Some of us turn out like Weston. He can be cold and unemotional, and granted, it isn't just because of his job. But he doesn't have an on-off switch like I do. He is the way he is, at work and in the rest of his life. Being somewhat detached makes him a good surgeon.

As for me, in the OR I'm almost robotic. I check my emotions at the door and keep a wall between myself and my patients. I see them as problems to be solved. It sounds bad to say I don't see them as people, but in a way, I don't. I can't. If I think about the guy on the operating table and wonder if he has a wife and kids who will miss him if I screw up, I'd buckle under the pressure.

When I leave the OR, I go back to being human again. Sometimes that transition is hard.

Tonight, it's hitting me like a truck. He's not the first patient I've lost, and I'm not sure why his death is leaving me so hollowed out.

I get home and feel a pang of guilt. I was supposed to be home for dinner, and now it's past Charlotte's bedtime. I've missed seeing her so often in the last few weeks. We're down a surgeon and until we get someone in to replace her, I'm working a lot more than usual. I know it's taking a toll on Charlotte. It's taking a toll on all of us.

Inside, I find Linnea on the couch and I'm surprised to see Charlotte curled up, asleep with her head in Linnea's lap.

"She wanted to wait for you," Linnea whispers, running her fingers through Charlotte's hair.

I'm feeling open and raw after my night in the OR, and seeing this beautiful woman lovingly stroke my sleeping daughter's hair undoes me. I sink down onto my knees in front of

Linnea and gently cup her cheeks. She smiles as I lean in and kiss her mouth. The feel of her lips is like cool water on a burn.

"Are you okay?" Linnea asks when I pull away.

I tuck her hair behind her ear. "I am now."

"Do you want me to take her upstairs?" she asks.

"No, I'll do it."

I scoop Charlotte into my arms and cradle her like a baby. I can't believe how big she's getting. There was a time when I could hold her like this with one arm. Now her head rests in the crook of my elbow and her legs dangle over my other arm.

She wakes up a little when I set her in bed. "Hi, Daddy."

"Hi, Bug. Sorry I missed dinner again."

"That's okay." She yawns and I pull the covers up to her chin. "Will you be home tomorrow?"

"For a little while, yeah."

"Okay. Night-night, Daddy."

"Night-night, precious girl." I kiss her forehead and make sure she's all tucked in, then turn off her bedside lamp and close the door behind me.

Downstairs, I find Linnea in the kitchen making tea.

"Are you hungry?" she asks. "There's leftovers from dinner."

I don't answer. I grab her, slipping my arms around her waist, and bury my face in her neck.

She hesitates for half a second, then wraps her arms around my shoulders. Her fingers slide through my hair as she gently massages the back of my head.

"Are you sure you're okay?" she whispers into my ear.

I nod, but I don't let go. I breathe her in while I hold her close. She smells faintly of vanilla. Her body feels so good against me and the tension in my back loosens at her touch.

Eventually, I pull away. She insists on feeding me, and considering I can't remember the last time I ate anything, that's probably a good plan. She has me sit at the table while she heats up leftover chicken and rice, then sits next to me with a mug of tea while I eat.

Food helps, as does the constant pressure of her hand on my leg. After I finish eating, I push the plate aside and pick up her hand, bringing it to my lips.

"Thank you." I kiss the backs of her fingers.

"Do you want to talk about it?" she asks.

I kiss her hand again. "I lost a patient tonight."

"Oh, Caleb," she says. "I'm sorry."

"It's not the first, and it won't be the last," I say. "It's part of my job. I can't save everyone. But sometimes it gets to me."

"Of course it does."

"Would you do something for me?" I ask.

"Yeah, what?"

"Will you play for me?" I ask. "Maybe something quiet, so Bug doesn't wake up."

"Why?"

"I love your music," I say. "And I don't get to hear you play often enough."

Her lips part in a smile. "Okay."

I take her hand and we go into the front living room, where the only furniture is her piano. I sit on the bench and pull her into my lap. My arms thread around her waist and I lean my chin against her shoulder.

She turns the volume down, then places her fingers lightly on the keys. I feel her take a deep breath, and she starts to play.

The music begins soft and slow. Her long fingers stretch across the keys, her touch gentle. At first, the melody is simple. But soon it gains complexity and her body moves with the rhythm of her song.

It's mournful and haunting, and the longer she plays, the more I feel her lose herself in the music. I hold her gently, giving her space to move. The song is achingly beautiful, and her expert fingers caress the keys. I let my eyes close and the music surrounds me like a cloud.

She sways, her graceful movements subtle. The song's intensity builds and even with the volume turned low, I feel its power. It stirs my emotions, making me feel a swirl of sadness and longing. And peace. Like the high note that carries above the darker melody, a sense of peace and tranquility steals over me.

The song ends and she pauses with her hands still resting on the keys.

"That was beautiful," I say softly into her ear.

"Thank you." She reaches up and rests her palm against my cheek. "Do you feel a little better?"

I breathe in the warm vanilla scent of her hair again. I'm calm and relaxed, the painful knots of tension in my back easing. But I'm so fucking exhausted. I can't remember the last time I had a good stretch of sleep. "Yeah, I do. Now I'm just tired."

"You should get some rest," she says.

"Will you sleep with me tonight?" I ask, still speaking quietly into her ear. "Just... sleep. I'm so tired."

She nods. "Of course I will."

We go upstairs and she ducks into her bedroom to change into a tank top. She crawls into my bed and I pull her against me, resting my hand on her belly. My exhausted body has reached its limit; I'm already falling asleep. The warmth of her body and the feel of her soft breathing unravels the last of the strain I was carrying.

Somehow, Linnea's softness—her gentle care—soothes me in a way nothing else can. With her in my arms, I drift into a deep sleep, my mind free of the stress of failure. Free of the weight of all the responsibility I carry.

20

LINNEA

Caleb's lips whispering against my back wake me. I'm still snuggled up against him, his arm draped over me. No light comes in through the cracks in the blinds; it must be the middle of the night.

His hand slides beneath my tank top and over my breast. My eyes are heavy, but his touch has me instantly aroused. My nipples tingle and I arch my back, feeling his thick erection pressing into my ass.

"Sorry, beautiful," he whispers, then kisses the back of my neck. "I should let you sleep, but you feel so good."

I am sleepy, but my body is coming alive. I shift my hips, rubbing against his cock. The heat building inside me is too much to deny.

Without thinking about what I'm doing, I reach behind me and wrap my hand around his hard length. "Maybe you should fuck me first."

He groans and I feel tension ripple through his body. "Jesus, Linnea. Say that again."

The combination of desire and half-sleep leaves me feeling uninhibited. I stroke his cock. "You should fuck me first."

With a throaty growl, he tosses the covers aside and pushes me onto my back. His hands are rough as he yanks my panties down my legs and pulls my tank top over my head. He holds himself over me, his muscular torso flexing, and leans down to graze his teeth along my neck.

"How about I taste your pussy first," he says, his voice low in my ear.

I gasp, but he's already kissing his way down my tummy. He works his way past my hips, his mouth leaving a trail of heat on my skin. For a second, I'm about to say something—I've never done this before—but he pushes my legs open and clamps his mouth down on me.

A few strokes of his tongue and I'm clutching the sheets, unable to think. I've never felt anything like it. He brings me to the brink of climax so fast, it takes my breath away. I ride the peak while he does magical things with his tongue. It slides up and down, caressing my tender bundle of nerves in a steady rhythm. He gently sucks my clit, groaning into me like he's enjoying this too.

I'm panting, my hips moving of their own accord. I whimper and moan, trying not to make too much noise. But I'm losing control. He sucks harder and runs one hand up my body to palm my breast. I almost cry out at the heady combination of his mouth on my pussy and the pressure of his hand on my sensitive nipple.

My body is totally in his control. He keeps me on the edge until I'm begging for release.

"Please, Caleb. Oh my god."

"Come for me, beautiful."

He releases my breast and slides two fingers inside me while his tongue works my clit. My eyes roll back—I have the fleeting thought that maybe people can die from too much pleasure—before the biggest orgasm I've ever had makes me stop breathing.

Wave after wave of hot tension rolls through me. My muscles clench around his fingers, my back arches, and my mouth drops open. My entire body lights up, like sparks of electricity are racing through my veins.

The pulses subside and I'm left breathing hard, my mind blank, my body quivering.

"What did you just do to me?"

Caleb crawls on top of me and wraps his hand around the back of my neck. "God, I love driving you crazy. Because you make me fucking insane, do you know that?"

"How do you want me?" I ask, my voice soft and breathy.

"How do I want what?" he growls.

I lift my head and lick my taste off his lips, earning another deep, throaty growl. "How do you want to fuck me?"

He kisses me hard, his hand tightening on the back of my neck, his tongue aggressive. I tilt my hips, trying to take him inside me, but he doesn't thrust in.

"Come here." He flips us around so he's lying on his back, his cock pointing toward his gorgeous abs. I straddle his upper thighs and despite the earth-shattering orgasm he just gave me, I already want more. I want his thickness inside me, stretching me, filling me. And I want it now.

He reaches over and grabs a condom out of his nightstand. This time I take it and roll it on for him. He watches, biting his lower lip, his brow furrowed.

I shift so the apex of my thighs is at the base of his cock and lean down with my hands on either side of him. "Show me what you like."

"Sit up," he says. "I want to watch you ride my cock."

I lift myself up to sitting, my legs around his hips. He grabs the base of his cock and holds it up while I place my opening at the tip. He groans as I slowly lower myself down, sheathing him inside me.

My eyes flutter closed and I lean my head back, reveling in the sweet pressure of him filling me. He grabs my hips and starts moving me back and forth. I use my legs to lift and lower, sliding up and down his cock. The ridge around the tip drags through my pussy, sending jolts of pleasure through me with every pass.

Instinct takes over and I roll my hips, grinding my clit against him each time I lower down. His fingers dig into my hips and he groans. I love it when he makes that sound.

I brush my hair behind my shoulders so it cascades down my back. The rhythm comes to me—the tilt of my hips, the pressure of my thighs. My nipples tingle in the cool air and I bring my hands up to caress myself. It feels so good to run my fingers across my hard peaks.

"Fuck, Linnea, keep doing that," Caleb says, his voice gravelly. "You are so fucking sexy."

I've never been so unrestrained, but Caleb brings out something in me. Without a shred of self-consciousness, I ride him, stroking my breasts while he watches.

He thrusts his hips up, burying his shaft deep inside me. I move faster, squeezing his cock with everything I have. Another orgasm builds, the pressure deep in my core. But I'm focused on him. On the groove between his eyebrows, the sharp lines of his jaw. The primal groans coming from the back of his throat. The sheen of sweat on his toned chest and gorgeous abs.

"Come here," he says, his voice demanding.

I lean down and he slides his fingers through my hair and takes my mouth in a kiss. We keep moving, thrusting, grinding together. This angle hits my clit in a whole new way and I find myself getting louder, moaning into his mouth.

All at once, he flips us over so I'm beneath him again. He drives into me and I clutch his muscular back.

I call out and he clamps his hand over my mouth.

"Shh," he says, but the wicked look in his eyes and the smile on his lips tells me he likes it when I lose control.

He keeps his hand gently covering my mouth, but that's the only part of him that's gentle. His hips thrust harder, faster. I run my hands down his back and press against his glutes. His cock pulses and I know he's close. The first tremors rippling through his solid length make my eyes roll back and my pussy clench around him.

"Are you ready for me to come inside you?" he asks.

I meet his gaze and nod. His dark eyes are clouded with lust and I get a thrill that it's me who does this to him.

The pressure in my core reaches a breaking point. He plunges in again, his body stiffening, his mouth dropping open as he starts to come.

He grunts and I cover his mouth like he's covering mine. The feel of him bursting inside me and the look of unbridled pleasure on his face sends me over the edge.

We groan into each other's hands, our bodies moving in sync as we come together. The clench and release of my orgasm surges through me, sweeping me away. He drives his hips until we both finish, then pauses, resting his forehead against mine.

He carefully moves his hand away and I wrap my arms around his neck. His lips come to mine and he kisses me tenderly—soft, slow, lazy kisses that turn my insides to mush.

"Be right back," he whispers.

I wait, my eyes heavy, my body languid, while he slips into the bathroom. When he comes back, I'm already half-asleep again. The warmth between my legs feels so good and my entire body thrums with pleasure.

He draws me close and pulls the covers over us. "Sorry I woke you."

I nestle against him and let my eyes drift closed. "I'm not."

His arms tighten around me and he kisses my neck. "Good night, beautiful."

"Good night."

~

I WAKE up for the day in my own bed. My alarm got me up early and I reluctantly slipped out of Caleb's arms. I don't know if he wants me to keep doing that so Charlotte won't find us in bed together, but it seems like I should. Sleeping by myself isn't nearly as nice, but I do drift off again.

Downstairs, I find Caleb and Charlotte eating breakfast together at the dining table.

He glances up from his cereal and a slow, sexy smile crosses his face. "Good morning."

"Good morning," I say and the way his eyes hold mine makes my tummy flutter. I swear he's picturing what we did last night.

He looks so much better than he did yesterday. His eyes are bright, his smile genuine. The tired slump in his shoulders is gone. He looks rested. Happy.

"I wanted to wake you up, but Daddy told me no," Charlotte says. "He said something kept you up last night. Did you have a bad dream?"

Caleb winks at me and I try not to smile too big.

"No, not exactly." I smooth down my hair and go into the kitchen to make tea.

I put the kettle on and feel Caleb come up behind me. He puts his hands on my hips and leans in to kiss my neck.

"Hi, beautiful."

I turn and he cages me in against the counter. My eyes flick over to the table where Charlotte is still eating her cereal. Her back is to us, but she could easily look over. I know Caleb talked to her the other day and told her we're dating. But so far, he's still been cautious about how he acts when she's around.

"It's okay," he says, brushing the hair back from my face. "I think it's all right if she catches Daddy kissing his girlfriend."

I smile as he leans in to kiss me. Our lips meet, just briefly, and he pulls away. But he moves in again for another kiss, and then another. It's like he keeps meaning to stop, but he can't get enough. I giggle a little as he kisses me again, and this time his lips linger against mine.

"Daddy, ew," Charlotte says.

He laughs. "Ew? What's ew?"

"You look like Alex and Mia," she says.

"You've seen Alex and Mia kissing?" he asks.

She rolls her eyes and shakes her head. "All the time when they think I'm not looking."

He laughs again and kisses my forehead. "Well, my two favorite ladies. I don't have to be at work until tonight. What should we do?"

Charlotte's eyes light up. "You can stay?"

"Yep," he says. "And if we eat a little early, I can have dinner with you."

Charlotte decides she wants to stay home, which doesn't surprise me at all. It's pouring down rain outside, and she often prefers to be at home anyway. She and I play a few songs on the piano while Caleb listens. He gives us both standing ovations, which makes Charlotte giggle.

Then we all snuggle up on the couch together to watch a movie. Caleb dozes off with his head in my lap while I run my fingers through his hair.

After the movie ends, Charlotte goes to play upstairs for a while. I stay with Caleb and enjoy the way he's relaxed against me. When he wakes up, he shifts to look up at me, giving me that slow, sexy smile again. He sits up, leaning over me, and kisses me—a deep, unhurried kiss that leaves me feeling dazed.

Charlotte's voice comes from the stairs. "Ew."

We both laugh and he leans in close to whisper in my ear. "You're so delicious, I can't help it."

Caleb orders pizza for dinner so no one has to cook. Soon after we finish eating, it's time for him to leave for work. He cuddles Charlotte at the door, holding her and softly rubbing her back. When he puts her down, she goes back to the living room to play with her stuffed animals.

He pulls me close and kisses me. "Thank you."

"For what?" I ask.

"Everything," he says.

After one last kiss, I watch him go.

21

LINNEA

Over the next few months, things between me and Caleb only get better. We trade off babysitting with Megan and James for date nights—they take Bug so we can go out, and we take Noah so they can go out. Charlotte and Noah are such great little friends, and they love hanging out together, so the arrangement is great for everyone.

Spring arrives, and with it, Charlotte's birthday. We celebrate by taking a trip to the zoo with Noah's family. Not long after, Caleb surprises me with a night at the symphony. We both get dressed up—he looks so sexy in a suit—and sharing that experience with him is wonderful.

With parent night less than a week away, I help Charlotte practice her song after school. I don't like to push too hard—she's still little—but I know the more she practices, the more comfortable she'll be when the time comes. Even if she's nervous, her fingers will remember what to do.

She plays her song beautifully. I'm so proud of her. Even more than that, I'm excited at how proud she is of herself. That was one of the biggest things music did for me—gave me something that made me feel competent.

"I think we're finished practicing for today." I plant a kiss on top of her head. "Daddy should be home any minute."

"And everyone is coming over later," she says.

"They sure are."

Everyone to Charlotte means her grandad and her aunts and uncles. We often get together at Ken's house, but this time Caleb invited them here. He thought it might be a fun change of pace, and there's plenty of room for everyone. And I think he's secretly hoping Charlotte might play a song on the piano for them.

She heads into the living room to finish building a puzzle she started this morning. My phone rings and I glance at the screen. It's my mother. She pointedly hasn't asked about Caleb again, and I haven't brought it up either. But there's so much weight in her silence on the subject. All she wants to talk about is how much I'm practicing, what songs I'm working on, and go over potential opportunities for auditions.

"Bug, I'll be upstairs for a few minutes." I answer the phone as I walk up to my room. "Hi, Mom."

"Linnea," she says and her voice is tinged with excitement. "I have the most wonderful news. I pulled some strings, and you have an audition with the Pittsburgh Symphony Orchestra."

My mouth hangs open and I don't answer right away. An audition? In Pittsburgh? I duck into my room and close the door. "You pulled some strings?"

"Yes," she says. "As it turns out, one of my colleagues is married to a woman who serves on the board of trustees for the Pittsburgh Symphony. I saw him again a few weeks ago at a conference, and the connection came up. He said he would talk to his wife and see if she might have some pull. I sent them your audition tape, and he called me this morning to give me the good news."

"Wow," I say, still trying to process what she's telling me. "When are they holding auditions?"

"Monday," she says. "You have a slot at eleven thirty."

"This Monday?" I ask. "Mom, that's just a few days from now."

"Yes, but if you're being honest with me about how much you've been practicing, you should be prepared," she says.

"Of course I've been honest with you," I say. God, she didn't hound me about practicing this much when I was a kid. "That's not what I mean. It's such short notice. And Charlotte is performing at her school on Tuesday night. I can't miss that."

"This is far more important."

"No, it's—"

"Linnea," she snaps. "This is the Pittsburgh Symphony Orchestra. It's one of the more prestigious and well-respected symphonies in the country. Do you have any idea how difficult it is to get an audition?"

"Yes, but—"

"And how many auditions have you gone to since you moved to Seattle?" she asks.

I sigh. "None. But that's because the only two pianist positions to open up recently were with, what did you call them? Small-time symphonies?"

"Precisely. And if you'd gone after a position with a small symphony, you wouldn't be free to pursue this," she says. "I'll book your flight for you."

"Mom, I can pay for my own ticket," I say. Last minute flights will be expensive, but I have money saved. And if I book it myself, I can make sure I get a flight back that will have me home in time for parent night.

"Linnea, this is so important for your career," she continues. "You'll very likely look back on this experience as the key turning point in your life."

"Yeah."

"See, what have I been telling you? Stay focused. Practice.

Put in the hard work, and doors will open. It won't be long and we'll be announcing our daughter is a pianist with the Pittsburgh Symphony Orchestra."

"Um, Mom, this is a lot to take in right now," I say. "It's very sudden."

"You have plenty of time to pack," she says.

"Yes, I know."

"Well, then," she says. "There's no problem. I'll talk to you soon."

After I hang up I bite my lip and stare at the wall. I should be excited. My mother is right, the Pittsburgh Symphony Orchestra is very well-respected. My classmates from college would kill for a shot to audition for them; an opportunity like this is rare. I expected I'd need to play with a much smaller symphony for years before I had a chance at a position like this.

This is everything I've been working toward. Why I went to college. Why I spend hours every day practicing while Charlotte is at school. This was always the plan. It's a much bigger opportunity than I thought I would get, and it's been dropped in my lap.

Only now, everything is so different.

Facing what this means leaves me frozen. If I get the position, I'll have to move across the country. Leave Charlotte and Caleb behind. The thought makes me sick to my stomach.

As does the thought of such a high-pressure performance. Playing in front of an audience makes me so anxious. I love music, and I love to play, but I've never loved this side of it. Not when I was younger, playing in the youth symphony, nor when I performed in college. Teaching is one thing—I love working with kids and sharing my passion for music. But the pressure of a performance is crushing. I often wonder why I do it to myself.

But that's what pianists are supposed to do, isn't it? Play?

Through my partially open door, I hear Caleb. I need to go downstairs and tell him. But I can't seem to move.

A few minutes pass and footsteps come up the stairs. Caleb peeks into my room.

"Hi, beautiful," he says. "Is something wrong?"

"No," I say. "Sorry, my mom called."

He comes in and shuts the door behind him. "Are you okay?"

"Yeah, she was fine." I take a deep breath. "Actually, she called because she helped me get an audition with a symphony."

"Wow," he says. "That's... that's great. Which one?"

"The Pittsburgh Symphony Orchestra."

He blinks at me, looking stunned. "Pittsburgh?"

"Yeah," I say. "It's... well, it's a prestigious organization. I didn't think I'd have a shot at a major symphony for years."

"When is the audition?"

"Monday."

"That soon?" he asks. "Do they really expect people to be prepared on such short notice?"

"It's last minute because my mom knows someone and they got me in," I say. "I didn't really get it on my own."

"Have they heard you play?" he asks.

"Yeah, she sent my audition tape," I say.

He looks at me for a long moment and I wish I knew what he was thinking. When he speaks, his voice is quiet. "Linnea, you're incredibly talented. If they heard you play, you did get this audition on your own."

I tuck my hair behind my ear. "I suppose."

"So, Monday?" he asks.

"Yeah," I say. God, this is happening too fast. "I'll have to leave Sunday."

"When will you come back?" he asks.

"Tuesday, and I'll make sure my flight gets in early enough that I'll be at parent night," I say. "I won't miss it."

"Okay." He rubs his chin and takes a deep breath.

"I'm sorry this is so sudden."

"No, don't be sorry. What are we doing?" He takes my hands and pulls me to standing. "We should be celebrating. Linnea, this is amazing."

"Yeah, I guess."

"You guess?" he asks. "This is what you've been working toward, isn't it?"

I nod.

"And like you said, it's a big symphony," he says. "This sounds like the opportunity of a lifetime."

"It is. A lot of musicians never get a chance like this."

We look at each other again, and I feel the weight of all the things I'm not saying. But he's not saying anything else either. He smiles and rubs his hand up and down my arm.

"I'm proud of you," he says. "You'll have to share the news with everyone tonight."

"Yeah, I will. Thank you."

"I'm going to go change," he says. "They'll all be here soon."

"Sure."

He smiles again and leaves me alone in my room.

22

CALEB

Linnea's news leaves me reeling.

I change clothes and go back downstairs. We're doing a casual get together—I'm ordering pizza—so I don't have much to do to get ready. But I'm restless, trying to figure out what to think. How to feel about this.

Pittsburgh. She's going to Pittsburgh for an audition.

It's no surprise her parents had something to do with it. They've probably been plotting to get her out of here since Charlotte made her *sleepover* comment. I'm frustrated at their meddling in her life. But at the same time, they're helping her get where she wants to be. Even if their motives include getting her away from me, I can't fault that they want her to be successful. So do I.

But fucking Pittsburgh.

My family starts showing up and I have to put it out of my head for a while. Alex and Mia arrive first, followed closely by Kendra and Weston. Linnea comes downstairs and sits in the living room, chatting with Mia and my sister. Alex, Weston, and I each grab a beer and hang out at the dining table.

There's another knock and I go to answer the door—it's

either my dad, or the pizza. We usually get together at my dad's house so he doesn't have to drive. I offered to come pick him up, although it's out of my way. But he insisted he'd get here on his own. We all help him out as much as we can, but he's been working hard to regain his independence since his back surgery. He's been doing really well.

I open the door and blink in surprise. It's my dad, but he's not alone.

"Hi, son," he says. "Sorry to spring an extra guest on you at the last minute, but this is my friend Jacqueline."

His *friend*? He grins at me, then at her. Holy shit, does my dad have a girlfriend? I open the door wider. "No, it's fine. Please, come in."

Dad comes in, leaning on his cane, and Jacqueline follows. She's probably in her late fifties—very pretty with a hippy or maybe yoga instructor vibe. Mostly-gray hair cut in a short bob. Bright blue and orange patterned dress with blue leggings and brown sandals. She's wearing a bunch of necklaces, but despite the different sizes and colors, they all seem to go together.

"Thank you so much for having me," Jacqueline says and her eyes crinkle with a pleasant smile. "I'm sorry, I thought Ken told you I was coming."

My dad chuckles. "I wanted it to be a surprise."

"It's fine, it's great to meet you." I raise my eyebrows at Dad but he just grins again.

I lead them into the house and we make the rounds of introductions. Mia stares at Jacqueline with her mouth hanging open until Alex nudges her. Kendra looks like she's ready to burst, but amazingly she doesn't start drilling Dad with questions. He calls Jacqueline his *friend* again, but the way they smile at each other makes it pretty clear she's a little more than a friend.

The pizza arrives soon after, and we all sit around the dining table to eat. Dad tells us how they met at his physical therapist's office. They were both patients and had regular appointments at the same time, so they found themselves in the waiting room together each week. Kendra and Mia don't bother to contain their sighs of awe as Dad recounts the day he got up the courage to ask Jacqueline if she'd like to have coffee.

Kendra sniffs and wipes under her eyes. "This is so sweet. I'm so happy for you, Dad." She starts crying harder and Weston hands her a napkin.

"This is amazing," Mia says. "Oh my god, Jacqueline, do you have kids? If you and Ken get married, we could have a bunch of new siblings." She stops and pinches her lips together for a moment while the rest of us shift in our seats. She adjusts her glasses. "Sorry… I didn't mean… I'll stop now."

Dad smiles at his daughter-in-law and his eyes light up. I don't know if I've ever seen him so happy.

"I do have one daughter, Gwen," Jacqueline says. "She lives nearby, so maybe you'll meet her sometime."

Mia makes a squeaky sound and looks at Kendra. She's still crying.

"I'm sorry," Kendra says. "I don't know what's wrong with me."

All eyes move to Kendra and as soon as I see the self-satisfied look on Weston's face, I realize what's going on.

"Kendra?" I say.

She wipes beneath her eyes and looks at Weston. He gives her that smile I've never seen him give anyone else, and nods.

"Well, since we're all here," she says. "I'm pregnant. We're going to have a baby."

The table erupts with congratulations and exclamations of happiness. Mia jumps up from her spot, knocking over her chair, and runs around the table to throw her arms around Kendra. Weston leans out of the way, looking a little bit alarmed.

Dad claps a few times, then takes Jacqueline's hand and kisses it. She smiles and leans close to him.

Charlotte is sitting next to me, and she stands up in her chair so she can whisper in my ear. "Is Kendra having a baby?"

"Yep, she sure is," I say.

"Does that mean the baby is my cousin?" she asks, still whispering.

I nod. "Exactly. You get a new baby cousin."

She smiles. "I hope it's a girl."

The excitement dies down and everyone goes back to their dinner. We ask Kendra questions about her pregnancy. She's due in January, so it's still early, and so far she's feeling fine—other than a propensity for bursting into tears. Weston absently strokes her hair and leans in frequently to kiss her temple.

Partway through the meal, Charlotte gets down and goes around the table to climb into Weston's lap. He eats around her like a pro, and despite everything else going on in my mind, it makes me smile. There was a time when I never would have imagined having this thought, but Weston is going to be a great dad.

Jacqueline chats comfortably with the rest of us. It's strange to see my dad with a woman. As far as I know, he never dated after my mom left. When we were kids, he was busy working and raising the three of us almost all on his own. Later came the struggles of his back injury—the surgeries, the financial stresses. It's easy to see why dating wasn't a priority.

I'm happy for him. There's a sense of relief at the idea that my dad might have found someone to share his life with. And Jacqueline appears to be nothing like my mother. Mom would have worn a suit and heels, and probably found a way to ruin Kendra's announcement with some sort of criticism. With Jacqueline's warm friendliness and eclectic style, she fits right in.

I glance around the table at my brother and sister, sitting

with their spouses. Alex and Mia are comfortable and secure—clearly crazy about each other. Kendra has that pregnant-woman glow, and Weston—who is basically an ass to most people—adores her. I'm happy for them too.

My eyes go to Linnea and I get a twist of pain in my chest.

I know I have to do the right thing for her. The audition in Pittsburgh could be a once in a lifetime opportunity. How could I ask her to pass that up? And for what? To stay here and take care of my kid? How selfish is that?

She's so talented. She plays with a beauty and artistry that takes my breath away. And I know how hard she's been working for this. How much she practices. How dedicated she is.

I can't stand in her way.

She's been quiet, and I wonder what she's thinking. I meet her eyes. "Do you want to say anything?"

"Oh, sure." She puts down her napkin. "I guess I have news too, although it's not as exciting as Kendra's. I have an audition with the Pittsburgh Symphony Orchestra next week."

There's a pause and all eyes are on her. Then on me. She shifts in her seat and tucks her hair behind her ear.

"It's an amazing opportunity," I say. "She's worked really hard for this."

"Wow, congratulations," Kendra says.

That seems to break the ice and more congratulations follow, although it's decidedly quieter than after Kendra's big announcement. Linnea smiles and thanks everyone. She talks a bit about the symphony—how it's well respected and she didn't think she'd have a chance with such a large group so soon. Charlotte asks a few questions about what an audition is like, but she doesn't seem concerned. I don't think she understands what this means. Or maybe she just can't imagine that Linnea would leave us.

By the time my family leaves, I'm just done. I'm tired from

keeping up the façade that everything is okay—that I'm nothing but happy for Linnea. Happy for my dad. Happy for my siblings and their fucking perfect marriages.

But the truth is, I'm pissed. Not at them. I'm angry at myself for letting this happen. For falling for a woman I knew I couldn't have—not really. She's just starting her life. I'm a widowed father with a kid, an established career, and a mortgage. I'm settled. She should be free.

I put Charlotte to bed and all I can think about is how shitty it's going to be when I tell her. How it's not just me who's going to be hurt. I should have protected her from that.

My dad's reasons for not dating when we were kids make a lot more sense, now that I'm in his shoes.

I have to be at the hospital early tomorrow morning, so I get the kitchen cleaned up and make an excuse to Linnea about being tired.

I don't invite her to come to bed with me. I head upstairs and close the door. Alone.

23

LINNEA

Sunday comes all too soon. I'm packed and ready to go, but I'm riddled with nerves. And it's not just the audition that has my stomach tied in knots.

Caleb has been distant since Friday when I told him I had to go to Pittsburgh. I'm not sure what I expected him to say. I suppose I should be glad he's been so supportive. He's only had positive things to say about it. He's proud of me. He's excited for the opportunity. He's sure I'll do well. They'd be crazy not to hire me.

In fact, he's told me how excited he is so many times, I'm starting to wonder if he *wants* me to go—as in, permanently.

I could convince myself I've been imagining the distance between us, if it weren't for the fact that I've slept alone the last two nights.

Is he pushing me away because he knows that if I get the position, I'll have to move? Or is it because he wants me to leave anyway, and this is an opportunity to break things off?

I thought Caleb and I had something special. Something real.

But my track record for understanding men is pretty poor. I

thought the same thing about my boyfriend in college—that we had something special. I knew he was applying to Master's programs out of state. I didn't think that would mean the end of our relationship. But just like that, as soon as he was accepted, he informed me that we were over.

I was so used to being pushed aside—to being the invisible girl—I simply accepted it. No one had ever wanted me in their life badly enough to fight for me. Maybe it's the same now.

Caleb insisted on taking me to the airport. The closer we get, the sicker I feel. I try to remind myself this will be a short trip. I'll go to the audition tomorrow, and I'll be back Tuesday. What I'll be coming back to, I'm not sure.

Caleb navigates us to departures and slows with the flow of traffic. I wish he wasn't being so quiet. He's hardly said a word since we left the house.

"Linnea?" Charlotte says from the backseat.

"Yeah?"

"Are you sure you'll be back for parent night?" she asks.

I turn around so I can look her in the eyes. "Of course I will. Do you remember what I promised, way back on my seventeenth day?"

She nods.

"I promised I'd be here for you. I always will, okay, Bug? I'll always be here. I promise."

She smiles and nods again. "Okay."

I reach back and squeeze her leg. "Okay. I'll see you in a couple of days."

We pull up to the curb and my tummy churns. Caleb and I get out and he takes my bag out of the trunk, then comes to stand beside me on the sidewalk.

He passes the handle to me and meets my eyes. "Don't promise her things like that."

I blink at him, stunned. "What?"

"Don't make her a promise you can't keep. You're not always going to be here."

My throat feels like it's going to close up and cut off my air. "No, I didn't... I'm coming back on Tuesday. I'll..."

The hurt look in his eyes stops me short.

"You're amazing." He squeezes my arm. "The Pittsburgh Symphony is going to love you."

I watch him get back in the car and drive away, feeling like I just got punched in the stomach.

I BARELY REMEMBER THE FLIGHT. Even the short layover in Denver is a blur. My back and legs are stiff from sitting in the cramped seat for so long, but otherwise, it's like it didn't happen. I get off the plane in a daze, rolling my bag behind me. A taxi takes me to my hotel, and between the long flight and losing three hours to the time difference, it's late when I arrive. I should probably eat something, but I'm too tired to care. I make it up to my room and fall into bed.

My phone wakes me early. Blinking the sleep from my eyes, I grab it and look at the screen. It's my mother. Knowing she'll gripe at me for it, I decide not to answer. She'll either complain that I missed her call, or complain that I was asleep when I should have been up already, so I suppose I'm just picking my poison. I set the phone back down, resolving to call her when I've had a chance to wake up.

After a shower and some tea, I'm awake, although I don't feel much better than I did yesterday. Thinking about how Caleb left me at the airport makes me tear up. *Don't promise her things like that.* I hate that he thinks I didn't mean it. I *will* be back for her performance at school. That's why I'm getting to the airport well before dawn for a flight at six in the morning.

But he wasn't just talking about tomorrow night.

The thought of leaving them and moving away is devastating. But this was always supposed to be the plan. I went to school for this. I've been practicing for hours every day for this. The Pittsburgh Symphony is highly respected. It's the opportunity of a lifetime.

And Caleb said I should go. He practically insisted.

I've never been so confused. If Caleb had asked me to stay, what would I have done? Would I have turned down the audition?

I guess it doesn't matter. He didn't ask me to stay. And this *is* what I've been working toward.

My phone vibrates with a text. I hope it's Caleb, but it's my mother.

Mom: Are you ready? Meet me in the lobby.

The lobby? Oh my god, is she here? I didn't expect her to come. I scroll back and realize I missed a text from her last night. She is here, staying at the same hotel.

This is not doing anything for my nerves.

I'm dressed for the audition in a long black dress with a V-neck and three-quarter length sleeves. I smooth it down and take one last look at my hair before I go downstairs. I have it up in a twist—partially because it looks nice, and partially so it won't get in my way while I'm playing. I put on some red lipstick and blot my lips. I'm nervous, but at least I look the part.

My mother is indeed in the lobby, dressed in a navy jacket and slacks, pearls at her neck. She's always kept her brown hair short, and her makeup is tasteful as usual. Her eyes flick up and down as I walk toward her—analyzing my outfit, no doubt.

"Are you sure about the shoes?" she asks.

I glance down at my red heels. They're my favorite pair of shoes, and they hardly show beneath my dress. I decide to ignore her question and hope she drops it. "I didn't know you were coming. Is Dad here too?"

"No, I'm afraid not," she says. "But I wouldn't have missed this."

That pulls me up short. "Really? You want to hear me play? I don't know if they'll let anyone in during the audition."

"Yes, I know. I've heard you play before," she says, and starts walking toward the front doors. "We should get there early."

"If you didn't think you'd hear me play, why did you fly all the way out here? Just to sit in the lobby while I go in?"

The doorman holds the doors open for us and we step out onto the sidewalk.

"No, I'm having lunch with Dr. Singleton and his wife." She gives me a knowing look as we turn toward Heinz Hall. "It's his wife who is on the board of trustees. This is all about who you know, Linnea. It's important to foster connections with the right people."

My heart sinks. For a second, I thought she cared about hearing me play today. But of course she doesn't. She's just here because she doesn't think I can do this on my own.

Heinz Hall, the beautiful venue the Pittsburgh Symphony Orchestra calls home, is just steps away from our hotel. In the 1920s, it was an opulent movie house, but fell into disrepair. It was almost demolished, but was eventually renovated for the symphony.

We step inside and my mouth drops open. I've seen pictures, but nothing is like seeing it in person. The lobby is stunning, with walls of cream and gold, huge columns, and a massive crystal chandelier hanging from the tall arched ceiling. It's like walking into a palace. The wide staircase is carpeted in red with a dark wood banister. Every inch of the place says luxury, wealth, and style.

"Close your mouth and stop staring," Mom says. "Where are we supposed to go?"

I close my mouth and look around. There's a sign on a black stand that says *auditions* with an arrow pointing left. I find a table with a woman seated behind it outside one of the doors to the main hall. She has an open laptop and a stack of folders next to it. My mother hangs back while I approach the table.

My hands are already trembling and all-too-familiar pings of nervousness roll through my belly. "Hi, I'm here for my audition. I'm Linnea Frasier."

She looks at something on her screen and clicks the mouse a few times. "All right, Ms. Frasier. They'll call you when they're ready for you."

I'm not the only one here. Several other musicians linger nearby. Most appear to be alone, although one woman is sitting on a padded bench holding a man's hand. They're all dressed professionally—everyone in black, or black and white. I glance down at my shoes again, wondering if red was a mistake.

My mother finds a seat and busies herself with something on her phone. I wander away from her, trying to get my pre-performance jitters under control. I feel increasingly like I might vomit. Taking slow, deep breaths, I walk and stretch my fingers. I don't know if they'll give me time to warm up before I have to play, and I want my fingers to be limber.

Two of the other musicians are called in, one after another. They're each gone for about ten minutes before coming out again. One has a look of triumph on his face; I can tell he's happy with his performance. The other looks more relieved than confident.

"Ms. Frasier?" The woman at the table looks toward me. "They're ready for you."

My mouth goes dry and I avoid looking at my mother. "Thank you."

Deep breaths, Linnea. Deep breaths.

The concert hall is even more intimidating than the palatial lobby. The walls are detailed in cream, gold, and red. A beautiful grand piano is on the large stage, its dark wood gleaming beneath the lights. Most of the seats are empty, but a small group of people sits front and center. The audition committee.

I've been to auditions before. I tried out for the local youth symphony in high school, and I had to pass a series of auditions to gain acceptance into the music program in college. But I've never faced anything like this.

The expressions of the audition committee are passive, even bored. They each have a folder in their hands and pens for taking notes.

I step up onto the stage and my heels click against the hard surface, the sound echoing in the acoustics of the hall. It feels as if every breath I take must be audible against the gaping silence. My heart thumps uncomfortably hard and my hands shake. I hope I can steady my hands so I'll be able to play.

When I get to the piano, I turn to face the committee and pause, waiting for the go ahead to begin.

"This is Linnea Frasier," a woman on the end says. The other committee members consult their paperwork. "You have one minute to warm up, Ms. Frasier. Then you may begin."

I nod, but don't trust my voice to speak. My throat is so dry. The room feels cavernous. I'm so small in comparison. So small and quiet. The invisible girl.

I slide onto the bench and rest my fingers on the keys. It's the most gorgeous instrument I've ever touched. My hands tremble and I swallow hard before tentatively pressing down. The C major chord rings out, clear as day. Just that simple sound is so breathtakingly beautiful it makes me gasp. The piano is exquisite, the keys smooth, the action utterly perfect. Every detail of the room is designed to enhance the music, letting the harmonic stream of those three notes played together fill the air.

With less than a minute to warm up my fingers and get used to the feel of this incredible instrument, I begin my scales. My fingers move up and down the keys in an exercise I've done thousands of times. The familiarity takes the edge off my anxiety, allowing my hands to relax. My stomach still churns with nerves and my heart races, but at least I know my hands work.

I finish my scales and pause, putting my hands in my lap. I look over to the audition committee and the woman on the end nods.

My piece is Schubert's Impromptu in G-flat, Opus Ninety, Number Three. I'm what conductors call an expressive pianist. My hands aren't large, but my fingers are fast, and Schubert's piece showcases my strengths.

As I begin, I close my eyes and let the music come. It originates deep in my chest, and flows through my body into my hands. The song soars through the room, ringing out even at my gentle touch. It's exquisite. My left hand plays the melody while my right softly plays the rapid notes of the accenting harmony, my fingers flying across the keys. I let my body sway to the sound as the music fills me.

I've never touched an instrument so perfect. Never heard my music in a venue so beautifully made. I'm overcome with the simple pleasure of playing—of creating something lovely and pure. I've played this song so many times, but never heard it sound like this. I'm swept away by the beauty of it. By my love for the music.

I pour all my fear, all my doubt, all my confusion over Caleb, and Charlotte, and this audition into the song. I let my emotions run free, expressing them in the music in a way I never could with words. I bare my soul in the notes I play, leaving nothing behind. I forget that anyone is listening, and for the space of one beautiful song, my anxiety melts away.

The song ends and I slowly open my eyes, bringing my mind back to the present. I take a deep breath and gently caress the keys one last time, brushing my fingertips across their smooth surface.

That's it. My audition is over. I stand and thank the committee, although my voice comes out so softly, I doubt they hear my words. I leave the hall and walk out into the lobby feeling dazed. It's like waking up in the middle of a dream.

"Linnea," Mom says, like she's trying to get my attention. I don't remember her approaching, but she's standing in front of me. "Linnea, how did it go? How did you play?"

I blink at her. "I've never played so perfectly in my entire life."

24

CALEB

I read Linnea's text for probably the hundredth time since I got it a few hours ago.

Linnea: My audition is done. I don't think I've ever played better.

I replied right away, to tell her how proud I am. Which is the honest truth. I'm so fucking proud of her. I know how nervous she was for this audition, and I wanted her to nail it. I wanted her to feel good about her performance.

But it also sucks.

I've heard her play. I know how talented she is. If she played her best—if she played better than her best—there's no way she's not going to get this job.

There's a knock on my door, so I put down my phone and get up to answer it. It's Weston, holding a brown paper bag.

"What are you doing here?" I ask.

He sighs and comes in, walking past me toward the kitchen. "Let's get this over with."

"Get what over with?" I close the door and follow him inside.

"Don't make it weird by talking too much." He pulls a bottle of Maker's Mark out of the bag and sets it on the counter. "Is Bug around?"

"No, I have to be at the hospital tonight, so she's spending the night at Alex and Mia's." I watch him get glasses out of the cupboard and pour two fingers of bourbon into each. He hands one to me, then wordlessly takes his drink over to the couch. I bring mine and sit in the armchair.

He takes a sip. "Pittsburgh?"

"What, Linnea?" I ask. "Yeah, she's in Pittsburgh."

"Why the fuck did you let her go?"

I set my drink on the coffee table; I have to go to work soon, so I can't drink it. "What kind of a question is that? She doesn't belong to me. I can't tell her what to do."

"Can't you?"

"No. This is her career we're talking about," I say. "If Kendra had some big conference to go to, would you stop her?"

"If it meant I was going to lose her, yes," he says.

I sit back in my chair. "That's interesting, coming from you."

"Why, because I've made mistakes?" he asks. "At least with Kendra I figured shit out before it was too late."

"This isn't the same thing," I say. "I didn't get in some stupid fight with her. She had an audition with one of the best symphonies in the country. It's what she wants to do with her life. I've known that from day one."

"Don't be a dumbass," he says. "This isn't about her audition."

"Actually, that's exactly what it's about," I say.

"No, it's about your relationship with her," he says. "Did you tell her you don't want her to leave?"

"Of course not," I say.

He shakes his head. "Why?"

"How could I? I can't ask her to pass up an opportunity like that."

"Why not?"

He's starting to piss me off. "What is she supposed to do? Stay here? Date a guy with a kid? Fucking make me dinner every night?"

"I don't know about dinner, but yeah," he says.

"How is that fair to her?" I ask.

"What exactly is so wrong with what you guys had?" he asks.

"Nothing was wrong with it," I say. "That's not the point."

"No, that *is* the point," he says. "You seem to think that moving across the country, alone, to play with the goddamn Pittsburgh Symphony is infinitely better than her relationship with you. And with Bug."

"She's twenty-two years old," I say. "How can I possibly ask her to give up on her dreams to be stuck with a family?"

Weston stares at me, his drink held loosely in his hand. "Are you kidding?"

"No."

"Why the hell do you think giving her a family is a bad thing?" he asks. "It's the best fucking thing in the world when all you've had is a shitty one."

I open my mouth to reply, but I've got nothing. The enormity of what Weston just said leaves me speechless. Because I know he's speaking from experience. Aside from his speech to Kendra at our brother's wedding, that's about the most heartfelt thing I've ever heard come out of his mouth.

Suddenly that bourbon seems like a good idea, but I leave it on the table.

"I'm the world's most unobservant person," he says. "Even I noticed how good you were together. That's how obvious it was."

"If she wanted to stay with me, she would have."

"Did you give her a reason to?" he asks. "Or did you pack her bag and drive her to the airport?"

"I..." Fuck, I did give her a ride to the airport.

"You're not her father," he says.

I glare at him. "Dude, that's creepy."

"Then stop acting like it," he says. "She doesn't need you to sacrifice your happiness so she can get a good job."

"Then what does she need me to do?"

"She needs you to be honest with her," he says. "Don't wall yourself off because you think it's what's best for her. She's an adult. She can decide what's best. Tell her the truth—that you fucking love her and she's perfect for you and you should be together. Don't hold that back because you think she'll regret it if she stays with you. That's her call, not yours. And you're selling her short if you don't think she's capable of making her own choices."

Fuck. How messed up is my life that *Weston* is telling me I have my head up my ass? "What am I supposed to do? She's there. She had her audition and she killed it. They're going to offer her the job."

Weston takes another sip. "If it were me, I'd text Mia and ask her what to do."

"Mia?" I ask. "She trips over her own feet. How will she know what to do about Linnea?"

He shrugs. "I'm just saying, she'll know."

I sit back in the chair and pinch the bridge of my nose. "Fuck."

"Yep. Love will fuck you right up." He stands and takes his glass to the kitchen. "I need to get home to my baby mama, so stop being a dumbass."

"Yeah, thanks," I say.

"Anytime."

Weston leaves and I pick up my phone. I'm questioning my sanity a little bit as I bring up Mia's number and send her a text.

Me: You have a second? I guess I need advice.

Mia: Of course. Did you know Bug loves Dr Pepper?

Me: Don't give her that! It has caffeine.

Mia: Um... too late. But don't worry. We'll just keep her up until she's tired.

Me: Please come talk to me before you have kids.

Mia: Why? So my advice is call her.

Me: I didn't ask anything yet.

Mia: Linnea, right? Call her. Now.

I start typing another text, but Mia texts back before I finish.

Mia: Stop.

Mia: Whatever you were going to say to me doesn't matter. Call her. Tell her.

Me: Tell her what?

Mia: Do you really need this much hand-holding? Tell her you love her and you want her to come home.

Me: Shouldn't I wait and talk to her in person?

Mia: Do you want to take that chance?

I blow out a breath and bring up Linnea's number. I don't want to take that chance. Weston's right, I should have told her how I feel. She deserves the opportunity to make this decision for herself. If she still wants to go to Pittsburgh, I'll let her go.

Or... figure something out. Jesus, why didn't I consider the alternatives? I can get a job anywhere. What the hell is wrong with me?

I hit call. It rings twice, but it isn't Linnea's voice who answers.

"Caleb?"

"Margo?" I ask. Why is Linnea's mother answering her phone? "What's going on? Is Linnea all right?"

"She's fine," Margo says.

"Okay... can I talk to her?"

"No, she's not available at the moment," she says.

I close my eyes and try to breathe. She has got to be kidding me. "Margo, I really need to talk to her."

"I don't think that's the best thing for her right now," she says. "You know Linnea. She's... delicate. She needs to stay focused on her audition."

"She already told me her audition went well," I say. "Can you hand her the phone, please?"

"Her audition went *very* well," she says. "She just got the call that they want her back for a second audition tomorrow."

Tomorrow? She's supposed to come back tomorrow. "That's um, that's great. But it doesn't change the fact that I need to talk to her."

"Caleb, what are you doing?" she asks.

I clear my throat. "I'm trying to call Linnea and inexplicably talking to you."

"You know what I'm referring to," she says. "Quite frankly, I'm shocked. If I had known you would stoop so low as to seduce my daughter, I never would have suggested she live with you in the first place. I didn't think you were the sort of man to take advantage of an innocent young woman."

"Take advantage?" I say. "That's not—"

"Don't play dumb with me," she says. "I don't know what it is about my daughters that makes you want to prey on them. You already ruined Melanie's life. I am not going to allow you to do the same to Linnea."

A searing flash of anger rips through me and it's all I can do to keep my voice level. "I did not ruin Melanie's life, Margo. She was my wife, and I loved her."

"Yes, obviously," she says. "You loved her so much, now you're sleeping with her little sister."

I ball my hand into a fist and grind my teeth together. "How I feel about Linnea has nothing to do with Melanie. And it's none of your goddamn business. Put Linnea on the phone."

"Caleb, if I have my way, and we both know that I will, Linnea will not be coming back to Seattle at all," she says. "I'm quite certain the Pittsburgh Symphony is going to hire her, and until it's time for her to start, she'll be coming home to Michigan with us."

"And you don't give two shits about Charlotte?" I ask. "You expect Linnea to just abandon her without saying goodbye?"

"I love my granddaughter, and I've accepted there's nothing I can do about the way you insist on coddling her," she says. "But Charlotte needs to learn to handle disappointment."

"Are you really this cold?" I ask. "How did someone like you produce a woman like Linnea? Because it's baffling to me. Linnea can make her own decisions about where she lives. I don't know where you get off thinking you can control her. She's an adult, not some little puppet child."

"Believe me, I'll make sure she sees reason," she says. "I won't let her make the same mistakes Melanie did."

God, I'm so mad I can barely think. "Put her on the phone, Margo."

"I think we're done here."

Click.

"Fuck!" I throw my phone across the room and it hits the wall with a loud crunch. "Goddamn it."

I run my hands through my hair, clenching my teeth. My back is rigid with tension and I'm so mad I can hardly see straight. She hasn't made me this angry since she was threatening to try to get custody of Charlotte. What the fuck is wrong with her?

This is a fucking disaster. There's a dent in the wall where my phone hit, and my phone itself is fucked. The screen is ruined and no matter how many times I press the power button, it won't turn on.

God, why did I do that?

I toss it on the table and go upstairs to change. I don't have time to get a new one. I have an overnight shift and who knows if I'll have time tomorrow.

What a shit-show.

And the worst part is, I have to tell Charlotte that Linnea isn't coming tomorrow.

25

LINNEA

My heart beats too fast and I take a deep breath to try to stay calm. I've been in the bathroom too long and I know my mother is going to ask me what's wrong when I come out. Our food has probably arrived by now. But I don't want to eat.

I met her for dinner, despite the fact that all I wanted to do was curl up by myself in my hotel room and mindlessly channel flip until I fall asleep. Not five minutes after we were seated at an outdoor table, I got the call. The symphony director wants me back for the second round of auditions.

You'd think my mother would have been ecstatic. Instead, she gave me a cool smile and said, "Well, now you'll have to keep yourself together for a few more days. Do you think you can handle it, or are you going to buckle under the pressure?"

I got up and excused myself to the bathroom.

The audition is tomorrow. My flight back to Seattle is early tomorrow morning. If I don't go back, I'll miss Charlotte's performance at school. If I do go back, I'll have no chance at this job. There are other people vying for the same spot. They'll just eliminate me and move on to the next person.

I stare at myself in the mirror. What am I doing here?

Is this really what I want? Playing with a symphony—especially one as high-profile as this—will mean facing the pressure to perform constantly. My audition went well, and it felt good to play such a beautiful instrument. But that was fleeting; a few moments of musical beauty. It was nice, but was it worth it? Would playing like that be worth all the anxiety and stress?

And why did my mother come? She didn't have to be here. My parents never cared about my music when I was growing up. They looked at it like an odd quirk, a fascination that I'd outgrow. They indulged me enough to pay for lessons, but I think they always expected me to come to my senses and become interested in something else. Something worthy.

It wasn't until my sister died that my mother paid attention to what I was doing in music. Suddenly I had talent that needed to be nurtured. She made me keep a practice log and show it to her each week. She fired the piano teacher I'd been learning from for years in favor of one who had connections at several universities. Going to college for a music degree had been what I'd wanted, but my parents pushed me to choose a college with a good reputation.

All that attention, all that focus, had always been on Melanie. With her gone, it fell squarely onto me.

My mother has always seen me as weak, and for the most part, I believed her. But as I stand here in the bathroom, wondering what I'm doing with my life, a thought hits me. Something I've never thought about before, and I can't believe it took me this long to realize it. I'm *not* weak.

Granted, I might not be the toughest girl around, but I think about all the pressure my parents have put on me over the last five or six years. Pressure that came out of nowhere, sitting on me like a lead weight. It came at a time when I was still reeling from the loss of my big sister, still struggling to simply survive every day at school. My life wasn't a cake walk before Mel died, and afterward it became almost unbearable. At home, I went from being nearly invisible to having a spotlight shined on my every flaw.

But I survived.

Did I stand up for myself to my mother? Did I insist my parents treat me like an adult? No. I didn't. I still haven't. But I also didn't let their expectations crush me. I didn't let them change me.

And I'm not going to let them change me now.

The truth of what I need to do is so simple, it almost makes me laugh. Relief floods through me. I dig in my purse to get my phone. I need to call Caleb. I need to tell him.

I need to tell him I'm coming home.

Where's my phone? I shuffle things around, but I don't see it. I must have left it on the table when I got up.

Well, I'll just have to talk to my mother first, and call him afterward. A few more minutes isn't going to change anything.

I take a deep breath and straighten, pulling my shoulders back. This isn't going to be easy, but I'm not letting my mother bully me into staying in Pittsburgh.

Mom is on the phone when I come out. I hear her say something—it sounds like *I think we're done here*—as I walk through the doors to the outdoor patio where we were seated. She puts down her phone, but slides it across the table to my spot.

Wait, that wasn't her phone. It was mine.

She meets my eyes as I walk toward the table, her chin lifted. She looks defiant. Like she's daring me to ask who she was talking to.

Something snaps inside of me and I stop next to my chair, staring at her. It isn't the feel of something breaking apart—the sharp crack of destruction. It's like two pieces clicking into place

—two sides that always had an unnatural gap between them finally fitting together.

Margo Frasier, if you think I'm going to lie down and die again, you have another thing coming.

I lower myself into the chair, my eyes on my mother. I'll ask her about the phone in a minute, but first I need to get this out before I lose my nerve. I'm strangely calm and when I speak, my voice is clear. "I'm not going to the audition tomorrow."

She raises an eyebrow. "Yes, you are."

"No, I'm not. I'm flying out in the morning. I'm going home."

"That man's house is not your home." Her precisely manicured hand clutches her water and she takes a sip. "You're staying here until the audition process is over, and then you're coming home to Michigan with me. If you land the job here, your father and I will help you get settled somewhere in the area. If not, you can continue to audition while you're living with us."

"No," I say.

"Linnea, I'm not sure where this little display of rebellion is coming from, but I've had enough of it."

"I'm not rebelling," I say. "And I'm not a child, so stop treating me like one. I'm making a choice. I'm flying to Seattle in the morning. I have to be at Charlotte's school tomorrow night."

"The only thing you have to do is stay focused so you can nail your call-back," she says.

"Perhaps you didn't hear me," I say. "I'm not going. I'm declining the position."

"And what do you think you're going to do with yourself?" she asks. "With that expensive degree your father and I paid for?"

"I'm going to do exactly what I want to be doing," I say, and I'm amazed there's no tremor in my voice. "I'm going to teach piano and take care of Charlotte. And if that expensive degree was such a hardship, I'll be glad to work toward paying you back."

"Now you're just being ridiculous," she says.

"I'm sorry you feel that way, but I've made my decision."

"If you think you can go back to Seattle and play house with that man, you are sorely mistaken," she says.

The venom in her voice makes my heart jump, but I'm determined to stand my ground. "I'm not playing anything. This isn't about Caleb. Don't get me wrong, I'm in love with him." I take no small degree of satisfaction at seeing her eyes widen. "I don't know if he's in love with me. Maybe he is, and maybe he isn't. But that doesn't change anything for me. I'm still going back."

"No, you're not."

"I absolutely am," I say. "I promised Charlotte I would be there. I will not break my promise to her."

"You need to stop pretending you're that little girl's mother," she says.

Anger bubbles up from deep inside, searing hot. "I'm well aware that I'm not her mother. I don't need to be in order to love her. And there's nothing more important than that."

"Your career—"

"My career is my business," I say, cutting *her* off for once. "I know I'm supposed to want to play with a symphony. But I don't. That's what *you* want. I'm going to teach music, because that's what I love to do. And I'm good at it. If having a daughter who is a nanny and a piano teacher means you can't brag about my accomplishments to your friends, that isn't my problem."

"This has nothing to do with my friends. We raised you to be better. To be more. To aim as high as you can and shoot for your dreams." She sighs. "Your sister..."

I wait, knowing how she was going to finish that sentence, waiting to see if she'll come out and say it. "What about my sister? Why don't you just say it? You wish I was more like Melanie."

"That isn't what I said."

"You don't have to," I say. "Ever since she died, you've been trying to turn me into another version of her."

"Linnea, that isn't fair."

"You're right, it isn't," I say. "It isn't fair to me. I know you don't understand me. You never did. I'm not like you and Dad, and I'm not like Melanie. I don't want attention and prestige. I want a quieter life, and I don't think there's anything wrong with that."

"Linnea, what has come over you?" she asks.

"I'm done, Mom," I say. "I'm done trying to be the daughter you wish you had. I'm done trying to fit your ideal. I'll never live up to it. If you can't be proud of me the way I am, I guess I'll have to live without your approval."

"Linnea—"

"Why were you on my phone?" I ask, not letting her finish.

She doesn't answer.

I pick up my phone and check my calls. My stomach drops. It's exactly what I was afraid I was going to see. "You talked to Caleb, didn't you?"

"Yes."

"What did you say to him?"

"I told him the truth," she says.

"Mother," I say, anger leaking into my voice. In the back of my mind, I can't believe I'm having this conversation with her. But after so many years of succumbing to fear, I'm done. "What did you say to him?"

"I told him you have another audition," she says. "And that you won't be going back to Seattle, regardless of the outcome."

"How dare you!"

"Linnea, lower your voice."

"I will not," I say. "I can't believe you would do this to me. It's bad enough that you treated me like I didn't exist for most of my life. Never made a single attempt to get to know me or show any interest in who I was. Then you lost your favorite child, so you had to try to turn me into someone else so you could love me. And now you're trying to ruin my relationship with the man I'm in love with?"

"He was married to your sister," she says. "How can you possibly think he's in love with you?"

"The world did not actually revolve around Melanie," I say. "It's been years, and there's nothing wrong with Caleb loving someone else. Honestly, I don't know if he's in love with me. But if he is, it doesn't change anything about what he had with her. That's not how this works. And it's none of your business anyway."

Standing, I grab my purse and phone.

"Where are you going?"

"Back to my hotel," I say. "My flight is early and I have some calls to make."

"Linnea, you are not giving up this opportunity," she says. "You might never get another one."

"That's fine. I don't want it. I'm going home." I start to walk away, then glance back at her over my shoulder. "By the way, I have a tattoo. And Caleb watched me get it."

Without another word, I walk away.

My hotel is across the street. Before I'm through the lobby doors, I hit call, trying to reach Caleb. It rings as I make my way toward the elevators. Keeps ringing. Voicemail. Damn it.

"Caleb, it's me. Don't listen to anything my mother said. I'm leaving in the morning. Just... don't listen to my mom. Please. I..." I falter. I want to tell him I love him, but it might not matter. If he doesn't love me back, there's not much I can do about it. "Please call me back."

Maybe it's overkill, but I hang up and send him a text, typing while I get in the elevator.

Me: I'm coming home. Please call me.

Back in my room, my hands start to shake and it feels like I can't catch my breath. All the anxiety I wasn't feeling when I was talking to my mother hits me at once. It makes me panicky, like the air is too thick to make it into my lungs. I pace around the room, just trying to breathe. Trying to stay calm.

I get a series of texts from my mother that I don't read. She calls, but I don't pick up. Every time my phone makes a noise, I feel like I'm going to jump out of my skin. I want it to be Caleb—desperately hope it will be him—but he doesn't call. Doesn't text. I don't hear a word from him.

Finally, I start to calm down. My heart isn't beating so furiously and my hands don't tremble when I type a message on my phone. I send an exceedingly polite email to the symphony director, thanking her for the opportunity and letting her know I have to decline.

I consider texting Mia and Kendra—and Alex and Weston, for that matter—asking them to tell Caleb to call me if they see him. But I know Caleb's schedule this week, and he's at the hospital overnight. He's so hard to reach when he's at work, especially because he's so often in surgery when he works nights.

Telling myself that's why I couldn't reach him—he's probably in surgery—I pack my things and call the concierge to arrange my ride to the airport. I have to get up at three in the morning in order to get to the airport on time, and there's no way I'm missing my flight.

~

Tuesday shapes up to be the worst day of my entire life. Or it will be if it keeps going the way it has so far.

I'm so anxious to get home I don't sleep at all. When my alarm goes off at three in the morning—midnight in Seattle—I'm out of bed in seconds. I'm already packed, so I change my clothes, stuff the last of my things in my bag, and head down to meet my ride.

The hotel shuttle gets me to the airport more than two hours before my departure time. I get through security quickly and wait at the gate to board.

And wait.

And wait.

Boarding time comes and goes, and there's an announcement over the loudspeaker that's hard to make out. Something about mechanical problems. They're waiting for another plane.

I spend the next hour trying not to panic.

There's no way I'm going to make my connecting flight in Newark. I talk to one of the gate agents and she assures me they'll be able to get me on another one. But she won't book my seat until they know when our flight out of Pittsburgh is departing.

So I wait some more.

My original flight had me landing by twelve-thirty, Seattle time. Parent night at Charlotte's school isn't until six. That would have given me more than enough time to get back. But as I sit in the airport and watch the time tick by, my chances of making it keep decreasing.

I have to get home. I can't miss Charlotte's performance.

Finally, the gate agent pages me. They have me on a different flight, with a layover in Denver. My first flight leaves in ten minutes, but she says she already called the other gate and told them I'm coming.

I race down the corridor, pulling my suitcase behind me.

The last few passengers are boarding when I rush up and hand over my printed-out ticket. The woman scans it and waves me through.

The flight is the opposite of the one I took to get across the country. I feel every second of it. I set my phone to Pacific time so I'll know how much time I have to get home. Between the delay and the longer layover, I'm going to be cutting it close.

My connecting flight is delayed even more. I feel like I'm never going to get home. I keep looking at my phone, as if somehow I'm going to find an extra hour. Or that Caleb will call me back. Neither happens.

When I land in Seattle, I'm exhausted, relieved, and in such a hurry I can't get through the airport fast enough. Thankfully I didn't check a bag, so I rush through the maze of corridors, past gates and restaurants and overpriced souvenir stores. I make it out to the curb and get in line for a cab.

I look at the time when I get in the backseat and give the cab driver the address. I have eighteen minutes before parent night begins. We're probably thirty minutes away, more if traffic is bad. This cab is going to cost me a fortune, but I don't care. All I can think about is getting to Charlotte's school.

"You in a hurry?" the cab driver asks.

"Yes," I say, my voice filled with urgency. "Please get me there as fast as you can. My little girl is waiting for me."

26

CALEB

I'm a few minutes early for school pickup, so I hang out near Charlotte's classroom door among a group of moms. It's been a while since I picked her up from school, and I feel like the women are all staring at me.

I touch my pocket, looking for my phone. It's like a reflex. But like an idiot, I broke my phone last night, and I haven't had time to replace it. I'm not sure when I will. We have to be back here for parent night, and somehow cell phone stores are like a black hole of time.

Several of the women are definitely staring at me. I shift on my feet and put my hands in my pockets, feeling like a wounded gazelle being circled by a pride of lions. I breathe out a sigh of relief when the teacher opens the door and kids start coming out.

Charlotte sees me and her face lights up. She runs over to me and I scoop her up, hugging her.

"Hey, Bug."

"Hi, Daddy," she says, giving me a big squeeze around my neck. "Is Linnea home yet?"

"No, sweetie, she's not."

"Okay," she says, her voice matter-of-fact.

I put her down and she takes my hand as we start to walk home. How do I tell her Linnea isn't coming tonight? And how is she going to react? She's made so much progress this year, and the fact that she wants to play piano in front of an audience—even a small one—is such a huge step. Is this going to derail her? Will she refuse to go?

"Bug, I need to talk to you about Linnea," I say. "Remember how she went to Pittsburgh to audition for a big symphony?"

"Yes."

"Well, her audition went really well," I say. "They liked her and they want her to stay longer and do another audition. So... honey, she's still in Pittsburgh."

"Pittsburgh is in Pennsylvania," she says.

"Yeah, it is."

"She's not in Pennsylvania," she says. "She's coming to parent night to see me play. I'm going to play piano just like her."

The confidence in her voice is like a kick to the gut. She's so certain. "I know she said she'd be here. I'm sure she wanted to be. But sometimes plans change. Linnea had to stay, which means she can't come tonight."

She stops walking, her hand still clutched in mine. I crouch down so I can look her in the eyes. This is killing me. I hate having to tell her something that's going to hurt her.

"But she promised me," Charlotte says. "A promise is like an oath and that means she has to come."

"I know. If she could be here, she would."

She tilts her head to the side and purses her lips. "Don't worry, Daddy. She'll be here."

I let out a long breath and Charlotte tugs on my hand, so I straighten and walk her the rest of the way home.

~

First grade parent night is held in the gym. It's a nice thing they do to share what the class has been doing all year. There are tables set up at the back with displays made by the students, and rows of chairs facing a stage on the other side. There's an old upright piano set at an angle on the stage. I glance at the program I picked up when we walked in. Among the list of children set to perform I see *Charlotte Lawson - Piano*.

I sigh and look down at her. She's wearing her favorite pink dress, with pink tights and a pair of shiny black shoes that Linnea bought her. Her hair is in a ballet bun, and honestly, she looks so adorable it makes my chest ache.

Her little hand is in mine and she glances around. Families wander through the tables with displays of students' artwork.

It's not a large group of people, and the rows of chairs don't make it look like the audience size will be too intimidating. But Charlotte still thinks Linnea will be here, and I'm worried about what she's going to do when she realizes she's wrong.

Linnea's friend Megan walks over with her son, Noah, and a guy in a button-down and slacks who must be her husband. I've met Megan a few times, and she seems nice. I'm grateful that she and Linnea decided to facilitate a friendship between Charlotte and Noah. It's made a big difference for Charlotte to have a friend in her class.

"Hey Noah," I say. Noah gives me the same almost-but-not-quite-smile I've seen on him before.

Charlotte says hi, and he does smile at her. Megan introduces me to her husband, James. We shake hands, and I can see where Noah gets his serious demeanor.

"Where's Linnea?" Megan asks.

I clear my throat. "She's at a symphony audition in Pittsburgh."

Megan lifts her eyebrows. "Really? Wow, that's... I guess it's good?"

"Yeah," I say. I've gotten good at pretending I'm happy about this. "It's an amazing opportunity for her."

"Huh," Megan says. "The Pittsburgh Symphony means... Pittsburgh."

"Yeah," I say.

She narrows her eyes at me. "Well, I guess I'll have to text her later and see how she's doing."

"I'm sure she'd love that."

I touch my pocket again, thinking about my phone, wondering if Linnea has tried to call me today. I'm so torn over her. I can't blame her for staying in Pittsburgh. What else is she supposed to do? Parent night isn't exactly as important as a callback audition for a top-tier symphony.

But to Charlotte, it *is* that important. I know I can't protect my little girl from everything. But I hate that she's going to get hurt. And it's worse that it's because of Linnea.

Well, it's my fault too. But that doesn't make me feel any better at this point.

Charlotte leads me by the hand to look at the displays. She shows me hers—it's a collection of pictures depicting the life cycle of a butterfly. She's been fascinated since they learned about them in her class.

Her teacher walks out on stage and announces that parents have about five more minutes until it's time to take our seats.

Charlotte tugs on my hand and my heart twists at the worried look in her eyes. "Daddy, where is she?"

"I told you, Bug, she's still in Pittsburgh. She's not coming."

She doesn't cry. Her eyes don't fill with tears and she doesn't cause a scene. Her eyebrows knit together and she gets a little groove between them. Her mouth presses closed and I can practically feel the tension rolling through her little body. I can see her struggling to process what this means as her eyes dart around the room—from me, to the piano on stage, to the floor.

Finally, her eyes lock on the ground. Her back is stiff and she clutches my hand in a tight grip.

I crouch down. "Bug. Baby girl, I know you're upset. I'm so sorry."

She doesn't answer me. Her eyes stay on the floor in front of her.

Her teacher comes over and smiles. "We need Charlotte over on the far side of the stage in a few minutes."

"Okay, we'll be right there." I touch Charlotte's chin and try to coax her into looking at me while her teacher walks away. "Bug? Sweetie, if you're going to play your song, we need to get you in place over by the stage, okay?"

I stand and nudge her, tugging gently on her hand, but she doesn't move. It's like her feet are glued to the floor.

Fuck.

The other parents file into the rows of chairs, taking their seats. The small group of kids who are performing begin lining up next to the stage.

Movement near the back of the gym catches my eye and I glance over. A woman who looks exactly like Linnea comes through the door and starts walking toward us. She has a handbag on one shoulder and she's pulling a rolling suitcase behind her. Her hair is down and a little messy, her blouse partially untucked and wrinkled.

It can't be.

"Bug," she says as she hurries to us.

Charlotte turns at her voice and instantly her demeanor changes. She drops my hand and gasps. "Linnea!"

I gape at Linnea as she crouches down in front of Charlotte.

"I'm so sorry I'm late," Linnea says. "I tried so hard to get here on time."

Charlotte smiles. "I told Daddy you were coming. You promised."

"I did promise," Linnea says. "And I meant it. I'm so sorry if I made you worry."

Charlotte throws herself into Linnea's arms. My throat feels tight as I watch her hug my daughter. She's here? Why isn't she in Pittsburgh?

"Are you ready to play your song?" Linnea asks.

"Yes," Charlotte says. She looks up at me. "Daddy, am I supposed to line up now?"

"Yeah, right over there with your teacher."

"You're going to do great," Linnea says. "I'll be right here watching the whole time."

Charlotte nods, then walks over to her teacher near the stage. I watch while Ms. Peterson gets her situated in line to wait her turn.

Linnea stands and brushes her hair back from her face. She rests her hand on the handle of her suitcase.

"Did you come straight from the airport?" I ask.

"Yeah," she says. "Flight delays and traffic and... I didn't think I'd make it but the taxi driver was some kind of wizard. He knew a shortcut that bypassed an accident on the freeway."

"I thought you had another audition." I know I'm staring at her like an idiot, but the sudden change, from thinking she'd let Charlotte down to seeing her burst in here at the last second, leaves me feeling like I have whiplash.

"It's kind of a long story." She glances at the stage. "I know this isn't the time, but can I talk to you?"

"Yeah," I say, feeling my brain start to work again. She's here. Holy shit, she's fucking here. This changes everything. I grab the handle of suitcase and lead her to the back of the gym, behind the display tables.

"Caleb—"

"Wait," I say. "I need to talk to you too. Let me go first. Please."

"Oh, okay."

I look into her beautiful blue eyes and I'm flooded with relief. "I don't know what happened in Pittsburgh, but I want you to come home. I want you to stay. No, I don't just *want* you. I *need* you. *We* need you. You're perfect for me, and you're perfect for Bug, and my god, Linnea, I am so in love with you. I should have told you before, but I didn't want to hold you back. And if this is your dream, and you have to move to Pittsburgh... fuck it. We'll move too. I'll find a job over there and we'll come with you. We'll find a way to make this work, because all that matters is *us*. The three of us are a family, and I'll do whatever I have to do so that we can be together."

Her lips part and she stares at me, her eyes glistening with unshed tears. She takes a trembling breath. "I... um..."

"What?" I ask.

"I practiced what I was going to say on the way here about a hundred times, but you just went and said all that and..."

I brush her hair back from her face. "Okay, well, say what you were going to say."

"I was going to say that I'm not moving to Pittsburgh," she says. "They called me back for a second audition, but I turned it down. I didn't want the job anyway. I don't want to play with a symphony. That's what other people expected me to do, and it took me way too long to realize I could follow my own path. I was going to say that... that I don't know if you love me, and if you don't I'll figure out how to live with it. But I love Charlotte and I want to live here and take care of her and teach piano. So please don't make me lose her too."

"Oh, Linnea, no."

"But if you... did you just say you love me? And we're... we're a *family*?"

I step close and slip my hands around her waist. "Yes. I love you so much. You and Charlotte are my world."

"I want to stay," she says, looking up at me, her voice soft. "I love you too and I want to come home."

Smiling, I lean in to kiss her. Ms. Peterson says something into the microphone, but I don't hear my daughter's name, so I don't worry about it. My lips find hers and I practically shudder with relief at the feel of her mouth on mine. I pull her close and slide one hand behind her head, my fingers tangling in her hair. I kiss her hard and deep, without a single fuck for the fact that we're in my daughter's school and it's completely inappropriate.

I kiss her like she's *mine*. Because she is, and I'll make sure she knows it's always going to be that way. I'm never letting her go again.

"And next up we have Charlotte Lawson, who is going to play *Twinkle, Twinkle, Little Star* on the piano."

We both pull away, gasping. Leaving Linnea's bag where it is, I grab her hand and we rush up behind the last row of chairs.

Charlotte walks out on stage and sits at the piano. She looks so precious and small. Linnea's grip on my hand tightens as Charlotte lays her fingers on the keys. She pauses, her body completely still. I hold my breath.

Her fingers press the first notes. Linnea claps a hand over her mouth and squeezes mine harder. Charlotte nods her head to the beat as she plays, both hands finding the keys. She doesn't just play the melody; she's learned how to play accompanying chords with her left hand, and the effect is remarkable. Several of the children in the audience start singing along.

I'm so proud of her I think I might burst apart. Linnea and I hold onto each other, our excitement growing with every note. She comes to the end and holds the last chord before lifting her fingers. The crowd applauds and she twists on the bench, her eyes instantly finding me.

Her mouth moves in a smile that is so big and so bright it makes me tear up—and I feel absolutely no shame. I clap, and

Linnea has both hands covering her mouth, her shoulders trembling. A few tears trail down her cheeks as Charlotte stands and curtsies, lifting her dress as she bends her knees and dips her head.

Charlotte descends the few steps from the stage and runs into my arms. I scoop her up and Linnea and I hug her between us. My little girl squeezes my neck and the woman I love has her arms around us both. For someone else, it might be a small moment, just an embrace. But for me, it's everything.

From the corner of my eye, I see Megan smiling so big she scrunches her nose. She gives me a thumbs up and mouths, *Yes*.

I couldn't agree with her more.

27

LINNEA

Four months later…

"No, we can't go inside yet." Charlotte grabs my wrist with both hands and leans back, digging her heels into the ground.

"Why not?"

"Because," she says. "We can't."

"Bug, Daddy's home," I say. We're in the driveway and his car is here. "Don't you want to see him? He probably wonders where we are. We were at Noah's later than we planned."

"We need to wait," she says. "Just a few more minutes."

I move closer to her so she's no longer pulling on my arm. "Charlotte, is something going on?"

"I don't know," she says.

We spent the afternoon at Megan's so Charlotte and Noah could play. We've been alternating playdate locations and this was supposed to be our week. But Megan insisted we come to her. She said it's because she's pregnant and felt like staying home.

However, something seemed a little off. I could have sworn Megan was trying to get us to stay longer. Every time I said I was going to tell Charlotte it was time to clean up so we could go, Megan found something new to talk about. If she'd only done it once, I wouldn't have noticed. But it must have happened four or five times.

And now Charlotte is acting strange.

I narrow my eyes at her. "What are we waiting for?"

She presses her lips closed and her eyes dart to the sky. "Mm… I don't know."

"I think you *do* know," I say.

Before she can answer, the door opens and Caleb comes out, smiling. "There's my girls."

"Hi, Daddy." She runs to him and he picks her up.

"Hi, Bug." He kisses her cheek. "Good work."

"Good work?" I ask as I walk over to them. "What's going on?"

He puts Charlotte down and pulls me in for a kiss. "You'll see. Close your eyes."

"Why?"

"Just close them." He moves behind me and places his hands gently over my eyes. "Okay, walk forward."

"Caleb, what are you doing?" I move where he leads me, his hands still covering my eyes so I can't see. I hear the door shut and the sound of Charlotte's footsteps.

"Oh, Daddy," she says, her voice soft.

"Shh," he says. "Not yet."

He walks me farther inside and my heart flutters with anticipation. What is he doing?

"Okay, are you ready?" he asks, his mouth close to my ear.

"Um, I think so."

His hands drop and I blink to clear my vision. Then I blink again, because I'm sure I must be seeing things.

A gorgeous Steinway grand piano sits in the living room. My mouth drops open and my eyes widen. For a long moment, I can't do anything but stare at the gleaming black wood and shiny keys.

"Well," Caleb says, "what do you think?"

I step up next to it and brush my fingers across the keys. "Oh my god. Caleb..."

"It's not brand new," he says. "But I did a lot of research and this is one of the best pianos on the market. I talked to the guy who owns Henley's Music, and he took a look at it for me. He said it's in perfect condition. We'll need to get it tuned because of the move, so I don't know how it sounds right now, though."

I turn to look at him and he gives me a hopeful smile. "This is the most incredible thing anyone has ever done for me."

"You like it?" He steps closer and slips his hands around my waist.

"I love it. I love you. I can't believe you did this."

He kisses me and I wrap my arms around his neck. I'm so overwhelmed, I don't know what to do with myself. I never dreamed I'd own a piano as beautiful as this.

"There's one more thing," he says, pulling away.

"Something else?" I ask. "You just gave me a piano."

"It's little," he says with a wink. "Bug?"

"Oh! I'll be right back." She runs down the short hallway and up the stairs.

"Why don't you sit," he says. "Try the bench."

I lower myself onto the bench in front of the beautiful instrument. My hands are a little shaky and I'm almost afraid to touch it.

Charlotte comes running back with a small pink gift bag. "Got it. It was still in the hiding place."

Caleb laughs. "That's perfect. Do you want to give it to her?"

"Can I?" she asks.

"I think you should."

She climbs in my lap and sits sideways, her legs dangling between mine. She reaches into the bag and pulls out a small black box.

My tummy flip-flops as she puts the box in my hand. It's square and velvety soft.

Caleb sinks down onto one knee next to me and Charlotte threads her arm around my neck.

Oh my god, is this happening?

"Open it," Caleb says, his voice low.

With trembling hands and a racing heart, I slowly open the box. My vision blurs as tears fill my eyes. It's a beautiful ring with a square-cut diamond surrounded by a halo of smaller, sparkling stones.

Caleb pulls out the ring and sets the box on the piano. "Linnea, Charlotte and I would like to know if you'll marry me, and make the three of us a family forever."

I'm not sure if I can answer without sobbing. I nod and manage to choke out the words, "Yes. Yes, I will."

He smiles and takes my shaking hand, holding it steady in his own, and slips the ring on my finger.

Charlotte throws her arms around my neck and hugs me tight. Caleb stands up enough to kiss me. When Bug finally lets go, he gently moves her off my lap and pulls me up. He slides his fingers through my hair and kisses me again. His mouth caresses mine and his tongue slides against my lips. I press my body against him, melting into his kiss. His arms wrap around me and I drift in the feel of him, letting what just happened sink in.

Caleb is going to marry me.

"Okay, Daddy," Charlotte says. "You're getting married, you can kiss her later."

We both laugh and draw Charlotte against us. She wraps her

arms around our waists and looks up at us with her sweet brown eyes.

"I love you, Bug," I say.

"I love you, too," she says. "Can I be your flower girl? I have experience."

That makes us laugh again. "Yes, you can definitely be our flower girl," I say.

~

WE SPEND the afternoon making phone calls to share our news. Of course Caleb's family already knew what he had planned. They're thrilled to hear it's official. Kendra starts crying as soon as Caleb gets two words out and has to hand the phone to Weston. When we talk to Alex, we can hear Mia squealing in the background. Ken says he can't wait for me to officially be his daughter, which makes me tear up all over again.

But the most amazing thing is when we call my parents. The three of us call on Skype, all sitting together at the desk with Charlotte on Caleb's lap. Bug tells them the news and holds up my hand to show them the ring. My parents smile and congratulate us, and there's no sign that they're anything but happy for me.

My mom and I never talked about what happened in Pittsburgh. It took a while before I was ready to speak to her again, but even with the way she treated me, I couldn't be too hard on her. She lost a child, and I can't imagine how devastating that must have been.

Ever since I stood up to her, she's treated me differently. Like a woman capable of making my own choices. Both my parents accepted my relationship with Caleb and haven't said another word about major symphonies or auditions. I'm not sure if it's what I said, or simply the fact that I finally asserted myself that made the difference. Whatever the reason, it's been a relief to start rebuilding a relationship with them—to feel like they're finally beginning to see me for who I am.

The three of us have dinner at our favorite restaurant to celebrate. After we get home, Caleb puts Charlotte to bed. She's tired after all the excitement of the day.

While he's upstairs, I close the lid on my new piano to dampen the volume, and play a few chords. It is a bit out of tune from being moved, but the sound is rich and deep. Closing my eyes, I begin the Schubert piece I played in Pittsburgh. It's still one of my favorites. I keep my touch light so it's not too loud, and drift with the music. It flows through me, thrumming through my chest, tingling my skin.

When I finish and slowly open my eyes, Caleb is standing next to me.

"God, I love hearing you play." He slides onto the bench and I scoot over to make room. "I think I bought this piano as much for me as for you."

"I still can't believe you did this," I say.

He brushes my hair behind my shoulder and leans in to kiss my neck. "I'm glad you like it."

I tilt my head as his lips press against the sensitive skin below my ear. He reaches out and closes the fall, covering the keys, then moves me in front of him. Grabbing my hips, he lifts me so I'm perched on top of the covered keys.

He stands and kisses me while he slides his hands up my thighs, beneath my dress. His fingers hook around the thin fabric of my panties and he yanks them off. My breath quickens. His mouth is insistent, his hands rough as he grabs my hips, hiking my dress up my legs.

"Get on top," he says. "I want to taste you."

He helps me up onto the flat lid and I lie back. Pushing my thighs open, he leans in and caresses me with his tongue. My eyes roll back as waves of sensual heat roll through me. I don't know how he does it, but his tongue is like magic. He sucks on my clit and I'm ready to burst apart. My hips move with his rhythm and I bite my lip to keep from crying out.

The orgasm sweeps through me and I'm practically vibrating with pleasure. Shock waves reverberate through my whole body and my breath comes in gasps. He growls into me and doesn't let up, drawing out my climax until I'm panting and begging him to stop.

"Oh my god, Caleb... please... I can't..."

He kisses my thighs while I catch my breath, then helps me sit up. "I really like this piano." He runs his hand around the back of my neck and draws me in for a kiss. Tasting my flavor on his lips makes me crazy, and he knows it.

"Caleb, I need you inside me."

"I'll give you everything you need, beautiful."

He stands and picks me up over his shoulder. I laugh as he carries me upstairs and tosses me on the bed. I finish undressing while he pulls off his clothes, revealing his strong arms, broad chest, and toned abs.

I love the way he climbs on top of me, nuzzling my breasts with his mouth as he moves up my body. His skin against mine is heavenly. I slide my arms up his back and wrap my legs around his waist.

He kisses along my neck, his cock teasing the outside of my opening. His voice is low in my ear. "I love you."

"I love you too."

I gasp when he thrusts inside me. I love feeling so close to him. With our bodies joined, we move together, drowning in bliss. The intensity builds and he increases the pace, taking us from slow and tender to fierce and rough.

No one has ever made me feel so needed. So beautiful. So

sexy. So alive. He makes love to me like he could never get enough.

I'm ready to detonate, on the brink of climax. His cock pulses, thickening inside me. He brings his mouth to mine and the simple pleasure of our tongues caressing sends me over the edge. I cling to him, moving my hips with the waves of my orgasm. He groans as he comes, a low noise in the back of his throat. His hips drive into me and his muscles flex. There's nothing like this moment, when we're overcome with the feel of each other.

He lingers inside me, slanting his mouth over mine in a slow, lazy kiss. When he slides off, he pulls me close, wrapping me in his strong embrace.

"I'm glad you said yes," he whispers.

I smile, nuzzling my head against his chest. "Well, you did butter me up with a piano."

He laughs. "Obviously it worked. There's just one problem."

"What's that?" I ask.

"I don't know how I'm ever going to top that," he says. "What can I ever give you that will be better than a grand piano?"

I lift my head and meet his eyes. "I can think of something."

He puts his arm behind his head. "Yeah? What?"

My mouth turns up in a shy smile and I look up at him from beneath my eyelashes. "A baby."

28

EPILOGUE: CALEB

"Almost done, Dad." I slide the end of the dark blue tie through the knot and pull it tight. Perfect.

He turns to the mirror and adjusts his jacket, then fusses with the knot again.

"It's straight," I say. "Quit messing with it."

Alex pats him on the back. "Caleb's right. You look great. Are you nervous?"

Dad blows out a breath, still eying himself in the full-length mirror in his guest bedroom. "Don't think I'd be human if I wasn't nervous. I'm about to get married."

Alex and I are both dressed in suits and ties, as is Weston. Our brother-in-law sits in a chair next to the guest bed, a little pink bundle in his arms. He has his six-month old daughter, Audrey, cradled in the crook of his elbow while he feeds her a bottle.

The wedding is here, at my dad's house, so it's not formal. Dad and Jacqueline have both been married before, and neither of them wanted a fancy wedding. But they did want a way to celebrate their marriage with their adult children—and grandchildren.

There's a knock and Kendra pokes her head in the door. "Are you guys ready?"

I put my hand on Dad's shoulder. "Let's do this, Dad."

We walk out to the backyard where the guests are waiting in folding chairs. It's a small gathering—a few of Dad's old friends, some of Jacqueline's friends and family, and several people from the physical therapy office where they met. Thankfully the weather cooperated, and the sun is out, with just a few wispy clouds in the blue sky.

Someone starts the music, and Weston goes first, carrying Audrey, sound asleep in his arms. I'm next, then Alex, and finally my dad. He walks with his back straight, and although he's leaning on his cane, his stride is sure. I feel a little choked up seeing him walking so well—up the aisle at his wedding, no less.

The women come out the back door. First Gwen, Jacqueline's daughter, followed by Kendra. Mia pauses to adjust her glasses and rests her hand on her very pregnant belly before walking up the aisle.

Behind Mia is Linnea, holding Charlotte's hand. Her blue dress drapes over her body beautifully, showing the swell of her belly. She's not as far along as Mia—who scared the shit out of everyone at dinner last night by having regular contractions for an hour. But the curves of her body have changed, and she's visibly pregnant.

My beautiful wife, pregnant with my baby.

Charlotte is wearing a pale pink dress with a big bow in the back. Someone curled her hair and she has the pink butterfly hair clip Jacqueline gave her as a flower girl present. She was extremely excited to add yet another run as a flower girl to her resume—her fourth, if you count Kendra and Weston's impromptu wedding. Which of course, Charlotte does.

Linnea and Charlotte come up the aisle, hand in hand, and I can't stop smiling at my beautiful girls.

The bride appears at the back in a long, strapless dress. Instead of white, it's turquoise with layers of purple in the skirt —colorful, and very Jacqueline.

It's a nice ceremony—short and sweet. Which is good, because Audrey wakes up before it's over and Weston has to walk up and down the side of the yard with her so she'll stay quiet.

When it's over, everyone stays for the reception—which is simply a lot of food and booze in the backyard.

Linnea and I sit with Charlotte at one of the tables set up for guests. Mia waddles over with Alex right behind. He holds her chair while she carefully lowers herself down.

"This kid must be ten pounds by now." She winces and shifts around, like she can't get comfortable.

Alex takes the seat next to her and draws his eyebrows in. "Really? You still have a few weeks before your due date."

"I'm exaggerating, but he feels huge." She presses down on her belly. "I think his butt is right here."

Charlotte giggles. "Can I feel the baby?"

"Sure, Bug," Mia says. She shifts again and blows out a breath while Charlotte goes around the table to sit next to her. "Right here."

Charlotte puts her hand on Mia's belly and her eyes light up. "I can feel him!"

Kendra and Weston sit down. Audrey is awake, but no longer fussy. Weston takes her from Kendra and perches her on his knee, facing out so she can see. Her little bit of brown hair is tied in a ponytail on top of her head—Kendra calls it her whale spout—and she has gray eyes like her dad.

"Linnea, how are you feeling?" Kendra asks.

"I feel good most of the time," Linnea says. "Just tired."

"When do you have an ultrasound?" Mia asks. "Are you finding out if it's a boy or a girl?"

"Yeah, we have a lot riding on this," Kendra says. "The girls finally outnumber the boys in this family. Are you keeping our streak alive?"

"Actually, with Audrey, and now Gwen, girls are ahead by two," Mia says.

"True," Kendra says. "But I still want to know."

Linnea and I smile at each other. We had an ultrasound a few days ago, but we haven't told anyone. Charlotte knows, because she came with us, but she's good at keeping secrets.

"You know, don't you?" Kendra asks. "Come on you two, tell us."

"Bug, do you want to tell them?" Linnea asks.

Charlotte smiles. "I'm getting a baby brother."

Mia and Kendra both "aw" at the same time.

I kiss the back of Linnea's hand, just below her ring. We had a small wedding—Linnea didn't want a lot of fuss. Charlotte stood with us, holding both our hands, as we said our vows in front of our friends and family.

Linnea's parents flew out for the wedding and to their credit, they were pleasant guests. I don't think I'll ever be their favorite person, but they seem to be doing their best to love their daughter for who she is. They doted on Charlotte, and I have to admit, it's hard not to feel some affection for people who love your kid.

I put my hand on Linnea's belly and she covers my hand with hers. I always love touching her, but since she got pregnant, I can't keep my hands to myself. If I could have my arms wrapped around her every minute of the day, I would.

Life is still busy. My schedule is hectic and the pressures of my job are still there. But I'm no longer facing it all alone. From the moment Linnea walked into our lives, she fit like she was always meant to be with us. Like she was meant to be with me.

Things don't always turn out the way we plan, and sometimes we have to travel a dark road to get to our destination. But I couldn't have imagined a better life than this. I'm the luckiest guy in the world.

TURN the page for a special bonus chapter. Just a little something I wrote as a treat for my readers, featuring a certain cocky asshole we all know and love. Enjoy!

BONUS CHAPTER: AUDREY REID

Weston

Kendra stops next to her car and looks back at me. "Are we sure about this?"

I move from the open doorway and walk down the porch steps to stand in front of her. "Yes. We're sure."

"Okay," she says, but I can tell she's not convinced. "But... maybe I shouldn't go."

Touching her chin, I lean down to kiss her. "It's one day. You'll be back tonight."

"I know, but this is the first time I'm leaving for an entire day," she says.

"Don't you think I can handle it?" I ask.

"No, that's not it at all," she says. "I know you'll be fine. I'm sorry, I'm just nervous."

I kiss her again. "It's okay. I'll miss you, but you should go. This will be good for you."

"Yeah," she says. "You're right. I know."

"Don't worry, baby. I've got this."

"Just... be nice if you're out and about, okay?" she says.

"Be nice?"

She smiles and puts her hand on my chest. "You know what I mean."

I wrap my arms around her, giving her one last hug before she leaves. I step back onto the porch, my hands in my pockets, and watch her pull out of the driveway.

I am going to miss her—I hate it when she's gone—but this *will* be good for her. She was invited to a large writer's conference to be a panelist in two sessions on editing. I'm so proud of her, but I understand why she's nervous.

After closing the front door behind me, I head into the kitchen and take a seat at the little round table.

"It's just you and me, Peanut."

My seven-month-old daughter, Audrey, looks up at me from the mess on her highchair tray. I left her with a few bits of very soft banana while I walked Kendra out. I had a feeling Kendra wouldn't leave if she had to say goodbye to her again.

The banana is smeared everywhere. I wonder if any got in her mouth.

I raise an eyebrow. "You're a mess."

She smiles, showing the two little teeth just starting to poke through her lower gums.

"I think Mommy is worried about leaving us." I get up and run a fresh washcloth under warm water, then wipe Audrey's face. And hands. And arms. And neck. Jesus, this kid is sticky. "But we'll show her, won't we? I'm a goddamn surgeon. I can take care of my own baby for a day."

I toss the washcloth onto the counter and glance at her again. Her bright gray eyes—which look just like mine—get bigger and her mouth closes.

"I probably shouldn't talk like that in front of you."

She smiles again and it gives me that warm feeling in my chest.

Despite my assurances to Kendra, I'm not sure how this day is going to go. I've never taken care of her by myself for more than a couple of hours. I came into this fatherhood thing without a clue as to what I'm doing. I've never been around kids, except for my niece, Charlotte. But I didn't spend any time with her when she was a baby. And my own dad certainly didn't set a good example.

Kendra is the most amazing mom on the planet, so together, we're doing pretty well. But with her gone, it's all on me.

"Come here, Peanut."

I get her out of the highchair and take a moment to just hold her. She always smells so good. I lean my face down to her soft head and breathe her in.

I didn't realize how much my life would change when I became a father. I was on board with getting pregnant—not that I knew it meant Kendra would turn me into a sperm factory for months. But I wasn't hesitant about it. Kendra was meant to be a mom. When I asked her to marry me, I knew this was part of the deal.

But nothing could have prepared me for the moment I saw my daughter for the first time.

Kendra had a few complications with her pregnancy, and needed a C-section. So, when our baby was born, the doctor handed her to me first. I had this tiny, wet, wrinkly little thing in my arms and all I could do was stare. She was the most beautiful thing I'd ever seen.

There was a lot of blinking and throat clearing on my part. If anyone suggests I cried at my daughter's birth, I'll tell them to fuck off.

Although maybe I teared up a little.

When Kendra said we should name her Audrey, after my mother, there was probably more throat clearing. But fuck, can you blame me? I'd just become a father for the first time, and my wife said we should name our baby after my mother who died when I was a kid. I'd challenge any man to get through that without a bunch of goddamn feelings. It's not like I don't have a soul.

Audrey is still in her pink pajamas; they zip up the front and have little bunny ears on the feet. When Kendra was pregnant, I swore we weren't going to dress the baby in pink all the time. But now that she's here, I'll admit, pink looks pretty adorable on her.

I kiss the top of her head. "Should we get you dressed? Or do you want to be like Mommy and hang out in your pajamas all day?"

She kicks her little feet.

"Dressed it is."

With Audrey dressed in a shirt that says *Daddy's Girl*, a soft pair of pants, and little slip on shoes, we head out. I toss her diaper bag full of all the baby shit we bring everywhere now into the back, and strap her in her car seat.

"See, Peanut? I've got this."

First stop is the gym. I've never brought Audrey with me before, but Kendra says she'll be fine in the daycare. There's a big window where parents can check up on their kids, but I'm still eying the whole thing with skepticism while I sign her in. I'm not sure I want to hand my daughter over to some stranger.

The girl behind the desk looks like she's twelve. I pass her the diaper bag. She shoulders it, then reaches for Audrey.

I hand Audrey over and she looks back at me. She seems fine —she's such a laid-back baby, it takes a lot to piss her off. Still, it's hard to walk away.

After changing clothes and warming up on the treadmill, I go back to the daycare window so I can peek inside. Another girl is holding Audrey, propped on her hip, while she walks around. I guess that's fine. She isn't crying or anything.

I go back to my workout, but after a couple of sets of pull ups, I wonder how Audrey's doing. I head to the daycare and look through the window again. They have her on a blanket on the floor. One corner of my mouth turns up a little. She's so good at sitting up on her own now.

But she's just sitting there.

"Hey," I say to the girl at the front desk. "Someone should give Audrey her taggy blanket. She likes the texture. It's in her diaper bag."

She glances back. "Oh, okay. Um, I think she's fine, though."

I stand there for a second, my hands on my hips, my eyes moving from the girl to Audrey. She does seem okay; she's watching a couple of toddlers. But if she gets bored, she doesn't have anything to play with.

"Taggy blanket. It's in the diaper bag." I turn around and go back to the weights.

About ten minutes later, I'm thinking about my girl again. Is she okay in there? I look through the daycare window and at first, I don't see her. Where the fuck is my kid?

I'm about two seconds away from losing it when I spot her. She's on the other side of the room, sitting on the floor, chewing on a blue plastic ring. Someone must have moved her; she's not crawling yet. But what does she have in her mouth? That's not one of her toys. What the hell? It's probably dirty. I don't want her trading slobber with some other little cretin.

Fuck this. I'm out.

I run to the locker room so I can change back into my dark gray Henley and slacks. At the daycare, I hand the card they gave me to the girl at the front. "Audrey Reid."

"Done already?" the girl asks, giving me a cheerful smile.

I don't smile back. "Yeah. Baby, please."

"Okay." She goes into the back and comes out with Audrey and our diaper bag. I grab Audrey first and then take the bag.

"Bye, Audrey," she says in a singsong voice.

We head back to the car and I get her strapped in. I have a patient to check on at the hospital, but I wonder if I should take Audrey home and feed her first. Or does she need a nap? I wonder what Kendra would do. I look at her for a second and she chews on her fingers, getting drool on her chin.

I'm not usually so indecisive.

"Okay, Peanut. Daddy has to do a little work today. Shouldn't take too long." I kiss her forehead, hoping I'm making the right call.

My patient is a post-mastectomy reconstruction that I performed yesterday. Surgery went beautifully. Strictly speaking, I don't have to go in, but I want to check on how she's doing.

At the hospital, I find a spot in the physicians' area of the parking garage. I get Audrey situated in the baby sling Kendra got me. It's black and goes over one shoulder, making a pouch where Audrey can sit in front. I could carry her around like this all day, and if she gets sleepy, it's easy for her to snuggle in and nap.

My patient is up on the third floor. We get out of the elevator and I absently rub Audrey's little hand while we walk through the corridor. It seems like everyone we pass stops and stares—the women, anyway. I don't know what the hell they're looking at. I'm pretty sure they've all seen a baby before.

A woman in blue scrubs comes toward me. "Oh, Dr. Reid." She reaches out to touch Audrey. "She is so precious."

I angle myself away so she can't get her hands on my baby. I don't like it when other people touch her. "Thanks."

She pulls her hand back and I walk past her toward my patient's room.

"Hi Dr. Reid." Christy McCormick, my patient, smiles at me from her bed.

I come into the room and log in at the workstation. "How's your pain today?"

"I feel okay," she says. "Sore, but it's not unbearable."

"Good. You've been out of bed?"

"Yeah, the nurse had me up twice today," she says. "It actually felt good to walk around."

I nod and check a few more things in her chart.

"Is this your daughter?" she asks.

"Sure is."

Audrey bangs her hand on the counter and makes some bubbly noises while I check over Christy's chart.

"She's beautiful."

I glance over at Christy and crack a smile. You bet your ass my daughter is beautiful. "Thanks. She looks like my wife."

"That's so sweet," Christy says. "I'm glad you brought her with you."

"Looks like you're doing fine," I say. "I expect you'll be ready for discharge tomorrow."

"Okay, thank you," she says.

A nurse in blue scrubs comes in. She stops in front of me and her eyes move from my face, down to Audrey, then back up again.

"Wow," she says, under her breath. "I never knew a baby sling could be so hot."

"They're not." What is with the women in this place?

She blinks at me, her face flushing. "Oh. Sorry. Hi, Dr. Reid."

"Looks like the patient is doing fine, but page me if anything changes," I say.

"Of course," she says, still staring at me.

I raise my eyebrows and glance between Christy and the nurse. "Okay, then."

Audrey babbles as I walk out into the corridor and I fiddle with her little fingers again.

A man walks down the hall toward me and I stop in my tracks. It's my father.

Considering he's the head of surgery here, I don't see him very often. But only about ten percent of my patients come to this hospital. I've only spoken to him a handful of times since I severed ties with my former partner, Ian. My dad lost a lot of money when I left Ian's practice, and I doubt he'll ever forgive me for that.

He knows I got married, but as I glance down at Audrey, I realize he probably doesn't know Kendra and I had a baby.

Huh. This should be interesting.

"Weston," he says, and the lines in his forehead deepen as he looks me up and down. "What is that?"

"*She*," I say, emphasizing the word, "is my daughter."

"Does she belong to that woman you married, or someone else?" he asks.

A knot of anger forms in my gut. "What kind of a question is that?"

"A reasonable one," he says. "A friend of mine is a family law attorney. If you get into trouble with child support issues, let me know."

"For fuck's sake," I say under my breath. "I'm not you, Dad."

"I didn't father any illegitimate children," he says. "I did the smart thing and had a vasectomy right after you were born."

I stare at him for a second and the hot flash of anger I always feel when I see him dissipates. He really has no idea what he missed. My entire childhood, I was ignored by him at best—treated like a burden at worst. I'll never understand how a man could have a child and not see the miracle of it. How he could be so wrapped up in his own bullshit, he failed at the most important job he ever had.

Looking at him now, feeling my baby girl's hand wrapped around my finger, I realize something. I'm not angry at him anymore. I feel sorry for him.

When I fell in love with Kendra, I fell hard. Before her, I hadn't experienced real love—at least, not since my mother was alive—and it was both addictive and life-changing. Now that we have Audrey, those two are my entire world. Loving them makes my life worth living.

What does my father have? A dead wife he didn't care about? A long string of girlfriends who never meant anything to him? He has money, I suppose. For all the good it does him.

"I'm sorry, Dad," I say. "You're missing out."

He furrows his brow. "Missing out on what?"

I kiss the top of Audrey's head. "Everything."

I don't bother to say goodbye as I walk away. There's nothing I can do to change my father. He'll probably never realize what an idiot he is. He has a beautiful granddaughter, and he's not going to be a part of her life.

Poor bastard.

I head home with my baby girl. Maybe I won't always know what she needs or how to best take care of her. I'll probably make mistakes. But is there anything more important for me to do than love her?

Even an asshole like me can do that—and do it well.

When she starts to cry while we're stuck in traffic, I don't let it get to me. I reach back to stroke her head and talk to her in a soothing voice. I know she'll be fine. There's no way I'm going to fail at this dad thing.

We get home and she's still fussy. I cradle her in my arms and feed her one of the bottles Kendra left for her. She falls asleep and I hold her for a while. Even as little as she is—she takes after Kendra, so she's petite—my arm eventually gets tired. I put her down in her crib so she can finish her nap.

We're at home for the rest of the day. She wakes up and I feed her again. I play with her on the floor for a while, then put her in the little bouncy saucer thing. She slobbers all over the toys. I give her some solid food for dinner and I think she wears more of it than she eats.

That's a problem easily solved by a bath. When she's clean and dry, I walk around with her for a while, smelling her hair. Soon it's time for another bottle and her sleepy little eyes close.

We're on the couch, so I stretch out and carefully move her so she's lying with her head on my chest. I could get up and put her in her crib, but I'm enjoying the feel of her warm weight on top of me.

Kendra's hand on my shoulder and her voice whispering my name wakes me.

"Hey." She strokes Audrey's hair.

"Hey." I didn't realize I fell asleep. Audrey is still sleeping soundly on my chest. "Did you just get home?"

"Yeah," she says. "I've been sitting here watching you sleep for the last few minutes. You two are so adorable, I thought I might die. How was your day?"

"It was good. How was the conference?"

"A lot of fun," she says. "I missed you, but I'm glad I went."

She smiles and I reach out to draw her in for a kiss. Her lips are soft, and I enjoy the familiarity of her mouth against mine.

"I love you, Kendra."

"I love you too." She gently lifts our daughter and cradles her in her arms. "I'll get her to bed."

With Audrey settled, Kendra and I undress and get into bed. I pull her against me and hold her close.

"Thank you." I kiss her forehead.

"For what?" she asks.

"For you, and Audrey. For this."

She tightens her arms around me. "Thank *you*."

And that's the thing, isn't it? This thing Kendra and I have, it goes both ways. I'd do anything—sacrifice anything—for my girls. My wife would do the same for me.

There's really nothing better.

A few hours later, we wake up to the sound of Audrey crying. I roll over and kiss Kendra's forehead.

"Go back to sleep, baby," I say. "I've got this."

HER BEST FRIEND

Sign up for Claire Kingsley's newsletter at www.clairekingsleybooks.com and get **Her Best Friend**, a short story about Caleb's daughter Charlotte, for FREE.

Noah Douglas and Charlotte Lawson have been best friends since first grade. Noah had a hard time relating to other kids, and Charlotte was painfully shy. But once they found each other, they were inseparable.

Now sixteen, Noah is starting to see Charlotte through new eyes. Maybe it's just a crush. Charlotte is talented, fun, and pretty. What guy wouldn't be attracted to her?

But the threat of someone else dating his best friend brings out deeper feelings Noah didn't realize he had. Can he risk telling her how he feels? Or are they better off as friends?

Her Best Friend is the sweet-as-sugar love story of Caleb Lawson's daughter, Charlotte, and her friend Noah, who meet as children in Hot Single Dad. It's a short story of approximately 6,000 words and is meant to be read after Hot Single Dad.

AFTERWORD

I always feel such a mix of emotions when I get to a highly anticipated story like this one. I love it when readers are excited for a character. There's a lot of buildup, and that makes the whole process fun. But there's pressure too. I don't want to disappoint my readers with a story that doesn't live up to their expectations.

We first meet Caleb in Book Boyfriend. He's Alex's younger brother, and he comes back to Seattle for what his siblings think is a visit. He tells them he's actually interviewing for a job, with the hope of moving closer to his family. He's struggling as a single father, raising his daughter Charlotte, while keeping up with a demanding career as an ER surgeon.

In Cocky Roommate, we see a little more of Caleb. He's an old friend of Weston—one of the few people in the world Weston can honestly call a friend. We learn a little more about the loss of Caleb's wife, Melanie, when Caleb tells his sister Kendra how Weston helped him out after Mel died. It's a surprising revelation for Kendra, and we get to see a little glimpse into Weston. But we're also reminded that Caleb suffered a tragic loss when his daughter was just a baby.

Caleb's story begins when Charlotte is six, just beginning

first grade. He's had a tough time finding a reliable caregiver, and Charlotte is struggling with shyness and anxiety at school. Caleb is feeling the weight of his responsibilities. When his in-laws insist their younger daughter, Linnea come to live with him to be Charlotte's nanny, he thinks he's getting more problems, rather than a solution. After all, the last time he saw Linnea, she was a teenager who barely spoke.

Of course, Linnea is no longer the quiet child Caleb remembers. She's grown up, and blossomed into a beautiful, talented young woman. And Caleb is struck by lightning the first time he sees her.

Linnea grew up in the shadow of her older sister. She's not like her parents, or Melanie, and she's never felt like she fits in with her family. After her sister's death, the pressure and expectations that had been reserved for her sister fell squarely onto her shoulders. She's been trying to cope with the weight of that ever since.

Moving to Seattle to be Charlotte's nanny gives her some much-needed breathing room from her overbearing mother. But she's still trying to live up to her parents' expectations, particularly when it comes to her career. She struggles with feeling abnormal, like she doesn't fit in with her peers. And despite her self-proclaimed insta-crush when she meets Caleb again, she sees him as unattainable/off-limits.

From her first day in Caleb's home, Linnea fits like a missing puzzle piece. She has a natural gift for nurturing others, and both Caleb and Charlotte are in desperate need of that sort of care.

But, of course, it's not all smooth sailing. Caleb struggles with all the reasons he believes they can't be together, despite his growing attraction to her. Linnea does the same. But, as Alex predicts, it was inevitable that it would all come out.

There were a lot of things I enjoyed about writing this story. I had a soft spot for Caleb from the moment I introduced him in Book Boyfriend. He's a sweet and gentle father who's doing his best for his daughter. He's suffered a difficult loss, but by the time his story begins, he's ready to move on. But a demanding job and the responsibilities of parenting make that difficult.

In Linnea, I wanted to explore a character who was both soft and strong—something that can be a challenge in a romance heroine. Linnea isn't sassy and no-nonsense like Kendra, nor is she awkward and quirky like Mia. But she has a quiet strength, and an ability to care for, and about, others without losing herself in the process. She can nurture both Charlotte and Caleb in the way they need, without sacrificing who she is.

And Charlotte. Oh, how I love that little girl. The sweet, shy thing with so much sunshine just waiting to come out. My hope was to incorporate Charlotte in the story enough that she'd be an enjoyable character, and you could see her growth as the story progresses. The trick was not letting her overpower the love story between Caleb and Linnea. Because let's be honest, some kid stuff is cute, but it's not exactly sexy. And we still want some sexy.

But between her dad's devotion and love, and Linnea's gentle encouragement, Charlotte does grow and you see glimpses of the girl—and young woman—she's going to become.

I love writing close families, and the Lawsons have become one of my favorites. What I love about them is that I didn't plan them that way. I didn't outline Book Boyfriend with the intent of creating this fun group of characters who'd be such integral parts of each other's lives. It all developed very naturally as each story progressed.

In fact, when Book Boyfriend begins, that closeness doesn't exist—at least not to the degree that it does later. Alex is a grumpy divorced guy working a job he hates, struggling to help his dad through a difficult time. Kendra is trying to find her place in the world, both socially and professionally. Caleb lives in another state, the distance keeping him from developing a close relationship with his siblings.

But as each of the Lawsons meet their person, their entire family is strengthened. Mia becomes best friends with Kendra. Weston embraces his new family, trading up from the crappy one he was born into, and develops real friendships with both Caleb and Alex. Linnea completes the circle, coming into Caleb's life and fitting in like she was always meant to be there. And loving Caleb and Charlotte fulfills Linnea in a way nothing else ever could.

I have to give a special thanks to my friend Nikki for her suggestion that Ken Lawson meet someone and have his own happily ever after. I can't take any credit for that idea, and it was perfect, wasn't it? The only thing I love more than a romantic happily ever after is a romantic double happily ever after. I was really glad I could write that in for Ken. He certainly deserved it, and I love the idea of him living out his own happy ending with Jacqueline.

And I know it's Caleb's book, but I can't end without talking about Weston. First of all, the beach scene in chapter seven. I know it seems like everyone is kind of ganging up on Caleb, but honestly, I put Mia and Weston in a scene together and hilarity ensues. From Mia calling Caleb a DILF, to Weston saying Caleb has a dad bod, to Mia and Weston's game of "real or not real"... I just can't even with these people. Seriously, that scene wrote itself.

I also had a TON of fun turning Weston into Kendra's sperm bank. It was a little bit of karma for the guy who man-whored his way through life for so long to suddenly feel like his wife is using him for sex. I tend to agree with Caleb; there's no way that isn't funny.

That was what prompted me to write Weston's bonus chapter. I knew he and Kendra would have a baby, and the temptation to write Weston as a father was too strong to resist. How cute is that asshole walking around with his daughter in a baby sling? I loved how he's oblivious to why the women are all staring at him (um, because a hot guy with a baby is sexy AF, Weston, get a clue). I also wanted to show that, despite the fact that he's a big softie for his wife and daughter, he's still Weston. He's short with the childcare attendant at the gym ("Baby, please.") and he doesn't like people touching his daughter (I could almost hear him saying, "Mine," when the woman in the hospital tried to touch Audrey). It was fun to revisit Weston from his point of view, and give him a little bit of closure when it came to his father.

Thanks for reading! I hope you enjoyed this book as much as I did, and that Caleb's story was everything you wanted it to be.

ACKNOWLEDGMENTS

Thank you first and foremost to my readers. You make this job worth doing. I love you so much.

Thank you to everyone who makes writing these stories possible. David, Nikki, and Tammi, for ideas, brainstorming, pep talks, and answers to stupid questions. Thank you to Elayne for cleaning up my words. I'm so lucky to have a great bunch of people around me. I couldn't do what I do without you.

Thank you to my fellow authors for writing beautiful stories and inspiring me to keep writing.